THE
MERMAID
LATITUDES
BARRY JAMES HICKEY

Also by Barry James Hickey

The Five Pearls

Chasing God's River

The Glass Fence

Waking Purgatory

The Water Lawyer

The Pendragon Prophecy

This is a work of fiction. All names, characters, places, and incidents either are the product of the author's imagination or are used fictitiously. Any resemblance to actual persons, living or dead, business establishments, events, or locales is entirely coincidental.

FIRST EDITION

BLACKMAIL BOOKS, LLC
ISBN: 978-1-64516-731-0
Printed in the United States of America.

SPECIAL THANKS TO MY FAMILY
AND FRIENDS FOR THEIR LIFELONG
SUPPORT OF MY ARTISTIC AMBITIONS

THE MERMAID LATITUDES

BARRY JAMES HICKEY

CHAPTER 1

George Chumley lived to a ripe old age and died suddenly, leaving behind a juicy mystery attached to his unique death.

It was a wet afternoon, typical of August in Chicago. Larry Settlebottom estimated two hundred open umbrellas along the string of black limousines being loaded at the curb of Holy Name Cathedral. Larry felt the dampness rising off the pavement under his gray trench coat.

It would take an hour for the funeral procession to reach Calgary Catholic Cemetery in Evanston. Dozens of police cars blocked intersections and efficiently led the long procession to George Chumley's final resting place.

Larry's benefactor was a beloved man. Dead at the age of eighty, doing what he loved best: staring at stamps. If it weren't for George Chumley, there would be no Chicago Numismatic and Coin

Museum on Michigan Avenue across the street from the Art Institute.

George and his scrappy wife Rosemary had always treated Larry like a cherished nephew. The Chumleys loved Larry with their money and he never really understood why. They had paid for his university education. They singlehandedly raised the necessary funds to open the museum, giving Larry a mission, a career and a fantastic salary.

Reaching their golden years, George and Rosemary sold off their beloved Chumley Confectioners to the highest bidder for a tidy billion dollars. Not bad for a pair of Irish immigrants who came to Chicago in the 1960s, their only belongings in canvas bags. While men landed on the moon, the couple sat in their modest Chicago apartment and dreamed of the future.

George learned how to make chewing gum. Chumley's Chews: spearmint, peppermint, cinnamon and bubble gum, all wrapped in gold foil. They were as recognizable as McDonalds and Coca-Cola worldwide. Rosemary worked with chocolatiers and invented Patty's Push-Ups, Leprechaun Gold Bars and Black Flag fudge.

The candies and gums took America's sweet-toothed youth by storm.

But this was a funeral. No one was eating candy or smacking gum today.

The revered Archbishop of Chicago read a final piece of scripture over George's casket from *Ecclesiastes 3:1-2.*

"For everything there is a season, and a time for every matter under heaven: A time to be born, and a time to die; a time to plant, and a time to pluck up what is planted."

After the casket was carried into the copper-wrapped mausoleum, the ceremony ended.

To some in the crowd, George's final resting place reminded them of a giant candy bar wrapped in gold paper. That was the way George wanted it.

Larry stayed back as Rosemary Chumley received condolences from well-wishers and friends. Everyone was invited back to the Chumley mansion to share their stories over the years about *Loveable Georgie.*

"But no button accordion music!" Rosemary promised.

George loved playing his accordion, loved singing dirty limericks passed down from his childhood in Dublin.

"There was a young gal name of Sally who loved an occasional dally

She sat on the lap of a well-endowed chap, crying, 'Gee, Dick, you're right up my alley!'"

As the crowd thinned, Larry approached the missus with an open umbrella.

Rosemary Chumley took his arm in hers. "Such a day, such a day!" she sighed.

Larry guided Rosemary to her waiting car. Her chauffeur stood by the open door as Larry helped her in the back seat. The woman had a mind as sharp as a penny nail but her body was frail. Larry tucked a quilt across her lap.

"Now Lawrence, you must come back to the house for the shenanigans! This is an Irish thing. The dead aren't gone until we say so."

"I wouldn't miss it for the world, Rosemary."

Her eyes fell on George's final resting place. "Oh, that damned Georgie and his stamps! I've always been jealous of them." She shook her head and stared at Larry. "I have something to show you. It's rather disturbing. "*Pornographic*, but in a tasteful sort of way. I don't know what to make of it."

"Mrs. Chumley!"

She patted him on the cheek. "Come now, Lawrence. We must be adults about such things. I'll see you at the house."

Her driver climbed behind the wheel and steered her away.

Larry closed the umbrella and handed it to an attendant. He climbed in the front passenger seat of a waiting limousine.

"Back to the South Side, sir?" said his driver.

"No, Homer" Larry said glumly. "Follow the northbound parade."

"To the Chumley mansion then?"

"Yes, whether I like it or not."

"How come you always sit in front, Mr. Settlebottom?"

"I'm a working stiff just like you, Homer."

CHAPTER 2

It was an uncharted island used to mocking hot winds and relentless sun.

Ismelda stood at the edge of the white cliff. She could jump and die on the sharp rocks below but who would take care of the old ones? She stared out to sea. No boats on the horizon. No rescue or death today, just a rolling blue expanse of nothingness to remind her how very alone she was.

An old woman approached. Her mottled, cracked skin was brown and baked from too many years in the sun. She stood next to the younger Ismelda, admiring her.

"So beautiful you are with your long black hair and bronze flesh!"

Ismelda raised the brim of her worn straw hat and smiled back at the old woman.

"You are just as beautiful, Calista."

“Me? I am a bag of bones,” said the old woman.

Ismelda held out her rough hands for the old woman to examine. “We are all just bags of bones.”

The old woman glanced over the cliff and stared at the sharp volcanic rocks below.

“It is okay to jump,” Calista said.

Ismelda shook her head. “I will never jump,” she promised.

The old woman sighed. “El Gordo waits. We must trim the plants.”

“Always the pulque,” said Ismelda.”

"There will be no drink for him in a few months,” said Calista. “What will happen then?"

"What always happens. He will hurt us or he will kill us.”

The women glanced towards the small village, a collection of leaning shacks made of tin, sheets of fiberglass and plastic. It was an ugly place. Above it ran a low-lying hill. Neat rows of agave plants ran up its spine.

“The harvest is too hard for you,” said Ismelda. “I will talk to the pig.”

The old woman squeezed her arm. “No! We cannot have trouble now. We are almost done!”

Ismelda heard a small noise, a pitiful squeak that came from a cactus plant near her feet. A small long-nosed bat was trapped between its spikes. She reached down and carefully pulled the bat free, releasing the creature to the wind. It dropped away, over the cliffs to find a hiding place away from the bright sun and heat of the day.

Ismelda's eyes followed a wide path away from the shacks, leading down through a break in the cliffs to a leaning dock barely erect on rotten pylons. It was the only accessible place to land on the island, the adjacent beach only two hundred feet across. There was no escape. No boats on the beach. No wood or debris to make a seaworthy raft. El Gordo had seen to that.

Ismelda raised an open hand over her eyes and stared out at the empty sea again.

How much longer, she wondered.

CHAPTER 3

Homer was a talker. Larry had come to expect it from the driver over the years.

"A beautiful service," said Homer. "Wish the sun came out, though. Mr. Chumley would have preferred it."

The limo inched ahead in heavy traffic. There was no police escort this time.

"You want a quick whirl past your old alma mater?" Homer asked. "Northwestern is only a hop, skip and a jump."

"Not today, Homer."

The driver glanced at him. "Yeah, to hell with it. Bygone days. What did you study there, Mr. S?"

"Business Administration."

The driver whistled between his teeth. "No kiddin'."

"No kidding."

Larry was certain Homer knew most of his history; that the Chumleys had paid for his college education, that he was almost married once but things went awry.

It was whispered by many of Larry Settlebottom's envious detractors that the Chumleys had built the Chicago Numismatic and Coin Museum to give Larry a carefree job to last his lifetime. It was probably true. Larry had never answered the argument in his own mind. He was afraid to. He was afraid of many things, most of all abandonment and worthlessness. There would be no crowds at his funeral. He wasn't amusing enough.

At an early age, Larry was raised by the Little Sisters of the Poor, the last Catholic orphanage in Chicago's Bridgeport neighborhood. The last child to leave at the age of fourteen, he was adopted by a pair of sisters who needed a house boy and errand runner. His first mother, Ann Settle, was a retired school teacher. Married briefly to a notorious Irish alcoholic who worked as a butcher, she left the arrangement after her fifth beating. Her sister, only a year younger, was Catherine Bottom, an elderly nun without any benefits who had worked in the orphanage kitchen for thirty years.

Substantial donors to the orphanage, Mr. and Mrs. Chumley were kind and generous. They chose carefully and wisely where to give their money away. Theirs wasn't *old money*, derived from railroads, steel, gas and oil. Theirs was *candy money*. They built their empire from the personal scrap of hard labor, never accepting the insults of competitors or the derogatory stereotype that they were lucky Irish micks. Mr. and Mrs. Chumley both embraced their gift of gab. They never talked themselves up, but always entertained with their views of individuals and society, especially when it came to Chicago politics. Rich or poor, the Irish were known for strong opinions.

The car turned north, houses turning to mansions hidden behind high stone walls.

"I love this area," Homer announced at the wheel. "Makes a man dream of bigger things. You want a mansion someday, Mr. S?"

"No. They remind me of museums. I work in a museum now."

Homer laughed. "And all those maids, butlers, chefs, groundskeepers, and drivers like me. I guess I wouldn't want the high life either. No privacy except maybe the bathroom."

The car passed a sign. They were in Lake Forest now. Homer turned onto Mayflower Road. Serious old and new money. Serious big houses.

Homer arrived at the gated drive to the Chumley mansion. The iron gates were flung open, a handful of valets attending to arriving guests. The limo pulled up in line.

Homer hurried to unsnap his seatbelt. "Let me get your door for you. Mr. S. There's still a little room left in this world for protocol."

Larry patiently waited for Homer to come around the car to open his door. He looked up at the enormous hand-crafted mansion. It resembled a British castle, designed in the Tudor style. It held twelve bedrooms, twelve baths, ten fireplaces, an extensive library, game rooms, and two elevators; one for servants, one to the master bedroom where Rosemary would sleep alone until her death.

Such an exquisite estate on six acres, built by famed architects and designers for another legendary family in Chicago's bright age before the Great Depression. The Chumleys bought the foreclosed property in the 1980's at auction.

"We didn't buy it, we stole it," George Chumley liked to say.

Beyond the mansion was a long strand of private beach on Lake Michigan below the cliffs. Visitors could ride the canopied tram down or take the winding wooden stairs to reach it.

Larry made his way up the mansion steps behind a gaggle of curious guests; members of Rosemary's bridge club, museum donors, valued old employees and top executives from the former Chumley Empire. Several people nodded at Larry. He was a common sight at Chumley functions, an acknowledged player with spurious credentials, somehow tied to big money.

Larry knew the widow Rosemary would not be standing at the door greeting the mourners. She would be inside, by the burning hearth, even in summer, holding a stiff glass of Jameson Irish whiskey in one hand while the other stoked the coals of burning cedar with a poker as she entertained a large group of sycophants with one of her Georgie stories.

"He hated potatoes," Rosemary was saying, "said they tasted like ass. Georgie abhorred oatmeal as well. '*Swill*,' he always said. Reminded him of growing up poor in Ireland."

"What *did* he like?" someone said.

"A fatty steak with asparagus, Cocoa Puffs cereal and a good chunk of Chumley's dark chocolate!"

There was a titter of laughter as her guests raised their glasses to his memory.

Larry snagged a ginger ale from the open bar and worked his way through the crowd to Rosemary's side.

She took his hand in hers and addressed her guests. "Now if you'll excuse me," she apologized. "Mr. Settlebottom and I have something to do. Back in a jiff!"

Mrs. Chumley led Larry by the hand down a wide hallway to a large study facing Lake Michigan at the rear of the mansion.

There was a familiar man inside wearing a dark suit. Claude Baker, security.

Strands of light filtered in from the tall windows, the drapes half-opened, reminding Larry that it was as gloomy outside as it was in the room. This had been George Chumley's private sanctuary for years.

"Anyone in or out of this room today?" Rosemary asked Baker.

"No, Mrs. Chumley."

"Thank you, Claude. We are not to be disturbed."

"I understand, Mrs. Chumley."

Mr. Baker left the dim study and closed the door behind him.

Larry admired the décor: Walls adorned with carved wooden figures in the paneling, tapestries of Irish heraldry mounted on the walls, and an elaborate plaster fresco on the ceiling depicting angels. Stacks of books of a former life in progress were everywhere.

"George read so much. I'm surprised he didn't go blind," said Rosemary.

Larry crossed to the shelves weighted down with rows of stamp books and coin booklets arranged in an order only George had understood.

"Oh, if walls could talk," Rosemary said. She finished her glass of Jameson and set it on a side table. "So here we are, Lawrence. The scene of the crime."

"A crime?" said Larry.

"*Infidelity*, dear Lawrence. It appears my husband was seeing another woman." She pointed at the desk. "Look for yourself. Under the microscope. George's latest acquisition."

Larry moved behind the sturdy oak desk and sat. There was a large illuminated magnifying glass clamped to it with an adjustable arm lamp and a diopter lens for increased magnification, the kind used in assembling electronics or performing needlework.

Next to the mounted magnifier were special foot-long tongs made of nickel-plated steel. The ends were small, flat and thin. George learned decades ago never to use tweezers with channeled teeth. They could ruin a perfect stamp. George never touched his stamps by hand. He dared not soil or damage them. He always washed his hands before he sat at the desk, careful not to deposit the oils from his fingers on anything.

There were a few hand magnifiers on the right side of the desk. They reminded Larry of something Sherlock Holmes, the famous detective of fiction might own.

Larry turned on the magnifier's lamp. A protective stamp mount comprising a pair of opposed transparent glass slides held a small rectangular image in place on the desk.

"Perhaps my team at the museum —" suggested Larry.

"In due time, my dear. I want your impression first."

Larry adjusted his seat and stared through the magnifier at the stamp. He pulled away briefly, somewhat embarrassed by what he was seeing.

"Some stamp, eh Lawrence?"

"It is quite unusual," Larry admitted.

"Now get over your Catholic guilt and look again, Lawrence. What do you make of it?"

Larry studied the image. "At first glance, I'm not sure that it is a stamp. No postal markings, no rough perforations on the edges, no nation of origin. Definitely not a flyspeck from a print run." He carefully turned the mounted glass plates over and studied the back of the image. "No adhesive backing that I can see." He turned it over and studied the image again. "It's quite unique."

"She's certainly beautiful," said the widow. "Even if she is made of ink."

"I hardly think you should be jealous, Rosemary. After all, this isn't a portrait of a woman. It's a mermaid posing on a rock."

"Keep staring, Lawrence. See more."

Larry adjusted the magnifying glass closer and moved his eye along the projected image.

"Precise work. I've never seen such detail on such a small canvas."

"Perfect breasts, flawless skin. Look at her eyes, Lawrence. What do you see?"

Larry moved the magnifier closer and looked into the eyes of the tiny mermaid. They seemed to be staring directly at him, revealing a lost and hungry soul.

"Fascinating," said Larry.

"I've seen those eyes before," shared the widow. "Guess where?"

Larry looked up from the image at her. "Where?"

"Those were your eyes when George and I saw you for the first time at the orphanage. The day before you were adopted by Mrs.

Settle and Miss Bottom. It's as if the subject is calling out to us, Lawrence."

"Like a secret code in Leonardo DaVinci's *Mona Lisa*?"

"Something like that."

"I've heard of many artists working in miniature but this inspired work has real technical genius. But why paint for the eyes of ants?" Larry scratched his head. "Where did George get this?"

"I don't know. He dibble-dabbled with collectors all over the world. I could never keep up. It was his hobby, not mine. My hobby is spreading gossip at the bridge club. There may be some evidence in this room to lead our search. Would you mind snooping around a bit? You have an entire forensics team available at your disposal at the museum should you find something. I have guests to entertain."

"Certainly, Rosemary."

She started towards the door.

"Rosemary? Why are you so obsessed with this?" Larry asked. "It's only a stamp."

"It was enough to kill my Georgie. But something else bothers me. I think the mermaid is reaching out, beyond the image. Her pose is not relaxed. She seems a prisoner."

"I'm only a bookkeeper, Rosemary."

"And my favorite person still breathing. Please, Lawrence, spend some time alone with her. As George did." She waved her hands around the room. "As for all these stamp books and coin collections? I want them all removed. George's final donation to the museum."

"It's an extensive inventory."

"And a huge tax deduction. George would want it that way." She glanced around the room. "Good old Georgie. He'll always be with us," she said pragmatically.

"Indeed, Rosemary."

"Mr. Baker will be guarding the door so you can maintain your privacy."

She left him alone in the study and closed the door behind her.

Larry studied the mermaid image again. Whoever painted it was a master at his craft. His eyes fell on her eyes once more. An overwhelming sadness overtook him. He felt helpless. Larry took a long deep breath and turned away. How could a stamp affect him so? Who was the model? He covered the stamp slide with a piece of red cloth and turned off the magnifier light.

Larry crossed to a panel of light switches by the study door and turned them on. The room filled with light from the overhead chandeliers. Temperamental stamps didn't like bright light but it would only be for a few minutes while he made his brief inspection of the room.

He started with the objects on the desk. Was there anything in front of him that might be associated with the stamp? A bronze bowl at the edge of the desk held an assortment of coins from around the world. Were any of the coins connected? The scattered handheld magnifying glasses offered nothing.

Larry found a thin desk drawer above his lap and opened it. Inside were stamp collector tools; adhesives, tape, a magnifying loupe, a plastic-handled philatelic cutter to separate toothless stamps, brushes. He found a yellowed envelope, handwritten to George. There was no postmark. No return address. Larry carefully opened it and found a handwritten note inside.

"G – Get ready to have your socks knocked off. The package should arrive next week. Believe me; it's worth every shilling you paid for it. - B"

Larry set the letter aside and walked around the room, searching for opened packages. There were a few discarded shipping boxes in a corner. All were several months old. Larry stared at the floor. He noticed a trash can under George's desk. He pulled it out and set it on the desk.

There was a foot long brown corrugated cardboard box inside. By its condition it had traveled a long way. He held the box to his nose and sniffed it. There was a slight hint of brine to it. Saltwater?

Larry carried the box around the room, looking for bottles. He found an unopened bottle of champagne. It was too long for the box. He tried two flasks of whiskey. They were too round. He noticed a green handmade rectangular bottle on the side desk, next to Mrs. Chumley's empty whiskey glass. He thought of fingerprints and spoiled crime scenes, found a napkin and picked up the bottle. He compared the rectangular bottle to the box. It fit inside nicely. He held it up to the light. There was an etching on the bottle's bottom. It might reveal its origin. Larry carried the bottle back to the desk and turned on the magnifying lamp. He held the bottle up to the bright light. The etching was a series of numbers engraved by hand.

19.76153,-108.369141.

Larry set the bottle down and compared its mouth to the width of the stamp. It could have fit inside easily. He picked through the trash can next to the desk, found a large cork and compared it to the bottle's opening. A perfect fit.

He leaned back in the chair and drummed his fingers on the desk.

Was the stamp actually *a message in a bottle*? How old was it? Had it floated across a great sea? *Who* did Mr. Chumley pay to get it? *How much* did he pay? Who was B? Larry prided himself on his detective work for the day. Sherlock Holmes would be proud of him.

He stared up at the angels painted on the ceiling. They were bright and cheerful, their wings flapping in a peaceful sky. They gave him solace.

Larry turned on the magnifying lamp and pulled the cloth from the mermaid stamp to study it one last time. The mermaid's image was etched in his brain now, never to be forgotten. His eyes met hers and he whispered under his breath, "Who are you? *What* are you? Are you lost like me?"

He covered the stamp and turned off the study lights. Mr. Baker was patiently standing guard outside the doorway when he came out.

"I have to join the party. No one goes in or out of this room, Mr. Baker."

"Understood, Mr. S." Mr. Baker pulled a key from his pocket and locked the door securely. "Did you find something then?"

"It's confidential," said Larry.

CHAPTER 4

The two women were on their knees, gathering up the long quiote flowers of the agave plants.

A hard wind blew in, tossing pebbles of hard sand against Ismelda's skin. She stood and stared in all directions.

Calista, working beside her, stared up. "What is it?"

"Someone is coming," said Ismelda.

"When?"

"Soon."

"Before the pulque is done?"

"Maybe."

"Is he big and strong?"

"He is brave enough. That is what matters."

Ismelda dropped to her knees again and filled a large basket with the flowers. She looked at the old people filling their baskets. Some of them were eating the quiote flowers. An old man, thin and weary, chewed on a stalk, drawing the sweet sap, the aguamiel, from it.

"Luis, he drinks the honey water early," said Ismelda.

Calista nodded. "It keeps him alive."

"And the fish from the sea," said Ismelda.

"And the cans sometimes," said the old woman.

Ismelda cut a finger on the sharp end of an agave. She stuck it in her mouth to stop the bleeding. "A sewing needle poked me."

Luis finished his quiote and returned to work, scraping along the sides of an agave with a flat edged rock, trimming off blossoms. "On the mainland, I would be a Jimador," he complained. "They have their coa knives. Here we use rocks to cut."

"It is Gordo's way," said Ismelda. "If he gave us knives we would try to kill him."

Calista shook her head. "We were not put here to suffer like this. When that nasty pig settles himself between your legs at night —."

"I have a place I go to in my mind," said Ismelda.

"Are there trees there?"

"Shade trees and a cool breeze."

"When he has you locked away with him, I will go there in my mind and wait for you," said the old woman.

Ismelda stood. She stared at the sharp-edged leaves along the tall mast of one of the taller agaves. "If El Gordo fell against this maybe he could die."

"His legs are like tree stumps. It would take five strong men to push him," said Luis. "But there are no strong men here, only me and the other old ones."

Ismelda stared at the rows of agave. "The flowers are almost cut. Soon the cabezas will grow fat with sugar and El Gordo will have his mescal from the pulque juices." Ismelda picked up her basket. She called to the others. "Come, everyone. Our work is done today. The pig waits for his dinner."

CHAPTER 5

The guests were finally gone, most outstaying their welcome into the evening with the taunts of free booze, food and the fodder of gossip. The cover of gray skies had cleared, revealing stars above the wet plain of Lake Michigan. Larry and Mrs. Chumley sat outside under the cover of the gazebo. They watched sailboats struggling in choppy waves, heading towards Chicago marinas to the south. The bright lights of the city guided them.

"Did you enjoy your sailing days?" Larry asked Mrs. Chumley.

"Hated them. But I did it for George until he was bored with it."

"I prefer public transportation."

"I rode my share of public trains when I was poor; the sound of grinding steel in the subway and on the elevated. Why do you like it?"

"Everyone is anonymous. Everyone is equal. Everyone pays the same fare."

"You spend too much time observing, Lawrence. That is no way to go through life. You need to participate, engage."

"Look at what happened the last time I tried engaging."

"That was over three years ago." The widow sipped from a whiskey glass. "You got tricked by a black widow, is all. Many men have made such a mistake."

"Mine was deadly."

"I told you from Day One that Alina was bad for you. But she was a beautiful psychopath. I saw it in her eyes. I was going to run a background check on her but George told me not to interfere. He said you needed the experience of love."

"I was going to marry her, Rosemary."

"That was *your* plan, but not hers in the end. That diabolical Eastern European bitch played you smart. She devoured you emotionally. After she poisoned your mothers with strychnine she attempted to clean out their bank accounts. And on the very day of their funeral Alina was pure evil."

"I suppose she was."

"And she almost got away with it. If that burglary hadn't happened, you'd really have a mess on your hands."

"The details are etched in the stones of my memory."

"And you were next, my poor little Lawrence."

"She certainly knew her menu of poisons, as the detectives explained to me when they visited her apartment after she died."

"What did they find again?"

"Cyanide, arsenic, curare, hemlock, black berries of Nightshade..."

"All the classics used by impatient heirs, all available online and shipped to your door. Hemlock reserved for Socrates, undetectable white arsenic served in fine wines for Napoleon, Simon Bolivar, and England's King George III. What was she going to poison you with again?"

"Copper arsenite, according to one of the detectives. She was planning to paint the wallpaper in my house with it. A slow death. Stomach cramps, diarrhea, convulsions."

"It took her weeks to learn Miss Bottom's handwriting. Quite the suicide note."

"It seemed real at the time."

"Poor Lawrence!"

"Poor me."

"If you weren't such an introvert, you might have noticed things earlier in the affair."

"I've never been a man of action."

"I'm not saying it's a personality disorder, but in the animal kingdom your standstill reactions could get you killed. But if you insist on being such an introvert, at least be an engaging and amusing one. Be more witty, Lawrence. Toss things at people. Be off the cuff. Maybe George and I were wrong, sending you to college for business. What we should have done was made you a missionary, sent you off to save lost souls worse off than you ever were. Maybe then you would have a greater appreciation of your slight plight in this complicated world. What is worse? Being an orphan or being in a family of twelve where no one has the time of day for you? Think of the lonesomeness in that!"

Mrs. Chumley picked up a bottle of Jameson and poured herself a stiff drink. She stood at the gazebo rail, facing the vast lake.

"Here's to you, Georgie! You will be missed!" She drank down the entire glass and tossed it off the cliff with celebration. She turned towards Larry. "My eventful and glorious life is coming to an end, Lawrence. It's your turn now."

Larry spoke softly. "I'm content."

"Content with *what*? Your boring job? Riding the subway?"

"I have a purpose, Rosemary. Running the museum is fulfilling."

"And boring as hell. What if you lost your job tomorrow?"

Larry flushed. He had never considered it.

"Come now, Lawrence," said the widow. "George is gone. He can't protect you against other members of the museum board anymore. Some of them have different interests for the future which may not include you."

"You can replace your husband on the board," said Larry.

"For a year, maybe two. Then I'll be dead. The only reason I would do that is for your benefit. But don't worry. You're positioned very well in my Last Will and Testament." She shook her head. "Oh, screw the money. You're in your mid-thirties, Lawrence. Mrs. Settle and Miss Bottom have been dead three years. Can I speak frankly?"

Larry joined her at the rail. "You always have, Rosemary."

"You need to get some balls, Lawrence. Stop living your life in the shadows."

She picked up the whiskey bottle and poured two drinks. She handed one to Larry.

"Tomorrow you will march into your little museum to find out all you can about the mermaid stamp."

"I really don't think it's a stamp."

"Then whatever the hell it is. Meanwhile, I'll dig into George's bank transactions for this mysterious Mr. B. Now drink, damn you!"

Larry drank the whiskey to appease her.

The widow smiled at him, her old face half-hidden in th e darkness. "Can you feel it in your balls, Lawrence?"

"It certainly burns the throat, Rosemary."

She poured him another drink. "Man up, Lawrence. You're my date for the evening."

He stared at the drink in his hand. "Can I ask you a personal question?"

"You can ask me anything. You've always known that."

"You and George had the opportunity to adopt me. Why didn't you?"

"We were unfit parents. Too much stink of money and chocolate. We served you better as aunt and uncle."

He looked down the cliff at the long dock jutting into the lake. A large sailboat was tied to it. There were no lights below.

"Why did you and George keep the boat, Rosemary?"

"Every couple of months, he and I liked to sneak down there. So we could fool around."

Larry remembered what his driver had said. The only privacy in the Chumley Mansion was to be found in the bathrooms.

Larry faced the widow. "It's been a long day. You need to get some rest, Rosemary."

"Homer will drive you home, Lawrence."

"Just to the elevated," said Larry. "I'll find my way from there."

Mrs. Chumley wrapped her thin arms around him and hugged him. "Such a strange little beast of a boy you are. Find our little mermaid, Lawrence. I won't rest until the puzzle is solved."

CHAPTER 6

It was dark now. Pharaoh Williams sat on the cool metal bench outside the 99th street Metra station in Beverly. He was big, black and burly – an opposing figure dressed in his midnight blue running pants and pullover. He had been at the station for two hours, waiting for Mr. Settlebottom. It was a ritual now. Every Monday through Friday at six o'clock Mr. Settlebottom stepped off the train. But not today.

Pharaoh had read the Chicago Tribune before the street lights came on. He read about the fancy Chumley funeral downtown. He was pretty sure Mr. Settlebottom had gone to it. He had never talked to Settlebottom, only made eye contact with him maybe twice. Both times he smiled at the man with his pearly white teeth on full display. Both times Settlebottom seemed to acknowledge him with a tip of his head before shuffling away to his safe nest on Prospect Avenue.

Pharaoh always followed him at a safe distance, a newspaper under his arm to look nonchalant until Settlebottom turned down his street.

Pharaoh smoked another cancer stick and sipped down the last of his warm Colt 45 wrapped in a paper bag. He stood and tossed it in a trash can by the station door. Pharaoh looked up and saw a blue and white crossing the tracks on 99th, slow enough to take note of him. Even in the dark, he recognized the burly cops inside. It was the sixth time they had passed him in two hours. He didn't bother to wave at them. That would just piss them off.

But Pharaoh hadn't done anything wrong. Not today. Black folk were a common sight in the safe haven of Beverly now. The days of redlining realtors refusing to sell to blacks were long gone in this South Side neighborhood. There were black teachers and lawyers living here. Black people were free to go about their business now. The only visible reminder of the old days was a handful of ancient housekeepers making their way east to what everyone knew was still the black side of the tracks. Even they were far and few between now, replaced by Mexicans. The tall drab concrete high-rise slums of the Robert Taylor homes along the Dan Ryan Expressway had been torn down years ago. Urban emancipation.

Pharaoh crossed to the yellow line at the edge of the wooden platform. He stared north. He could barely make out the bright headlight on the nose of a train pulling to a stop at the 95th Street station.

"My last train," Pharaoh decided. "If he ain't on it, I'm gone."

He moved away from the platform, leaned his large frame against the freshly-painted brown station and waited.

Six minutes later the silver double-decker commuter train arrived. A handful of passengers exited, most carrying briefcases, umbrellas and rain coats draped over their arms. They were the last bunch of mostly white stragglers who worked in the tall office buildings in downtown Chicago. Pharaoh guessed they were bankers, lawyers, brokers or secretaries.

Standing six-feet-six, Pharaoh had no problem seeing over their heads. He knew what Mr. Settlebottom looked like; tall and almost thin, a full head of neat brown hair. Settlebottom walked with his shoulders hunched, his chin low on his neck, a man busy in his thoughts. He always wore or carried a gray trench coat, rain or shine, even in summer.

The exodus from the train was over in thirty seconds. Mr. Settlebottom was a no-show. As the train pulled out for the next station south, Pharaoh decided his next move.

"I could run west up to Janson's drive-in for a Chicago dog or I could run east to Vincennes for an Italian beef."

He still had two hours before his shift at the Kitty Kat lounge, a blues and jazz club on Halsted. Big black bouncers were in high demand on the violent South Side.

Pharaoh walked east. When he reached Prospect Street he turned north and cruised past Settlebottom's house.

It was a nice house. Neatly kept. A pair of flowering Sugar Maple trees hid most of the house from view.

Behind the house, on Charles Street, there was a vacant lot. A house had burned to the ground there five years ago. Tall wooden fences with burn scars stood on either side of the property.

Three years ago Pharaoh and his accomplices snuck through the lot and climbed over the back fence to burglarize the Settlebottom house on Prospect.

Nobody was supposed to be home.

Pharaoh and his accomplices had read the obituaries. The two old ladies who had lived there had committed suicide. There was a funeral that morning. Nobody was supposed to be in the house.

Stupid bitch. Why was she there? Why wasn't she at the funeral with her boyfriend Larry?

Pharaoh kept walking. Traces of steam from an earlier rain rose from the sidewalk. He caught a few glances from people looking out their windows on the quiet street.

"Damned bedroom community," Pharaoh whispered to himself, "everybody on guard for stranger-dangers. Then again, they got a right to be. Three women died on this street back in the day."

Pharaoh reached 95th Street and turned east again. He crossed the tracks at Beverly Boulevard and stared at the ugly buildings ahead. Everything east of the dividing line known as *the tracks* was worn out. Black territory. Home. The real South Side with the highest murder rate in the country. It wasn't just black folks killing each other anymore. The Puerto Ricans and Mexicans with their own drugs and guns were on a rampage.

Pharaoh's city was going to hell. He wanted out. He wanted his freedom. He wanted a new life.

But first he had to make his amends to Mr. Settlebottom.

Pharaoh wasn't a killer. He was just big, black and stupid. He recently found God and he knew, just knew that he had to reach out to Settlebottom for forgiveness any way he could.

He wanted to sit with the man and explain the details of the burglary: Why he tied Settlebottom's whining girlfriend to a kitchen chair, why he put duct tape over her mouth to stop her from bitching at him. He didn't know she had a breathing problem. He didn't expect her to die in that chair from asphyxiation. He wanted to tell Mr. Settlebottom what he did to Dwayne Jones and Bobby Brown when they met to settle up later, how he broke their bodies over a bagful of trinkets.

Did Mr. Settlebottom ever receive the stolen jewelry Pharaoh had left on his porch a week later? He had set it just inside the screen door with a note at three in the morning.

Pharaoh passed a food truck selling fresh tamales and tacos. He hated the smells coming from it, hated the damned Mexicans and Puerto Ricans moving in to his 'hood.

It had taken fifty years to move most of the white folks out to make room for black folk here. But nobody saw the swarm of illegals coming. They were everywhere now, in just one generation, with their hand-painted storefronts, corner churches and garish cars. English was becoming a second language here.

Pharaoh would never get his mother and sisters out of Chicago working three nights a week at a nightclub. Not enough cash to escape the city.

He wanted to work, could work, with his hands mostly. Give him a shovel and he'd dig a ditch a mile long until his hands bled.

Put him on a loading dock and he'd load fifteen tons a day. He wanted work. But there was none to be had on the South Side. He didn't like being a bouncer. Facing off with drunks and druggies was a dangerous occupation. Just about everyone carried a hidden blade or a pistol now. It was just a matter of time before he would get shanked or shot in a scuffle.

So far, Pharaoh was a lucky man with a clean record. He wasn't stuck in prison like his old man. Never peddled in drugs or prostitutes. Never owned a gun or shot one. He was on the straight path, thanks to his Lord and Savior Jesus Christ.

Pharaoh saw a stray dog down an alley, digging through a garbage can.

"I feel for you, brother. I really do."

CHAPTER 7

The morning sun was drying out the city pavement.

Larry found an empty seat on the lower tier of the train heading downtown. He set the plain brown box on his lap and rested his hands on it.

As the train left the 99th Street station, the conductor moved down the center aisle, punching day tickets or scanning passes with a handheld device. It was always the same conductor on the morning run, a disengaged spirit with dead eyes performing his drab daily routine.

Larry looked out the side window at the passing city. Most of the other commuters were into their newspapers, electronic books or gadget phones.

Larry's routine was organized. He spent nine hours a day at the museum. Forty-five minutes each way on the train. Twenty minutes a day walking from the LaSalle Street station to work and twenty minutes back to the depot again. Fifteen minutes in the morning from his house to the 99th Street station. Fifteen minutes from the station to his house on Prospect at day's end.

There was no clutter in his life. Larry had an assistant at the museum for all of his correspondence to protect his privacy. He didn't have cable or satellite television at home and dumped his cell phone after the murders. All he cared about now was his collection of old records and a cabinet stocked with fine wines. The outside world seemed not to notice him.

The train made three more stops before its final leg into LaSalle Street station. It had once been a great train station, carved in wood with great pillars and oval arches. It had served some of America's most illustrious train routes, including the 20th Century Limited and the Rocky Mountain Rocket. Scenes from Alfred Hitchcock's *North by Northwest* and *The Sting* were filmed here before it was turned into a new terminal of cold walls and metal that came to its final destination under the Chicago Stock Exchange high-rise.

Several prominent buildings stood nearby. The Chicago Board of Trade and the Insurance Exchange loomed overhead.

Larry carefully tucked the cardboard box under his arm and exited the station. He walked seven blocks east on Van Buren to

Michigan Avenue and turned north, passing the Chicago Architecture Foundation.

Tourist buses were parked across the street, waiting for the doors of the Art Institute of Chicago to open for daily tours.

The Chicago Numismatic and Coin Museum also offered tours, but only twice a week. The American public did not grasp the magic of stamps, coins and paper money nearly as much as the naked statues and paintings across the street.

The museum took up the second, third and fourth floors of the tall commercial building. The building's soaring brick profile was Egyptian inspired. It was the last building of its kind before the city discovered the art of building skyscrapers. The Monadnock building, as it was called, had an eternal fragrance from the smell of limestone mortar and bricks. One member of the museum board said it had the smell of Barbasol shaving cream.

Larry turned down the alley next to the museum and entered through the employee entrance.

Moe, an arthritic security guard wearing a gun belt with pouches for pepper spray and a flashlight greeted him. Moe had been guarding the side door since the Democratic National Convention in the 1960's.

"Good morning, Mr. Settlebottom. I didn't expect to see you today, given the circumstances."

"I'm a guardian of the public trust," said Larry. "I have a duty."

"Just like the post office, come rain or shine," said Moe.

Larry rode the elevator to the fourth floor and strode down the polished hallway to his office.

Carol, a woman in her sixties with a dead husband and forty years of experience opening mail and fielding calls was already at her desk. She was his assistant since the museum opened its doors ten years ago. Mrs. Chumley had picked Carol personally. Carol was an excellent gate-keeper. She didn't like gossip and always kept her docile boss at arm's length from predators.

"Good morning, Mr. S."

"Good morning, Carol."

"How was the funeral?"

"Tears and laughter as expected."

"That's good," said Carol. "I'm sure Mrs. Chumley enjoyed the spectacle."

"She did."

Larry opened the door to his office and set the cardboard box on his desk. He called out to Carol, "What time do our philatelic researchers come in?"

"Vivian and Andrew have titles, Mr. S. They're called Collections Managers."

"Of course, of course."

Carol glanced at a wall clock. "They should be in the stamp lab now. Why? What's up?"

Larry removed his trench coat and hung it on a peg. "I have a special project from Mrs. Chumley. I also have a major announcement. Can you put something together for next week? I want the entire board and all the troops there."

"George Chumley's private stamp and coin collection?"

"Yes. His study is wall to wall with the stuff. Rosemary has no use for them. I think we just increased the museum's value twofold."

Carol whistled. "You'll be the new star of Michigan Avenue. Too bad we're a non-profit."

"I didn't ask for it. The Chumley's have always been our most generous donors."

"Talk about job security."

"And call Nancy. Have her meet us in the research lab when she arrives."

Larry sat at his desk. He was elated. His job security for the next ten years was only an armored car delivery away. He was already the youngest director, president and CEO of any major museum in the entire Midwest. The latest Chumley acquisition would provide him years of carefree weekends, listening to his jazz and blues records behind the closed curtains of his house on the South Side.

He pressed his hands together and said a small prayer. "God bless Rosemary Chumley!"

CHAPTER 8

Larry rode the elevator down a floor, the brown cardboard box tucked under his arm. He rarely visited the museum's research departments. At the far end of the hallway were two large offices. The one on the right was for coins and paper money. The glass door to his left held the stamp research and restoration department. Larry entered the clean white lab. The lights were turned down low, the soft rumble of an air purifying system working overhead.

An illuminated glass table stood in the center of the room. A camera was mounted on it, displaying a magnified image on a computer screen hanging over the table. Around the edges of the room were a photo enlarger, two flatbed scanners, a large format printer for making posters and a dozen flat tables with rows of sliding drawers under them.

47

Vivian Link and Andrew Licker were studying the enlarged image of a Chinese stamp featuring a sitting black monkey in the forefront of a red background. The number 8 was prominent in the lower right field. Chinese writing appeared on the upper left corner. Vivian and Andrew were two of the best researchers in the country with forty years of philatelic studies between them. The researchers wore white lab coats and protective gloves.

Larry approached. "What have we here?"

Vivian pointed at the enlarged image. "A new donation. A perforated 1980 Red Monkey stamp."

"Issued in the Year of the Golden Monkey," said Andrew.

Vivian continued. "In Chinese culture the number 8 and the color red are both seen as lucky. It's one of the most sought after contemporary stamps in Asia, designed by Huang Yongyu and Shao Bolin."

"Printed with photogravure and recess printing methods," said Andrew.

"Value?" said Larry.

"Only ten bucks American," said Andrew. "Five million copies were printed."

The door opened behind them. The museum's conservator entered. Nancy Grace was a small woman, all of five feet tall and a self-proclaimed hippie from the seventies. She found a pair of white lab coats on a rack and handed Larry one.

"You know the rules, Larry."

Larry set his package on the table and slipped on the offered coat.

Nancy stared at the box. "News travels fast. From Mrs. Chumley?"

"Yes," said Larry. "Perhaps you can shed some light."

Nancy slipped on latex gloves and opened the box carefully. She pulled out the bottle and mounted stamp. Andrew and Vivian leaned in, curious.

"The stamp was being viewed by George Chumley when he died," said Larry. He pulled the yellowed envelope from his pocket. "I believe this came with it. No postmark. No return address."

He opened the envelope and put the handwritten note on the table for all to read.

G – Get ready to have your socks knocked off. The package should arrive next week. Believe me; it's worth every shilling you paid for it. – B.

"Any conclusions?" said Larry.

"The writer of the note used the word *shilling*," said Nancy. "It was a common coin once used in the British Empire."

“Which may imply the writer of the note is Irish, Scottish, English, Australian, or even an American,” said Vivian.

“American?”

“The shilling was frequently used in the thirteen colonies before we devised a gold standard,” added Nancy.

“The writer has a sense of humor,” said Andrew, “probably an older person.”

Larry nodded. “Mrs. Chumley is tracking down the source of the note. We believe whoever wrote it was paid by her husband.”

Nancy rubbed her hands together. “Now for the contents of the box.”

Larry took up the bottle with a latex glove and showed the others the hand-engraved numbers, reading them aloud. “19.761534,-108.369141. I have no idea what they mean.”

“I can run some algorithms,” said Andrew. “I’ve seen wide-mouthed bottles like these before. Central American, maybe Mexico. By the shape of it, the bottle didn’t come from a major production run. It isn’t machine molded. Looks like it came from a small batch.”

Larry picked up the cork and held it to Nancy’s nose. “Salt?”

Nancy sniffed the cork. “Yes,” she said.

“My guess is the stamp was shipped inside it,” said Larry.

"Like a message in a bottle?"

"Exactly."

Andrew leaned in and studied the bottle. "It has a wide mouth. Rectangular in shape. More like a jar than a bottle. Could have been used to store honey or fruit preserves."

"Could be ornamental," said Vivian. "Potpourri or bath salts."

"May I?" Andrew asked Larry. He took the bottle and sniffed inside. "I detect alcohol." He dragged a pen along the bottle. "This bottle was exposed to high humidity or water. When it dried out the salts in the bottle leached out and caused these crusty deposits of hard alkaline on the surface. Notice the crizzling? These fine cracks reduce the transparency of the glass. It's known as Glass Disease. A fault in the chemical composition of the original glass formula."

Nancy looked at her researchers. "Thoughts?"

Andrew scratched his head. "What we have here is a mystery wrapped in a mystery."

"A very vague mystery," said Vivian. "But let's run with this a bit. In the 16th century, the English navy used bottled messages to send information about enemy positions ashore. Shipwrecked sailors often wrote their last words and set them adrift. Many were found years later in all parts of the world. Scientists still use floating bottles to determine ocean undercurrents."

"But as is often the case, a message in a bottle can take decades at sea before they are discovered," said Nancy.

"In all likelihood," said Vivian. "May we examine the stamp, Larry?"

"By all means."

Vivian carefully picked up the mounted stamp and laid it under a projection magnifier. The image of the stamp was projected on a large screen. The researchers gathered together and studied the image.

"Oh my!" said Nancy.

"What have we here?" said Andrew.

"It's beautiful," said Nancy.

"Such detail!" said Vivian.

"Makes me horny," said Andrew.

"You haven't been horny since George W. Bush was in office," said Vivian.

Larry stood behind them. As he had done before in the Chumley study, his cheeks blushed from seeing the mermaid image.

"Is it a stamp?" he said.

Vivian rubbed her chin. “I don’t think so. Nancy?”

“Not a stamp,” said Nancy. “But we’ll call it one for lack of a better name.”

“I’ve never seen such detail in a work of miniature art,” said Andrew. “Who could have drawn such a thing?”

“It is quite exquisite,” said Nancy.

“Maybe priceless,” suggested Vivian.

“Can you tell its age?” said Larry.

“It will take some time,” said Nancy. “We have several ingredients to consider. What kind of ink was used on the stamp? What is the material of the stamp itself? Who could draw with such skill? Where did the bottle come from? Who wrote the note?”

“And is the stamp a message?” said Vivian.

“What do you mean?” said Larry.

Vivian’s eyes fell on the image of the mermaid. “Just look at her, the way she stares at us, pleading.”

“I had a similar reaction when I first saw it,” said Larry.

Andrew rubbed his chin. “What I see is a woman asking to be rescued.”

“She’s a *mermaid*,” said Vivian.

"Is she?" said Andrew. "Or just a model painted like a mermaid?"

Nancy turned off the overhead projector. "Marching orders, Larry?"

"Put all available resources on this. I promised Mrs. Chumley we'd get to the bottom of things. She'll find our note's author. You'll discover the rest."

"Vivian will start with the forensics first. We'll get a date on the stamp. Find out the ingredients," said Nancy. "Mind if we get a few friends involved? We'll be discreet."

"Who do you have in mind?" said Larry.

"Barb Woodley, a personal friend at the Field Museum, and our dear Hillary Griffith across the street at the Art Institute. Her team is the best in the nation. The artist of the stamp? He or she obviously painted before. We might find a link."

"I'll spend my time with the bottle," said Andrew. "See if I can narrow down the origin."

"Thank you everyone," said Larry. "And no mention of the Chumleys."

"Our lips are sealed," said Nancy.

Vivian zipped her fingers across her lips. "Shut tight. I am the mistress of misdirection."

Andrew raised his hand. "My vow of professional silence."

Larry took off the lab coat and hung it by the door. "Just one more thing — Rosemary Chumley is donating George's entire coin and stamp collection to us. Do you realize what this means for the museum?"

"The Chumley wing is about to get a whole lot bigger," said Nancy.

"With lots of overtime for us," said Vivian.

"And a free pack of Chumley's Chews with every admission ticket," said Andrew.

"Keep me informed," said Larry.

He spent the rest of his day speaking with the museum's legal counsel. An audit of the Chumley donation was necessary to determine its value.

Larry called Rosemary Chumley in the afternoon and reported his progress. An armored car was arranged for the following day to collect the new assets.

"What was the reaction of your team when they viewed the stamp?" said Rosemary.

"They are enamored of it," said Larry.

"Did anyone blush?"

"Just me — again," Larry admitted.

Rosemary Chumley laughed over the phone. "Oh, Lawrence! Such a prude! Georgie used to make me blush. He said it was a sign of a great lover."

"I wasn't blushing at her bare breasts, Rosemary. It was something else."

"Like what?"

"Guilt, maybe a sense of helplessness. I don't know."

"Let's hope we can get to the bottom of this," said Rosemary. "By the by, I have a lead on who sent the stamp."

"Oh?"

"A wire deposit was made from one of George's hobby accounts to a bank in Guatemala recently. My accountant is tracking down the recipient."

"What was the dollar amount?"

"A hundred thousand dollars."

"Only a few rare stamps bring that price," said Larry. "But then again, we're not dealing with a stamp, Rosemary."

"What then?"

"A rare work of art."

CHAPTER 9

Pharaoh Williams stood on the platform outside the 99th Street station, waiting for the six o'clock to arrive. He was perspiring from the muggy summer heat. He had decided that today he would make his first real contact with Settlebottom. He had rehearsed his story several times, often stopping to press his hand on a Bible for strength. He saw the train moving south on the tracks towards him. Pharaoh touched the silk tie on his chest, adjusted the stiff collar of his white shirt, felt the weight of the briefcase in his hand, filled with old classified ads offering jobs he could never get.

The train slowed and came to a stop. Pharaoh knew which set of steps Mr. Settlebottom would exit the train from. He always rode in the third car. Pharaoh cozied up to the side door and watched several pairs of feet reaching down the steps; a beige lady's shoe — slip-on brown loafers on a man's swollen ankles — white nursing shoes — now a polished size ten black lace-up shoe. Mr. Settlebottom's shoe.

Catlike for his size, Pharaoh lowered his head and bulled his way past the opening as Mr. Settlebottom stepped down. His shoulder met Settlebottom's midsection and carried him off the train, sending him sprawling sideways on the wooden platform, away from the train.

Pharaoh reached down for the man, offering a hand up. "Terribly sorry about that, sir. My mistake."

Mr. Settlebottom took Pharaoh's hand. Pharaoh pulled him to his feet and brushed him off with a handkerchief.

"Sometimes I get in such a hurry, I don't see where I'm goin'," Pharaoh apologized.

"Quite alright. Mistakes happen," said Larry. He adjusted his trench coat and attempted to step away.

Pharaoh stepped in front of him, wiping at his lapels. "At least you didn't fall under the tracks," said Pharaoh. "Hell of a way to die, gettin' run over by a commuter train."

"I can't imagine it," said Larry.

Pharaoh took a small step back, looking up and down at Larry with a canny eye. "Say, I know you! You live on Prospect Street. I see you turn there every day. You got a long step."

“Yes, well...”

Pharaoh turned to let Mr. Settlebottom pass, then charged up next to him, walking stride for stride.

“Let me see if I can keep up with you today. Just this one time.”

Larry nodded. They walked side by side for a quarter of a block.

“Yeah, this feels good,” said Pharaoh. “I like the longer steps. Makes the blood flow. Say, you work downtown?”

“Yes,” said Larry.

“I’ll bet you’re a banker,” said Pharaoh.

Larry smiled self-consciously. “No. No banker. I work in a museum.”

“No shit!” Pharaoh said with all the surprise he could manage. “What you got there? Dinosaurs? Fish? Inventions?”

“Stamps and coins, mostly.”

“No shit!” said Pharaoh. He took a few large steps, got in front of Larry and walked backwards. He reached into his pocket and pulled out a two-dollar bill. “I carry this in my pocket for luck. Had it two years now. My mama, she says it’s worth a lot more than two dollars. Can you look at it for me?”

Larry slowed down and stopped. He took the bill from Pharaoh’s hand and studied it. “It was printed in 1976. Not old enough or rare enough to be a collectible.”

Pharaoh came alongside Larry. "Turn it over. Look what's on the back."

Larry studied the back of the bill.

"Look at all those men signing the Declaration of Independence," said Pharaoh. "Now that's worth sumpin'."

"They called the 1976 series bicentennial twos." Larry offered the bill back to Pharaoh. "Still only worth two dollars."

Pharaoh stared up at the sky and let out an exaggerated sigh. "Some luck I got — I thought I was carryin' my ticket outta Chicago."

They started walking again.

"Guess where I want to go?" said Pharaoh.

"I have no idea," said Larry.

"Florida," said Pharaoh. "I want to live on a beach where the sun shines every day. You ever been to Florida?"

"No," said Larry. "I'm not much of a traveler."

"Me neither," said Pharaoh. "Got too much work to do here. Got to feed my family. You got family? A wife and kids?"

"No," said Larry.

"Oh!" said Pharaoh. "You is proudly single like me."

"But you said you have to feed your family," said Larry.

"I mean my mama and sisters," said Pharaoh. "My daddy, he's in prison for drugs."

"Oh."

Pharaoh stepped ahead of Larry again and came in for another block. He offered his hand. "Name's Pharaoh Williams."

Larry shook his hand. "Lawrence Settlebottom. Or Larry."

"A pleasure, Larry. Nice meeting someone new in the neighborhood."

Larry blushed. "Oh, I'm not new."

They walked another block. Mr. Settlebottom wasn't the inquisitive type. Pharaoh had to drive the conversation.

"Me? I'm a bouncer at a nightclub," said Pharaoh. "Fights every night. No problem. I'm good with my fists."

Larry nodded.

"Now if anybody picks on you? You just holler. Pharaoh Williams is your man."

"My life is rather organized," said Larry. "I don't see many fights in my future."

"You can say that, but danger is everywhere," said Pharaoh. "Happens in a stroke from a stranger. I know these streets better than anybody."

They reached Prospect Street.

"I turn here," said Larry. "Nice talking to you, Pharaoh."

Pharaoh stopped and watched Larry walk away. "Hey, it was nice meeting you, Larry. We'll do it again sometime."

Larry waved back at him. "Thank you," was all he said.

Pharaoh crossed the street and headed east.

"Well, I finally met him face to face," Pharaoh told himself. "He's an odd one to be sure. Didn't even notice my suit."

CHAPTER 10

The walk-in pantry off the kitchen was now a pedestrian wine cellar. Larry decided on a twenty dollar Merlot for his evening concert. Corkscrew and glass in hand, he opened the door to what was once the main bedroom where his mothers had slept. The room was a repository now. There was a distinct aroma in the room, the fragrance of paper sleeves and color printed card jackets, shellac wax, lacquer and vinyl.

After burying his mothers, Larry had followed three Catholic mourning traditions. The first was an intense deep mourning period. He wore only dark dress shirts and black suits for three months, turning down all social engagements. The following two months, during half mourning, he carried a white handkerchief in the breast pocket of his dark suit and sported a white shirt with dark ties. In the final stage of mourning – light mourning – his dress was hardly noticed, fitting closely to his everyday attire; black or gray suits with thin white pinstripes and usually a pale pastel purple shirt.

In further homage to his deceased mothers, coupled with the sudden death of his conniving and deceitful betrothed, Larry did not date nor consider offers to dinner or the theater.

There was a constant parade of women available to him; well-bred women mostly, a few artistic types from the downtown museums. All with credentials of stellar schools, all aware that perhaps Larry Settlebottom might be a secret heir to the childless aging Chumleys.

But Larry had no interest in anyone. He claimed he had no time for love, that he was still grieving. But the truth was that he was too busy perfecting this sound-proof room, investing in a personal musical library with a sound system to rival the most prolific audiophiles in the country. He had the turntables, the speakers, amps and headphones. Depending on his mood he could rattle the walls with jazz or tear them down with the blues.

Larry's turntables could spin any record from any era in the war of the speeds between 331/3 RPM, 45 RPM, 78 RPM and beyond. LPs, EPs, maxi-singles, 10 inch, 12 inch, 7 inch, it didn't matter.

He was still an amateur diamond needle doctor, but Larry's search for vinyl records had taken him to a slew of used record shops across Chicagoland in his hunt to build a high-fidelity collection of music with the warm, mahogany-rich sound that vinyl was famous for. He had narrowed his record collection to music recorded in analog. Mostly jazz and blues with a dash of Broadway, teasing movie soundtracks and a short stack of marching band music from John Philip Sousa, America's March King.

Larry remembered his first exposure to jazz and the blues. It was on an Ash Wednesday when he was a boy. A new nightclub had opened a block down from the orphanage. When night fell, the sweet but disturbing sound of a lone saxophone echoed down the street and up to his window perch.

Larry ventured out in the cold, drawn to it. He stood under the neon sign of Tiny's Hideaway and saw a black man through the smoked glass window, standing on a small stage blowing his heart out on the sax. A hunched drummer, bent over a small snare between his legs started adding rat-a-tat-tats, and then a man started plucking away with rough fingers on a stand-up bass.

Larry had stood there, transfixed, oblivious to the cold, his steamed breath fogging the window between him and the magic until the men were but a blur. The resonance of the music moved the glass like a faint heartbeat. Larry put his hand on the window and felt the music enter his body. He stood there until the men finished their set and climbed off the stage to get their free drinks from a bartender. Larry slipped inside the doorway of the music lounge and stared at the upright saxophone leaning on a stand.

A man's deep voice spoke down to him with apology. "Sorry, kids ain't allowed after dark."

Larry remembered pointing at the saxophone, polished as bright as any priest's Sunday chalice.

"What is that?" Larry had asked the bouncer.

"Why, that's an axe, son. A saxophone."

"I never heard anything like it," said Larry.

"The man who plays it, he says it's an artificial heart. It can make people cry, make 'em laugh, make 'em dance. Depends on the night and the crowd. Tonight it's makin' people cry."

Larry couldn't remember walking back the distance between Tiny's Hideaway and the orphanage. The streetlights arced yellow and looked like saxophones. The roofs of cars were snare drums. Windows on buildings resembled fret boards on a bass. When he returned to his sleeping dormitory, Larry stood at the end of the long hallway. Chunks of children were hidden under their blankets, lined up like a row of corpses. Larry stood and listened a long time, past the snoring and sniffling until he thought he could hear their uncommon heartbeats in what he would learn was a syncopated rhythm. Though they were dispensable and unwanted, the sleeping children were very much alive in the world.

Now Larry had this sound library, a treasure trove of American sounds. A million heartbeats together in one room with an entire wall stacked with vinyl records from floor to ceiling. Everything in the room was born in the United States in the 20th century, all works by the masters of jazz and blues: sounds to confront the poverty of the soul, blue notes, syncopation, swing, call-and-response, polyrhythms, improvisation, movie soundtracks, military marches, Broadway, jams, freedom!

In here, listening to his music, Larry was cool and hip. He could scat on his fingers with trumpeter Wynton Marsalis or feel the real pain of a broken heart following Satchmo's wailing cornet.

Larry knew his Dixie, too! Never a better trumpet or clarinet solo than the tracks on *Potato Head Blues*!

In the groove, he refilled his wine glass, listening to the free jazz of John Coltrane.

He spun another record. Duke Ellington banging on the piano. Such a cool cat!

Another record. Thelonius Monk.

"You poor broke genius! Bebop it! Smart it up! Free it up! Man, oh man!"

He tossed Dizzy on the turntable. "Nail those high notes! Put me on the moon!"

And so the night went. An orgy of beautiful sound.

It was almost ten. The bottle of Merlot was empty now. Larry slipped the last record on the spin table; soft jazz, calm and smooth, linear with poetic license. It didn't wobble.

He thought about the man he had met at the train station: Pharaoh Williams. Did he know his jazz and blues? Did he think of it as racist as some did? A reminder of the oppressive umbrella of white society? Did Pharaoh know about the Chicago Style developed by white musicians like Bud Freeman and Eddie Condon or Benny Goodman and Gene Krupa with their big band swing? They both came out of Chicago in the 1930's. They also included black musicians in their bands.

He thumbed through a stack of records. Tomorrow was Ladies' Night. Ethel Waters singing "Stormy Weather" followed by Billie Holiday, Ella Fitzgerald, Dinah Washington, Abbey Lincoln, and Anita O'Day.

He already had his weekend planned. He'd be taking the A train with the Big Band sounds of Count Basie, Cab Calloway, and Duke Ellington.

Old George Chumley liked his stamps. Larry liked his music. His private collection was growing, hidden in a bedroom on a quiet Chicago street, the walls insulated for sound. It was Larry's sanctuary to explore deep-seated emotions never brought to light until now.

CHAPTER 11

Andrew Licker sat on a stool in the lab. He loved a good challenge. In some ways he was a cultural anthropologist, digging into human history. That's why he was drawn to the world of numismatics and stamps.

The glass bottle offered a similar challenge. Andrew was fascinated by the beauty and functional elegance of glass. Glass had a fascinating history as well.

The bottle definitely smelled of alcohol. Andrew added water to the bottle and shook it vigorously. He poured the liquid into a glass beaker and sealed it. He would overnight mail the sample to a water testing lab. Maybe there was a clue in the water's chemical composition and trace elements.

After work, he visited a large liquor store downtown and cruised the aisles. Spirits were stored in all shapes and sizes. The odder-shaped bottles contained liqueurs and tequilas. He showed a photograph of the mermaid bottle to a store clerk.

"You ever see a bottle like this?"

"Looks handmade," said the clerk. "We only buy our liquor from the major distilleries."

Andrew visited a fragrance store next and found several handcrafted jars. Some held candles, others contained potpourri. Similar shapes. Nothing definitive. Since he was a middle-aged single man, Andrew indulged himself in the purchase of a cinnamon-scented candle.

When he arrived at his apartment near the Lincoln Park zoo, Andrew turned on his laptop. He leaned the photograph of the mermaid bottle next to it and spent two hours looking at bottle and jar images from Central America and Mexico. Once a year Andrew vacationed in Costa Rica at a timeshare he owned. He knew he had seen bottles like the one in the photograph before.

He researched bottle manufacturing. Such beautiful things made by man, from recipes of sand, limestone and soda ash melted in furnaces and shaped into molten glass. From there the glass was cut into gobs and formed into beautiful, functional containers. After the glass was formed it was reheated and gradually cooled to relieve stress and strengthen the glass. Perhaps the mermaid bottle had a signature in its design.

He made a short list of bottle manufacturing plants in Mexico, found the emails of their executives and sent queries to them with an attached image of the bottle.

I work for The Chicago Coin and Stamp Museum. We are trying to determine the manufacturer of this bottle. Can you help?

Gracias,

Andrew Licker – Collections Manager

He typed the numbers from the mystery bottle into a search engine and did a random search. There were no results. He took out the commas and periods between the numbers. Still nothing. He typed the numbers in from last to first. Nada. He took a wild leap and searched winning lottery numbers. Nope.

Satisfied with his day's progress, Andrew poured himself a glass of Chianti, sat on the small deck of his apartment and listened to the distant voices of distraught animals in their cages echoing up from the zoo. He wondered what might happen if all the animals were freed. How long would they survive on the wild streets of Chicago? He was an educated man, smart enough not to leave his apartment after dark. There were lions and tigers and bears out there with human faces lurking in the shadows of the concrete jungle.

CHAPTER 12

The morning sun beat down on the dry scrabble island.

El Gordo appeared in the doorway of his metal shack. He stood over seven feet tall, weighing close to five hundred pounds. His hands and feet and toes and fingers were large and thick. His jaw was prominent. So was his forehead. He had a huge flat nose on his broad baby-face. He was only thirty but he seemed older, his face bloated and splotched with pockmarks. He wore his hair long to hide his disfigurement. When he spoke, his words always came out swollen and distorted.

Gordo focused his eyes around him for the long day ahead. He did not see well. Things far away were a blur. He knew what boats looked like. He knew the shapes of human bodies, the stooped backs of the old ones under his control.

Wood was scarce on the island. What was available would be needed to fuel the fires for the pulque soon. The fence rails surrounding the shacks had been torn down and stacked in piles.

Wooden chairs and tables had been gathered and smashed. Wooden planks had been torn away from walls and roofs, replaced with pieces from dead people's boats. Things that did not burn. Sheets of plastic, fiberglass, and metal. The once promising little village had turned ugly. Gordo didn't care. He wanted his pulque.

He wiped the sweat from his forehead with a dirty rag. Today's headache was as bad as yesterday's. There were two plastic jugs on the table under the tin awning of his shack. He picked up one of the jugs and drank from it. A vent of red liquid dripped down his chin. It was a cheap table wine and not very good. He finished off the contents and tossed the empty jug into a pile of discarded cans, bottles and other jugs.

El Gordo picked up the second jug and smelled it. He needed water in his body. He drank it grudgingly. Finished, he walked up to a line of fish hung to dry. Gordo was sick of fish. Fish in the morning, at night.

"Woman!" he yelled towards the shack. "Food!"

Ismelda appeared at the entrance of the shack. A thin soiled sheet was draped over her naked body. There were bruise marks on her arms and face.

"I have a name," she said.

"You are just a thing to me now," the pig said.

She returned to the shack.

Around Gordo's neck, on a chain, were several keys. He took off the chain and went to a locked metal locker leaning against his shack. He found a key and opened the locker. There were cans on the shelves. He couldn't read the labels but there were pictures of cured ham, corned beef, chicken and potted meats. He took a can and set it on the plastic table.

Ismelda came out, wearing a thin, worn dress and sandals.

Gordo held up the can. "What is this?"

Ismelda read the label. "Chinese food. Sweet and sour chicken."

"Is it good?"

"No."

Gordo grunted and tossed the can on the ground. He reached inside the locker and pulled a handful of freeze-dried bags from a shelf. There were no pictures.

"What are these?"

Ismelda read the labels. "Chili mac with beef, chicken and dumplings and beef stroganoff with noodles."

"Gringo food," he said.

"Just add water," she said.

"How much water?"

"Just a little." She stared off at the smaller shacks on the nearby hill. "The old ones are working hard. Give them something besides fish and flowers to eat."

He handed her the bag of chicken and dumplings. "They can eat the Chinese can, too," he said. He handed her a freeze-dried bag of beef stroganoff.

"You feed me first."

He went inside the shack and returned with a pair of binoculars. They helped him see much better.

"We will have new visitors soon. More gringos in boats lost at sea. They will bring us things to burn, food, whiskey and beer. Clothes for the old ones, maybe guns and bullets." He turned and stared at Ismelda. "You would like a gun, so you can kill me."

Ismelda ignored his comment. Of course she wanted to kill him. Everyone on the island wanted him dead, especially her.

"But you cannot kill me," Gordo laughed. "I am a giant made of stone."

"You are just a thing like me," said Ismelda.

CHAPTER 13

Larry entered the museum lab. Nancy, Vivian and Andrew were at a table drinking their morning coffee. Larry slipped on a lab coat and joined them at the table.

Andrew slid a paper cup in front of him. “Green tea with honey,” he said.

“Thank you,” said Larry. He sipped the tea. It was good. “Any luck with the bottle?”

“I shipped an ingredient sample to a lab. I also sent several inquiries to bottle manufacturers. Waiting on the results.”

“And the numbers on the bottle?”

“Nothing yet. Give me some time.”

“We have a busy day planned for you,” Nancy told Larry. “Vivian will take you to the Field Museum this morning to analyze the stamp’s composition, then you and I have a date at the Art Institute.”

Barb Woodley waited on the bottom steps of the Field Museum, a neoclassical enormity south of the Chicago Loop. The natural history museum was world renowned for its academic research across many disciplines of study. Woodley, an attractive woman in her thirties, waved to Vivian and Larry as they exited the yellow cab.

"Right on schedule," Barb called out.

She led them up the steps, past tall pillars through wide glass and bronze doors.

Barb Woodley flashed her security pass to a guard. "VIP's," she announced.

Standing over them in the rotunda were the fossilized remains of Sue, the world's largest known skeleton of a Tyrannosaurus Rex.

"Sixty-seven million years old and sex unknown," said Woodley. "Based on her fetching smile, we assume she's female. Careful, Larry, I hear she's biting today."

They turned down a long hallway crowded with permanent exhibits and dioramas depicting mammals from Asia and Africa. The most notable exhibit was the infamous Lions of Tsavo, a pair of stuffed man-eating lions reputed to have attacked and devoured workers building a railroad bridge in the Kenyan savannah. The stuffed lions had been on display for over a hundred years.

"Well worth the $5,000 purchase," said Barb. "Their killing spree was greatly exaggerated. One of our biologists studied the chemical composition of the lions' hair keratin and bone collagen and measured the ratio of carbon and nitrogen isotopes. He estimated they only ate about thirty-five workers."

They passed through Grainger Hall, a large collection of diamonds and gems from around the world. Some of the jade artifacts were eight thousand years old.

"I saw you at the Chumley mansion after the funeral," Barb said in a near whisper to Larry. "I didn't have a chance to say hello. The widow whisked you away before I could grab you."

"She's on a mission. Miss Woodley. Which is why I'm here," said Larry.

"This stamp business," acknowledged Barb. "Everyone on Michigan Avenue is talking about it."

Larry looked at Vivian.

"Don't look at me," she said. "My lips are sealed. Remember?"

Barb tugged at Larry's sleeve. "You must know, Larry. There are no real secrets when it comes to Chicago's elite. They gossip more than children."

They turned down a new hall, past several permanent exhibits.

"Two million people visit us annually," said Woodley. "We have to keep things fresh and full of biodiversity in our collections. Our academic research is the best in the world when it come s to anthropological collections. We've been to every nook and cranny of every continent."

"And brought it all here," said Larry.

Barb smiled. "We have twenty-four million specimens and objects of interest between these walls. I can't even count how many books, journals, and photo archives are in our library. Everything imaginable from evolutionary biology, geology, archaeology, ethnology and material culture. Are you asleep yet?"

"Almost," said Larry.

"Forget the politicians. We're the true stewards of the future."

They turned into the Pritzker DNA Discovery Center, a working research lab. A dozen high school students stood at a large plate glass window watching researchers performing experiments on the other side of the glass. Large screens overhead displayed a moving image projected from a microscope. It looked like a piece of orange string pulling a fuzzy green ball along a strand of carpet.

"What is that?" Vivian asked Woodley.

"It's a myosin protein dragging an endorphin along a filament to the inner part of the brain's parietal cortex. We think it creates happiness." Woodley smiled. "Who says molecular biology isn't exciting?" She swiped a card next to a closed door and gained access to the lab. "We have a few methods at our disposal here. The ink on your stamp will give us some clues as to its origin. Plant or animal, all life has a DNA signature."

"Will your tests harm the stamp?" said Larry.

"No. We use imaging."

She led them past the scientists in public view to a back room filled with state-of-the-art equipment.

A young biologist wearing a lab coat pulled himself away from a microscope and greeted them with a firm handshake. "Tom Fargo. At your disposal."

Woodley turned to Larry. "The stamp?"

"Yes, of course," said Larry. He fished through his jacket and pulled out a clean handkerchief. The mermaid stamp was inside, sealed in its protective glass.

Fargo took the stamp from him and mounted it on a microscope. "The tree of life is quite diverse but we have lots of tools at our disposal. Photo imaging, CT and laser scans, photogrammetry. The DNA genetic sequencing should find a barcoded species match in our digital registries."

"It's boring stuff," said Woodley. "Lots of DNA helixes to sift through. You can tour the museum or grab a cup of coffee at the Bistro while you wait."

Larry looked to Vivian for a decision.

"You go play, Larry. I'll stay here and guard the stamp,"

Woodley handed Larry a wireless pager. "We'll buzz you when we have something."

He left the lab and wandered the hallways of the museum. Not much caught his eye. The complex world of natural history held little interest to him. His life was simple, organized. No confusion.

There was a swarm of kids and their corralling teachers ahead of him. Larry found a stairwell to avoid the crowd and ascended the steps.

On the next level he found a quiet gallery shrouded in dim light. The wood-trimmed room was cooler than other areas of the museum. Inside was a collection of embalmed animals mounted in glass cases marked EXTINCT. It was a haunted room. A cemetery.

One case held a Sumatran tiger. Another held the skeleton of a black emu. Dozens of odd specimens were in various stages of completion from whole taxidermy examples to partial skeletal remains. Lemurs, lions, rats, birds, fish. Dead things. Gone things. Forever lost. Some died from natural events. Cold spells, volcanoes, drought. Most were driven to extinction by the encroachment of humans, the hand-maidens of agriculture and growing cities.

At the far end of the room stood a case featuring a tall skeleton. From the torso up it appeared to be proportionally human. Below the torso it had long extended giraffe-like legs and hooves.

Larry bent over and read the plaque aloud. "World Columbian Exposition - 1893. Real or fake?"

"It's fake," said a voice behind him. Larry stood and saw Barb Woodley. "I tried to page you. Your battery must be dead."

Larry studied the skeleton again. "It seems so real."

"We've seen hundreds of hoaxes come through the museum over the years. Even had a special exhibit dedicated to them. Every hoax under one roof. Aliens made from moose bones, a petrified giant carved from gypsum. My favorite was the mummified Fiji mermaid. It had the torso and head of a juvenile monkey sewn to the back half of a fish. She also had teeth, tits, fish scales and animal hair. It's amazing what you can do with chemicals, stains and acids."

"I'm surprised the museum carried such a shoddy exhibit."

"We were sold out for a month. People want the fantastic."

Larry handed her the dead pager. "Are the results in?"

"They are. Not what you might have expected, I'm sure."

They started towards the exit together.

"Are you still single?" said Woodley.

"I don't have time for relationships," said Larry.

"Well, if you ever find the time, start with me."

Larry almost tripped at the words. She was an attractive woman. Worldly.

Woodley grabbed him by the arm and dragged him along. "Don't be so shy, Larry. You're a grown m an. Good-looking too, I might add."

Andrew Licker checked emails on his cell phone. There were two replies from bottle manufacturers. One of them did not know the manufacturer of origin and suggested it was a homemade bottle. The second email from Alibaba Industries was more interesting. The rep wrote that the bottle was made by *Perro Grande*, Big Dog Bottling located in Guadalajara, Mexico. The company made short runs of cheap bottles shipped mostly to small villages around the state of Oaxaca. The bottles were purchased by small-run makers of mescal and tequila, mostly used for local festivals. "Like backyard hooch or American moonshine," suggested the rep.

Andrew left the museum and walked to his favorite hot dog stand under the elevated tracks at Wabash and Madison. He ordered a Windy City classic hot dog with all the trimmings, found a clean bench near the stand and gobbled down the dog. With time to kill, he walked along the busy shops, first on Wabash, then down Michigan Avenue back towards the museum. His eyes were drawn to a window display at a map store. Inside was an assortment of world globes rotating on their stands. Behind them, on the wall, was a large modern world map painted in fresco.

Andrew tried to remember his high school geography lessons. The horizontal lines on the map indicated latitude, the angular distance, in degrees, minutes, and seconds of a point north or south of the Equator. There were five main parallels: The Arctic Circle, Tropic of Cancer, the Equator, the Tropic of Capricorn and the Antarctic Circle.

He looked at the odd numbers associated with them. The Tropic of Cancer's numerical identity was 23°26′13.8″ N.

The vertical lines on the map indicated longitude, points east or west of the Prime Meridian in Greenwich, England. The meridians were not parallel. They came together at the Poles.

"Interesting," said Andrew.

He entered the map store and purchased a folding world map. He found a booklet intended for a child in elementary school which explained the mechanics of map-reading. A second purchase.

Bag in hand, Andrew returned to the lab and laid out the map. He compared the sequence of numbers on the bottle and referred to the booklet for insight. 19.761534,-108.369141. After two frustrating hours, he determined the first sequence of numbers 19.761534 indicated latitude. The second set of numbers after the comma - 108.369141 - referred to longitude. He looked at the numbers as minutes and seconds.

"Sixty minutes in each degree. Each minute is divided into sixty seconds. Seconds are divided into tenths, and so on —."

He triangulated the latitude numbers with the longitude numbers and marked his spot on the map with a post-it note.

"That's it!" he realized. "An absolute location."

Larry and Barb Woodley returned to the DNA testing lab. Vivian and Fargo were sitting on stools, studying print-outs with a handful of specialists pulled in from the Regenstein Pacific Conservation Laboratory upstairs.

"Ah!" Fargo said to Larry. "We thought we lost you!"

"I found him in the frozen food section," said Woodley.

She pulled up a pair of stools and sat with Larry across from the scientists.

Fargo slid the encased mermaid stamp across the table to Larry. "That's quite the artwork there," said Fargo. "I could stare at it all day."

"What did you find?" said Larry.

Fargo looked at his notes. "You want the science geek or the layman's version?"

"Layman, please."

"Okay, first of all, the image wasn't drawn with any plant-derived ink. I saw that the minute I blew up the image. It was blood."

"Blood?"

"Bat's blood," said one of the scientists. "More specifically, the blood of a long-nosed bat."

Fargo took over the conversation. "The blood contains traces of certain fish and insects found in marine waters along the western coast of Mexico. It also contains hints of nectar found in the flowers of Agave plants."

"That specific?"

"Dead on. Long-nosed bats, *myotis vivesi,* are known to frequent small islands. Their range is naturally fragmented and limited. The long-nosed bat prefers to roost in caves or under rocks during the day. Your mermaid's ink also has traces of bat guano."

"Shit," said Woodley.

"I know what guano is," said Larry.

Fargo continued. "Depending on the bat's diet, their guano comes in many colors; red from eating crustaceans, black from eating fish. Green and brown guano are a result of feeding on algae and insects. The colored guano provided your artist with some variation in his drawing."

Fargo slid a map in front of Larry and circled an area with a thick pencil. "We narrowed it down for you. Based on species and diet matched to our databases, we believe the blood ink came from one of these remote islands two hundred miles northwest of Puerto Vallarta, Mexico."

"Out in the Pacific ocean?" said Vivian.

"Yes. Below the Gulf of Mexico, also known as the Sea of Cortez."

"So my message in a bottle theory makes sense," said Larry. He wrapped the encased stamp in the handkerchief and stuck it in his pocket. "Can I keep the map? To show Mrs. Chumley."

Barb Woodley rolled it up and handed it to him. "Consider this a gift from the Field Museum."

Larry thanked the scientists profusely and hurried out of the museum towards a waiting taxi with Vivian. They rode north up the magnificent mile of Michigan Avenue towards downtown.

"And I thought stamp research was exciting. What do you think?" said Vivian.

"Heady stuff," said Larry.

"We're in the minor leagues compared to the staff at the Field," said Vivian.

They arrived at their own museum. Vivian paid the cab fare and hurried after Larry into the building.

Andrew and Nancy were waiting inside the lab. Andrew's package had arrived. The returned sample vial was on the table with results from the water testing lab.

Larry turned to Andrew. "What did you find?"

Andrew glanced at the lab results. "The salt content in the bottle confirms a concentration of seawater. There are also hints of soil and bacteria found only in the Gulf of California and areas south."

Larry rolled out the map he had taken from the Field Museum. "Which supports what we learned earlier." He pointed at the map. "The Field team believes the ink on the stamp came from one of these small islands west of Mexico."

"But it's not a true ink," said Vivian. "It's blood. *Bat's blood.*"

"Interesting!" said Andrew.

"You gotta be kiddin' me," said Nancy.

"The area on the map matches my research," said Andrew. "The bottle was made by *Perro Grande*, Big Dog Bottling out of Guadalajara, Mexico. I also took a geography lesson today." He unfolded the world map he had purchased earlier. "The numbers on the bottle? They indicate longitude and latitude. Puts us right here."

He pointed to a dot on Larry's smaller map. It was inside the circle Doctor Fargo had drawn.

"Nice work," said Larry.

"We have our what, where and when," said Nancy. "Now all we have left is our missing artist."

"Our *who*," said Larry. He hurried for the door. His associates stared after him, amazed looks on their faces.

"Is that the Larry Settlebottom we know?" said Vivian.

"I've never seen him so excited!" said Nancy.

Larry opened the door and looked at Nancy. "It's your turn. The Art Institute beckons."

CHAPTER 14

Hillary Griffith was beautiful, educated and flirtatious. She wore the latest clothes pictured on the front covers of fashion magazines.

"Thanks for having us," said Larry.

"Oh, I haven't had you yet, Larry," Hillary smiled coyly.

She led Larry and Nancy to a large studio. A handful of scholars, conservators, and researchers from the Ryerson Library and Department of Contemporary Art were waiting.

"Thank you all for coming," Griffith announced to the room.

"Oh my *gawd*," Nancy whispered to Larry. "The big fellow with the Van Dyke beard and the cane is Theodore Ash. He's the five hundred pound gorilla of art!"

Ash, a Canadian who had never held a brush or a chisel was famous for his keen eye, barbed wit and a thorough knowledge of art history. He wore a bold pastel suit on his rotund body that made him look like a ripe peach. His weight was supported by a willow cane. Ash was currently the E.C. Chadbourne Chair of art history, theory, and criticism at the School of the Art Institute of Chicago. His critiques and reviews were published in newspapers, magazines, books, and on web sites worldwide. His opinions stirred debates. They made or broke artist careers. Like the others in the room, he had been drawn to the street talk surrounding the stamp.

Griffith introduced Larry and Nancy to everyone. "We have all heard the buzz by now," said Griffith. "Mr. Settlebottom possesses something unusual. What everyone is calling '*The Mermaid Stamp*'. But is it a stamp or something else? A work of microscopic art? A masterpiece? A fraud? Something commercial? Something valuable?"

"All works of art have a value," said Nancy.

"Even stamps?" said Griffith.

"Stamp collecting is the most popular hobby in the world," said Nancy defensively. "Stamps are not just pictures on little pieces of paper. Stamps represent people, places and historical events."

"I'm curious," Griffith asked. "What is the most expensive stamp in history?"

Nancy answered. "The 1986 British Guiana One-Cent Black on Magenta. It bears the image of a three-masted ship and the colony's motto in Latin: '*We give and expect in return.*' It's blemished, battered and cut. Its value comes from its history. It began in the hands of a young Scottish boy, passed through a killer's hands. It recently sold at Sotheby's in New York for $9.5 million. One billion times the stamp's original face value."

"A tidy sum for a stamp," said the art critic Ash.

"Yes."

Griffith asked Larry, "Do you think your little mermaid is a stamp?"

"No," he said bluntly. "And neither will anyone in this room when you see it."

"Let me share its provenance as far as we know it," said Vivian. She told them what information her team had gathered so far; about the bottle and its origins, details of the ink used to draw the stamp, what radiography and infrared imaging revealed. "This artwork is recent. I doubt you'll find anything like it in your catalogues, archives, collections or dealer records. Our final piece of the puzzle is our missing artist."

"Well, you came to the right place," Griffith smiled. She crossed to a slide projector and turned it on. "Your stamp, please."

Larry felt the encased stamp in his breast pocket. "The stamp may be susceptible to light," he warned.

"This projector has a flat piece of heat-absorbing glass in the light path between the condensing lens and the slide. It will be fine."

Larry handed Griffith the encased stamp. She placed it on the flat surface of the projection screen. The image was a blur. An intern came to Griffith's aid and adjusted the focal points of the lens.

Nearly everyone present gasped at the clear concise mermaid image.

"Where should we begin?" Griffith asked Nancy.

"We're stamp and coin people. Educate us."

"What are we drawn to first?" Griffith asked the experts.

"The eyes," said an observer.

"Why?"

"The artist led us there."

"I agree. What next? The breasts or the tail?"

"The breasts are admirable," said Ash, "but the extended tail touching the sea widens the landscape of the work. The mermaid longs to return to the womb, perhaps?"

"On and on we can go," said Griffith, "building or demoting the value system of the piece. Values of light and dark, source, scale, tints, hue."

"Come now," said Ash. "Art isn't rational. Only a few works are considered commodities. Purchased art appeals to only one percent of the world's population. Wealthy people. Why the royal family of Qatar purchased Paul Cezanne's 'The Card Players' for $250 million dollars I have no idea. It destroyed the baseline for art values."

"I agree," said Griffith. "There is no standard of supply and demand. Over the years, the art world has invented unwritten variables as a starting point to determine prices. How big or small the image? What is the medium? The more difficult the medium, the higher the selling price."

A researcher rubbed her hands together. "Quality is a subjective term. This mermaid painting, *which it is*, defies the standards, encourages, and mystifies. It is magnificent in detail; time-consumed, a brilliant labor of love and madness. The superb miniscule strokes and effort of the artist is obvious. But to paint this magnificent thing on a miniscule canvas, put it in a bottle and set it adrift! Why, it boggles a rational mind."

"Perhaps the artist is one of the rare few who doesn't care for acclaim or fortune," said Ash with an odd confidence. "Maybe he or she has already achieved it. Take Picasso after his worldwide prominence. He would sit outside a café, draw a funny face on a napkin and sell it to the woman at the table next to him for thousands of dollars."

"Only if he signed it," joked Griffith.

"Or we have a tortured artist," said an art scholar. "A modern Vincent van Gogh, an ignored mad genius, an unsound eccentric mind."

Theodore Ash stroked his white beard and pointed at the enlarged image with his willow cane. "Quite often, a work of art's value is driven by the public's perception of the artist himself. This artist is serious and mysterious, He has a back story. He was once a smart fox, but now he is crazy." Ash went on. "Later in life, the great writer Oscar Wilde walked the streets with a lobster on a leash. Charles Dickens fought off imaginary people with his umbrella. Salvador Dali liked to paint himself blue and wear a loaf of bread on his head. Were they crazy? Not in a clinical sense. They were not disconnected from reality. They were just weird. Then you have the disconnected geniuses. Charlotte Brontë. Emily Dickinson. Edvard Munch, Voltaire. They escaped society to their own creative refuges to produce works of art that defined them. As loners they were free of criticism or ridicule. They accessed their rawest emotions and rubbed elbows with their closest demons. Some contemplated suicide until their art freed them and gave them new life. What we have here in this mermaid portrait is such a man."

"A *man*?" said Larry.

"A very simple man on the surface, a most complicated man under the skin," said Ash.

"Do you know who he is?" said Ms. Griffith.

"I am certain of it. My modern-day Michelangelo. None other than Jack Douglas."

"The Canadian?" said Griffith.

"He even signed the piece. May I?" The astute art critic approached the enlarged work. "I have followed his work from his humble beginnings in Newfoundland." He used his cane as a pointer. "Notice the left-handed brush strokes? As distinctive as handwriting. See these dots and dashes in the lower right corner? It's Morse code. Dot, dash, dash, dash is the letter J for Jack. The dash, dot, dot is a D for Douglas. Jack Douglas was prolific in painting, sculpting, ceramics, and prints. He started using the dash and dot signature on his sculptures."

"No one has heard from Douglas in several years," said Griffith.

"Until now, apparently," said Ash.

"Tell us more about him," said Larry.

The critic leaned on a stool and addressed his contemporaries. "He was born in St. John's, the provincial capital of Newfoundland, a cold nasty place. As a young man he bled our Canadian soil, our seas, our air. He had pugilistic tendencies and liked to fist fight; a good thing working in the fisheries of his youth. His father was a sea captain. Jack spent his youth beheading and gutting fish in the factories. As an artist he was self-taught. Jack started his career painting oils of the sea and the coastal villages. He sold them to local pubs for drinking money and cigarettes."

"And then Tandy Parsons discovered him," said an art critic.

"Yes. Tandy Parsons was a teacher from The Toronto School of Art. She was on vacation in St. John's. She saw one of Douglas's paintings hanging in a booth in a local tavern. Mrs. Parsons scoured the town's pubs and purchased all the paintings she could find. Then she sought out Jack Douglas, working at one of the fisheries.

"The rest as they say is history. She was quoted in a review that when she first laid eyes on Jack Douglas, it was like seeing Adonis.

He was draped in a leather apron, his body covered in blood and guts and sweat with arms of steel. He reminded her of a god, with his blonde beard, long hair and blue eyes.

"Though married, Tandy Parsons gave Douglas free room and board and paid for his first three semesters at the Toronto School.

"Douglas, like his father, was an occasional alcoholic. In a fit of rage, he destroyed all of his earliest works claiming they were not fit for human digestion. Tandy Parson's husband, jealous of Douglas's good looks and natural talents and possibly suspecting an affair between the young artist and his wife, had him arrested for Destruction of Property since the Tandys now owned Douglas's works.

"Jack spent three months in jail. When he came out, he found himself homeless, broke and alone. He wandered the streets of Toronto, sketching daily life on the streets and in local taverns. As before, he sold his sketches to local pubs and soon gained notoriety.

"A middle-class art lover who owned a machine shop offered up his metal scraps and welding equipment to Douglas to create his eclectic *Tin Lizzies*.

"Douglas previewed his work to a handful of local artisans and was offered a solo exhibition at a local gallery. *Tin Lizzies* took

Toronto by the balls. The six wild metal sculptures depicted Her Majesty Elizabeth II at different stages in her life. They were grotesque pieces of the Queen Mother.

"Douglas claimed the *Tin Lizzies* were a form of topographical art. They had to be viewed from all sides to be understood. There was no collective opinion of the work. One critic said the surreal work was treasonous. Another likened the gargoyle-like sculptures to the overbearing weight of responsibility that takes its toll on the human body. Jack was smart enough to never offer his own interpretation.

"The self-absorbed provincial Toronto art community was ecstatic over the trouble he caused. You might say he single-handedly put Toronto on the international art map. You couldn't turn on the news for a month without a Jack Douglas sighting. The newspapers covered him like a rock star.

"Still, he never spoke of his art, nor offered his own interpretation. He took to street painting next; giant surrealistic murals on city walls depicting gruesome monsters lurking in the shadows of alleys adjacent to city streets, unseen or unnoticed by pedestrians. His critics said the monsters were politicians. Who knows?

"Jack Douglas escaped to Montreal next, causing a new uproar with a sensational birch wood sculpture called *Canoe*. Fifty feet long and raised twenty feet in the air, clear tubes with water dyed red ran along the length of the canoe into a circular red pool below.

"Some critics interpreted it as homage to the bloody history of the Canadian Voyageurs who opened the frontiers searching for animal pelts. Others claimed it was a slap in the face against the Canadian government and the genocide of aboriginal tribes."

"What was in the canoe?" said Larry.

"Rotting pelts and blankets," said Ash. "You couldn't see them from the ground. After three months, *Canoe* was ordered destroyed by the mayor because of the stench and hazard to the city's air quality. He even ordered the rotting blankets be examined to see if they carried Smallpox.

"Jack returned to painting. A New York art dealer created a bidding war for his canvases and Douglas was never poor again. He was compared to Picasso. Dipped his brush in Pop Art, Minimalism, Abstraction. He won the Grand Prize at the Venice Biennale for his work *Bowl*.

"I offered Jack unwavering support over the years. I saw his genius. He was maddened by the mundane. Obvious in his surrealistic *Mutilated Fish*. I bought some of his early paintings;

Atrophy, The Great Sad, String of Chains. I sold them for ten times my cost. Wish I had kept a few. They're worth a hundred times what they were then.

"Jack never cared about the art world – the exhibitions, the galleries. He just wanted to paint or sculpt or play with materials. Anything his hands touched became a form of art. We were sitting in a café once, just watching passersby. As usual, Jack was bored. He started playing with a glass jar filled with toothpicks. Thirty minutes later he'd built a teepee with two stick Indians standing in front of it. A passerby saw the work and gave him two hundred bucks for it. Such was Jack with his obsessional art, some made for the long term, others mere contrivances made in the moment.

"He visited Vancouver next, expanding his reach across all of Canada. At a fundraising banquet there he took to the microphone for the very first time and gave a short speech about the perils of modern society overrunning indigenous peoples, ruining the land for profits of land, minerals and water. He mentioned he was leaving Canada to chase what was left of us. Like a magician in a puff of smoke, Jack Douglas seemed to disappear forever. Until now."

"That's quite a story," said Nancy.

"Just my own interpretation of events," said Ash.

"And now we have this!" said Griffith. "Jack Douglas alive and well, apparently living off the coast of Mexico."

Ash turned to Larry. "Would you like to sell the piece?"

"It isn't mine," said Larry.

"Tsk, tsk," said Ash. "Like Jack's other works, it will bring millions at auction. Certainly worth more than the British Guiana stamp."

Larry crossed to the projector and returned the encased stamp to his suit pocket. He thanked the group. "You have been most helpful. I will put in a good word with my benefactor Mrs. Chumley. I'm sure she will continue her generous support of your museum."

"What now?" Ash asked.

"I expect Mr. Douglas will not remain anonymous for long," said Larry. "If he is still alive."

Ash came up to him and whispered privately in his ear. "If you ever find Jack, give him my regards. All his life, he seemed afflicted with an indescribable *aloneness*. Maybe it started on the desolate eastern shores of Newfoundland. Who knows? I hope he has found his peace."

Returning to his office, Larry called Mrs. Chumley. "Most of the puzzle is solved. The only missing tidbit is the person who sold your husband the mermaid stamp."

"I have an answer for that," said the widow. "Come to my house for lunch tomorrow and we'll put all the pieces together. I'll have Homer pick you up at noon."

Larry hung up and leaned back in his chair. It had been an exhilarating day, an unusual day, a cause for small celebration.

His thoughts returned to the artist Jack Douglas. Did they share something in common? That indescribable *aloneness*? It was different than loneliness, a choice really. But while Douglas exercised his demons with creativity, Larry did not. He didn't create music, he merely collected it.

CHAPTER 15

Larry stepped off the train at the 99th Street Station. He was surprised to see Pharaoh Williams waiting for him. The big man was wearing sweat pants and a pullover. He had a large brown bag under one arm and a bottle in his hand.

"Hey there, Larry. You remember me? Pharaoh Williams, the dude who knocked you down the other day. I want to make up for it. Thought we could break bread together. Actually, it's ribs from Barbara Ann's Bar-B-Que. Best in the city." The smiling younger man showed Larry the bottle. "Got us a nice wine to go with it."

"That wasn't necessary," said Larry.

Pharaoh was a fast talker, a young man with too much energy. "We can eat on your front porch. I got plates, napkins and forks; coleslaw, too. Don't even need to go in your house."

Larry answered uncomfortably. "Really, Mr. Williams. You didn't have to go to the trouble."

Larry and Pharaoh walked towards Prospect Street.

"Ain't no trouble," said Pharaoh. "I say when a man does a wrong, no matter how small, he needs to make things right. It's a good way to live."

He handed Larry the wine bottle. Larry read the label. "A 2007 Chateau Ste. Michelle Eroica."

"A good Riesling," said Pharaoh. "Cleans the palate."

"Are you a connoisseur, Mr. Williams?"

"Naw, I'm a freshman when it comes to fine wines." Pharaoh knew Settlebottom liked wine. He had picked through his curbside trash once. "And don't be callin' me Mr. Williams. Everybody calls me Pharaoh. You want me to call you Lawrence or Larry?"

"I'm not sure," said Larry. "Lawrence is so, so..."

"Important," said Pharaoh. "Like Lawrence of Arabia or the St. Lawrence Seaway. I prefer Larry. Makes you real."

"That's fine, Pharaoh."

"How was work today?"

"Atypical," said Larry.

"What does that mean?"

"My life is usually very routine and regimented. But not today."

"Oh yeah? Somethin' big happen? Somebody try robbin' your museum?"

"Nothing like that. I imagine to a layperson my day would still be very boring."

"You feel like sharing?" said Pharaoh.

"Not at this time," said Larry. "Confidentiality agreements and all that."

"Damn, if you don't sound like a lawyer!" Pharaoh laughed.

Larry was quick to change the subject. "And you? Did you *bounce* anybody last night at your club?"

"Naw. It was a quiet night. No blood spilt."

They walked another block. Pharaoh nodded to an old woman watering her front lawn. He yelled to a younger man waxing a sports car in his driveway. "You got a lady killer there!" Pharaoh shouted.

The younger man smiled back at him.

"Are you always so friendly with strangers?" said Larry.

"We all in this together," said Pharaoh. "Ain't nobody better or worse than the rest of us. Everybody just got a different set of dice to roll for their circumstances."

They turned on Larry's street.

"You ever notice there ain't no kids on this block?" said Pharaoh. "Why is that?"

"Nobody wants kids anymore in this uncertain world."

"And they cost too much to raise," added Pharaoh. "If I had kids, my life would be ruined. I can barely make it on my own. Still, maybe someday...."

They came to Larry's house. Larry walked up the steps to the porch, his house key in his hand. He looked back at Pharaoh, still standing on the public sidewalk. Pharaoh was staring at the house apprehensively.

"You coming in?"

"Just on the porch, like I promised," said Pharaoh. "A man needs his privacy."

What Pharaoh didn't say was that he thought he saw an apparition of Larry's dead girlfriend staring at him through a crack in the blinds.

There was a patio table and two chairs on the porch. Larry set the wine down and gestured for Pharaoh to take a seat.

Pharaoh took a deep breath and marched up the porch, joining Larry at the table. He opened the bag of barbeque and laid out the contents.

"We need wineglasses," said Larry. "And some music. I'll be right back."

He went to the front door and opened it with a key.

Pharaoh thought he saw Larry's dead girlfriend come flying out of the house with a butcher knife in her hand. She seemed to spit at Pharaoh as she raced down the steps. She stayed on the front lawn, jumping up and down like a wild woman in front of him, thrashing at the air with her knife. He couldn't take his eyes off her. He pulled a quarter from his pocket and threw it at the female apparition, hitting her in the head.

"Go on now! You go! Skit! Skedaddle."

The apparition spit at the quarter and ran into the street. She stood over a sewer manhole cover and vaporized to nothingness.

"Yeah, bitch. There you go!" said Pharaoh. "Back to the sewers where you belong!"

Larry returned with the glasses and a bottle opener and sat across from Pharaoh. "Were you talking to someone?"

"Naw, I thought I saw an old acquaintance go by."

"Oh. Do you like Gershwin?" said Larry.

Pharaoh turned his attention to the sounds of "Rhapsody in Blue" coming through the door.

"Who doesn't love great jazz?" said Pharaoh.

Larry uncorked the bottle and poured two glasses. "Listen to the steely rhythms, the tink-a-tank, rattle and bang. Just like the train I ride to work! A musical kaleidoscope."

Pharaoh raised his glass and offered a toast. "May the road rise up to meet you and the wind be always at your back."

Larry finished the phrase. "May the sun shine warm upon your face; the rains fall soft upon your fields and until we meet again, may God hold you in the palm of His hand."

They tapped their glasses together.

"How you know that one?" Pharaoh asked.

"I was raised Irish Catholic."

"Settlebottom is Irish?"

"Well, actually my last name was derived from my mothers, Mrs. Settle and Miss Bottom."

"That don't make no sense, Larry."

After he had gotten his first gig as a bouncer in a popular club, Pharaoh had spent an entire afternoon reading up on body language behaviors. He could tell when a person was lying by his or her chemical or physical reactions. Pharaoh learned to ask off-the-wall questions to trigger involuntary fight-or-flight reflex responses triggered by the sympathetic nervous system which activated a person's adrenaline. He thought it would come in handy picking up on chicks, checking I.D's at the door, or for ruling out gangbangers wanting to start shit in his club.

He called his body readings *ticks and tricks*. The vibe he got from Settlebottom was that the man was a straight talker. He blushed easily when asked a question that required an uncomfortable answer, but he didn't lie.

Larry enjoyed a sip of wine and actually smiled. "You must forgive me. I am very opaque at times. I was adopted when I was fourteen. Mrs. Settle was my elementary teacher at the St. Vincent DePaul Orphanage near the Chicago stockyards. Miss Bottom was her younger sister and a nun there. This was their house."

"Was?"

"They died a few years ago under tragic circumstances. I'd rather not talk about it. Bad memories serve no purpose."

"What about good memories?" asked Pharaoh.

Larry studied his glass, trying to find a feasible answer. "I can't say that I had many of those either."

Pharaoh shook his head. "You're complex, Larry. Deep."

Larry sipped from his glass and came up with a loud laugh. "I'm nothing of the kind. I lack substance and I'm humorless."

"And you dress in drab colors so you won't stand out in the crowd," said Pharaoh.

"There you go!" said Larry. "My secret is finally out."

"You got abandonment issues like me," said Pharaoh. "At least you like good wine and fine music."

"Oh, there's plenty of that to go around in this house now," said Larry. "When my mothers were alive, all you'd hear inside was chorale music performed by my orphanage choir."

"Did you sing?"

"I was too busy cleaning the hallways."

"Were you an altar boy?"

"I was an excellent altar boy at St. Vincent DePaul Church. Funerals every Sunday."

"What about weddings?"

"I never did weddings. The priests thought I looked too scrawny and pathetic for celebrations of life. Oh well, days gone by. The orphanages are gone now, swallowed up by government agencies and the foster care system. Mrs. Settle used to tell me I was the last institutionalized orphan adopted under the old system."

"So you don't really know what or who you are!" realized Pharaoh. "You might be German or Polish or Italian."

"Not Italian," said Larry. "I sunburn easily."

Pharaoh laughed. "Look at that! You got a sense of humor."

Larry raised his finger, waiting for a change in the music. "Here comes the next paragraph! Listen!"

The heavy sound of piano keys thundered from the house.

"Isn't it beautiful?" said Larry. "To create something like Gershwin?"

Pharaoh handed Larry a plate. "Come on now, we got ribs to eat. Music for the tongue."

They sat on the porch, time measured by two more bottles of wine Larry brought out from the house. The men moved from the chairs to catch a better breeze on the porch steps, watching the fading sun wrap anonymous passersby in golden silhouettes.

"You know your neighbors well, Larry?" said Pharaoh.

"I don't know anyone well," Larry said.

"I used to have a lot of friends," said Pharaoh.

"But not anymore?" said Larry.

"Some are dead, some I said good riddance to. Thought I'd start over."

"And how's that going?"

"Well, I'm here, ain't I Larry?"

CHAPTER 16

Larry sat in a parlor of the Chumley mansion, surrounded by antiques and priceless paintings. Rosemary was across from him, pouring tea.

"Tea always tastes so much better when served in a Tiffany teapot," she said.

Larry admired the tea set; a silver and ivory teapot, creamer, sugar bowl and a tray all stamped with German hallmarks.

"What did this set you back?" Larry asked.

"Two or three hundred thousand dollars," said Rosemary. "I can't remember. But screw the pot. It's all about the tea."

"And the price of this cup of tea?" said Larry.

"It's off the shelf Lipton's," she said, "the delicious trappings of the middle class. Like me and George, Sir Thomas Lipton came from humble beginnings. He started with grocery shops in Glasgow in 1871. Bought his first tea fields in Ceylon and brought tea to the masses by cutting out the middle men. His affordable tea came with bagpipes and brass bands when they first arrived in Glasgow. Good old Tommy was a marketing genius. He even invented tea leaves in tea bags. What he did for tea, we did for chocolates and gum."

Larry added a lump of sugar and a splash of milk to his tea and sipped.

"A perfect cup," he decided.

Rosemary handed him a finger of shortbread for dipping.

"As you like it," she said.

Larry came to the reason for his visit. "So what have you learned, Rosemary? Who is our mystery man who sold the Cinderella stamp to George?"

"It wasn't much of a mystery to solve, not like yours," she admitted. "A wire deposit was made from one of George's hobby accounts to a bank in Guatemala. One hundred thousand dollars."

"And the recipient?"

"None other than Basil Philbin."

"The Master Chocolatier?"

"He took Chumley's Chocolates to a whole new level. Basil was a tempering genius. He gave our chocolates the perfect color, shine and snap. And the mouth feel! You always knew when you had a

Chumley on your tongue. George paid Basil very well for our secret recipes."

"So Philbin lives in Guatemala now?"

"On the Pacific coast. I managed to get him on the telly. We had a lovely conversation. Basil owned a cocoa plantation for a while but between revolutions and hurricanes he could never make a success of it. He's been studying Mayan cultures as of late. Their love of chocolate goes back two thousand years."

"How did he come across the stamp?"

"Basil lives in a fishing village called Champerico with his hand in everything: the fish market, coffee and sugar coming down from the hills. Basil says the locals are always bringing him things to buy; Mayan and Aztec pots made a thousand years ago or yesterday, human and animal skulls, exotic insects, even albino monkeys. One day, a fisherman, fresh off the sea, approached him with the bottle. It was caught up in his fishing net. Basil paid him fifty dollars. He knew George would flip over it."

"And the rest is history," said Larry.

"My history, at least."

"The bottle's private sea voyage fits what we've learned," said Larry. "Found on the Pacific coast, carried with the currents. It's amazing that it was ever found at all."

"A very small discovery as far as human history goes, unlike the Rosetta Stone, which deciphered ancient Egyptian hieroglyphics or a child's discovery in the caves of Lascaux, France which revealed a far different history before modern humans ruled the land."

"What was in the cave?" said Larry.

"Wall paintings of ancient peoples, bulls, stags, rhinos, and giant cats. In Europe, mind you! There is still a great wonder in the world to this day, Lawrence. This stamp of ours? It has a long reach. We must follow its path."

"What do you propose now?" said Larry. "Hire a team for Mexico to follow what we have learned to its conclusion and find our missing artist?"

"There is only one man I can think of that I entrust to the task."

"Who do you have in mind?"

"*You*, my dear boy."

Larry leapt to his feet. "*Me*?"

"The vacation of a lifetime on the sandy beaches of Puerto Vallarta."

He paced the room. "Rosemary, I don't travel well. You know that. I'm fixed in my ways. I take the morning train downtown; I ride the evening train home. I eat red meat on Sunday, fish on

Friday, salads and oatmeal the rest of the week. That is what I do best."

"I could train a dog to do that, Lawrence."

Larry stumbled in his reply. "There is no passion to me. I'm boring Larry Settlebottom, the last child adopted from the orphanage. A yard boy. A man of necessary functions. I am incapable of doing anything remotely out of the ordinary."

Rosemary politely set down her cup of tea. "But not today," she decided. "You will go to Mexico. You will find this Jack Douglas and learn the history of the mermaid stamp. Who was his model? Why did he paint it? All the details. And when you have the answer, you can return here to your mundane world and its routines and I can die in my sleep knowing the truth of things. Straightforward and simple."

Larry sat across from the widow. "I hear Mexico is a precarious place. I could be at risk being in the wrong place at the wrong time, what with drug smuggling and human trafficking."

"Then we'll hire a bodyguard for your protection."

Larry resigned himself to the task. "I'll look into it myself," he said. "If I'm going to risk life and limb over a stamp, I may as well have someone I can trust."

CHAPTER 17

Larry exited the train and saw Pharaoh standing on the platform. The big man had a newspaper tucked under his arm.

"How was your day?" said Pharaoh.

"Not what I expected. Yours?"

"I spent some time at the library," said Pharaoh. "I love the smell of books."

He didn't want to bother Larry with the real purpose of his library visit; five hours reading up on orphan personalities. Orphans had control issues. They felt alienated from society. They feared abandonment. They had secret hostilities kept close to the vest. They coped by blocking their impulses. Larry didn't seem to have any real feelings about anything. No strong opinions. He was present but he wasn't really in the moment.

"Can we talk?" Larry said.

"That's why I'm here," said Pharaoh.

"Be honest with me now, Pharaoh. Do you have a criminal history?"

"None reported to the police."

Pharaoh's mind flashed back to the Settlebottom burglary three years earlier; the church wine, worthless art and cheap jewelry, the mean bitch with the foreign accent tied to the chair, kicking and trying to scream. The Chicago Tribune article about a botched burglary ending in the death by asphyxiation of one Alina Milosevic, an Eastern European. He got away with that one.

"Do you have a passport?" said Larry.

"No, but I can get one."

"I have to go to Mexico," said Larry. "Museum business. I need a bodyguard. Someone I can trust."

"And you thought of me?"

"Yes."

"I'm flattered, Larry, but you don't know me all that well."

"I have been authorized to pay you five hundred dollars a day plus expenses."

Pharaoh took a step back and fanned himself with the newspaper. "What is it we'll be doing in Mexico?"

"We have to find a missing artist."

Pharaoh pictured himself visiting art galleries. “Sounds dangerous,” he said. “Some sleuthing, I’m sure.”

“We start in Puerto Vallarta. Where it takes us after that I’m not sure.”

Pharaoh counted dollars in his head. “Could take weeks, maybe months.”

“Or maybe just a day or two,” said Larry. “Are you up for it?”

“Oh, I’m up for it.” Pharaoh smiled. “Question is, are you?”

They walked to Larry’s house and sat on the front porch together. Larry retrieved a bottle of wine from the house and went over the history of the stamp for Pharaoh.

“Sounds like an easy enough assignment,” said Pharaoh. “A muscle job; bash a few heads, break some bones.”

After finishing a second bottle of a 2006 Oyster Bay merlot, Pharaoh saw the dead Serbian woman across the street, hiding behind an elm tree. She kept yelling at him, “He’s mine! That’s my play! Larry was my sucker!”

“You see that?” Pharaoh asked Larry.

“What?”

“Across the street. You see anything?”

“What am I looking for?” said Larry.

“Never mind,” said Pharaoh. “Just my imagination.” He changed the subject. “They got palm trees in Mexico?”

“I’m sure they do,” said Larry.

“Always wanted to see one,” said Pharaoh.

Pharaoh thought of other things he wanted to see in Mexico, especially señoritas At five hundred dollars a day, he could afford a few dirty girls.

CHAPTER 18

The morning sun had already started baking the island. Ismelda helped the old man place the heavy basket on his head.

"Go easy," said Ismelda. "There is no hurry."

There were tears in the old man's eyes as he gripped the basket. "Why do I bother to work? I am a dead man anyway," he said.

Ismelda saw something fluttering out of the corner of her eye. It was Calista waving her hat, pointing out to sea.

Ismelda turned and saw a white pleasure boat bouncing over the stiff waves as it came towards the island's sagging dock. She saw the blue canopies, a pair of small bodies at the bow. Children?

No, please God! No children!

She left the old man and started to run. She saw El Gordo far ahead of her, hiding a machete behind his back as he strutted down the path towards the sagging dock.

The captain of the pleasure boat was cutting his engines. A pretty woman in her thirties appeared from under a canopy and picked up a coil of rope off the bow. She was wearing a sun dress like Ismelda's but hers was fresh and clean.

El Gordo was on the unsteady dock now, his huge frame braced steadily on the uneven boards as he treaded forward.

Ismelda waved her arms as she ran along the white cliffs. "Go away! Go away!" she screamed to the people in the boat. But she was too far away, the wind scattering her voice.

The happy woman leapt off the boat and tied it to a dock post. She reached back and took the hands of the two children as they joined her.

El Gordo moved towards them, a painted smile on his ugly stone face. He was shouting something to the people. What he always said, "Welcome to la isla!"

A handsome man in white shorts and tee shirt came off the boat last. He stretched his arms high in the air and shook himself loose, happy to be on land again. He put his arms around his children and wife.

Ismelda kept shouting. She looked like a mad woman as she ran, her arms flapping. "Run!" she screamed. "Run!"

The pig reached the family. "Anybody else with you?" he said.

"No, just us," smiled the captain. "We're the McKinley clan from Seattle. Mind if we take a quick tour of the island? Stretch our legs a bit?"

Ismelda reached the end of the dock. Her throat was dry, her voice hoarse. "Run!" she screamed. "Run!"

The entire family stared at the mad woman with the dirty face in the dirty dress running towards them.

The steel machete swung out from behind El Gordo's back. He chopped at the husband's neck first. Blood shot out, drenching his family. As his body sagged, his wife tried to scream as she struggled to hold him up. "No!"

The pig swung again. The machete dug deep into the wife's neck this time. El Gordo pulled it away slowly and stared down at the two children. A boy and a girl. Lovely kids.

Ismelda was nearly at the pig's back, screaming, "Not the children!"

El Gordo raised the machete and made lazy chops against the flesh of the children, like a man dicing onions.

The four bodies of the dead family slumped against the wet wood of the sagging dock in a pile.

Ismelda jumped on Gordo's back, kicking and screaming, tugging hard on his long matt of hair.

The pig reached back and tore her loose. He held Ismelda out like a rag doll in the air, stared at her with contempt, and tossed her into the sea. He waited for her to surface, changing the deadly machete from one hand to the other.

She came up, gulping and gasping for air.

"This is my island!" he screamed at her. "Mine!"

He bent over the dead family and wiped his blade clean on the hem of the mother's dress. Her eyes were still open, seeming to stare at him in wonder.

Ismelda swam along the dock to the shore and pulled herself out. She stood there, watching as the pig climbed aboard the cruiser. Gordo disappeared under the blue canopy and returned a minute later, a bottle of tequila in his hand. He was smiling.

He yelled towards Ismelda, holding her place at the edge of the dock.

"They have food and drinks, blankets and clothes. Go get the others!"

Ismelda did not move.

He raised his machete high in the air. "Get the others now! Move woman, before I kill you!"

"I am already dead," said Ismelda.

She shook her head and started back up the path. She saw Calista coming, the old people behind her.

"What has he done?" Calista cried.

"What he always does. There were children this time." Ismelda brushed past the old people and ran away as fast as her legs could carry her.

When she reached the shacks, she turned south, following a narrow path that led along the edge of the steep cliffs to the southern end of the small island. There she reached a series of narrow steps carved in the rock. They were too narrow for El Gordo to ever use. She groped her way down them, using the occasional outcropping of stone in the cliff for added support. The steps ended ten feet above the crashing surf. She placed her hands on an old rope hung from a metal stake pounded into the cliff face long ago. She felt the rope in her swollen hands, gripped it securely and lowered her body down to a large flat rock made smooth by the sea. A small wave of white foam danced across her feet as she released her hand from the rope.

There was an opening here, the entrance to a cave with a shiny marbled face of smooth black and white rock. She came here to cry and to fight the urge to kill herself while the pig cleaned up his messes.

First the pig would inspect the boat for guns. His big fat fingers could not pull the triggers. He would smash the guns to pieces and dump them in the sea.

Next he would stand on the dock and sip from his new bottle of tequila while the old ones stripped the boat clean of anything useful; drinking water, cushions, tarps, clothing, food, gasoline, pieces of fiberglass and chunks of wood. While the old ones carried the bounty up the hill to the village he would rip out the navigation system, smash cell phones, and rip down antennas. Then he would untie the boat from the dock, turn it to face the sea and tie it to the dock again. Next, he would toss the dead bodies on the boat and throw them in the cabin.

Next he would fetch one of the old men and put him in the captain's chair. El Gordo would start the boat's engine and push the controls to neutral. With his machete he would go to the ship's keel, lift the cover to the bilge and stab large holes through the floor until a fountain of water sprang up.

Once the ship started flooding, he would leave the boat and order the old man to shift the boat's throttle into gear. When the boat lurched forward the old man would hurry to the rear and dive into the water while El Gordo cut the boat free from its rope tether to the dock.

The pig would stand there on the dock, drink his tequila, and watch the boat drift out to sea until it sank. Something he called *a lovely sunset.*

Satisfied, Gordo would stagger up to the shacks on his drunken legs and sift through his booty. He would lock most of the canned food in his lockers. Things he did not like or need he gave to the old ones, nothing that might float and carry them out to sea.

After the sun went down, when the tequila bottle was empty, he would sit on a large rock and call out Ismelda's name. When she finally returned he would beat her, and if not too drunk he would rape her. He was an evil pig.

Standing at the cave entrance, Ismelda stared down at her feet. There was a pile of fish bones above the waterline, well-picked by seabirds. She listened to the distant sounds of a hammer tapping against rock in the cave. She saw the faint flicker of a light dancing from deep within.

Ismelda called out, "Hello in there! Is it a good time to visit?"

The tapping stopped.

A man's brittle voice answered with tired enthusiasm. "You are always welcome. Come in, come in! The walls are alive! And I am more alive than ever!"

Ismelda lowered her head and entered the cave. She could not leave the island but she could hide herself here for a time, exchanging one kind of madness for a better kind.

CHAPTER 19

Rosemary Chumley's influence had a long reach. Passports were expedited in three days. Mrs. Chumley's driver Homer picked Larry and Pharaoh up at Larry's house and drove them towards O'Hare airport. Larry sat in the back seat for a change, next to Pharaoh. Pharaoh had never been in a limo before. He stared at the champagne on ice.

"Is that for us?" he asked Larry.

"Bon voyage complements of Mrs. Chumley," Homer announced through the partition.

Larry pulled the bottle from the ice bucket. "You like French?" he asked Pharaoh.

"What is it?"

"A 2002 Blanc de Blancs Le Mesnil-sur-Oger."

"Expensive?"

"Very."

“Then I think we better drink it,” said Pharaoh.

Pharaoh settled back in his seat and enjoyed the ride. “It don’t get any better than this,” he realized. “Limos and fine wine. Your employer, she thinks highly of you.”

“Like an aunt I never had,” said Larry. He popped the cork and poured them each a glass.

“Wish I could find me an aunt like her,” said Pharaoh.

Homer handed a thick envelope through the partition to Larry. “Spending money,” he said. “Fifty grand large. You know how Mexico is.”

“I’ve never been to Mexico,” Larry told Pharaoh. “I’ve never even left the United States before.”

“You’re shittin’ me!” said Pharaoh.

“Nope.”

“But you been to Florida? California?”

“Nope.”

“But you have all those international stamps at your museum.”

“The stamps come to us from collectors.”

Larry handed Pharaoh the cash envelope.

“You trust me with it?” said Pharaoh.

“You’re my bodyguard. I trust you with everything.”

Pharaoh stuffed the envelope in his coat pocket. He turned away, staring out the window, stifling small tears stinging the corners of his eyes. He didn't know what to make of things. Larry was the real deal, but a dope, trusting him. Pharaoh had killed his fiancée, robbed his house. Now he was in charge of covering Larry's ass in a foreign country. Pharaoh blotted his eyes with a sleeve and sipped from his glass.

The limo arrived at the airport terminal. Homer pulled to the curb behind a waiting limousine.

"Mrs. Chumley wants to see you off," announced Homer.

He opened the back doors for his guests and popped the trunk to remove their luggage.

Larry walked up to the second limo and saw Rosemary inside. She leaned her head out the window and stared back at Pharaoh Williams.

"He'll do," said the widow.

Pharaoh approached her window and smiled at her. "Thank you for the opportunity," he said.

"You were Larry's idea, not mine." She looked at Larry. "Enjoy your adventure. You may never have another like it. And one more thing, Lawrence." The widow pitched a golden coin at him. Larry caught it midair. "For luck," she said.

Larry stared at the shiny dollar in his hand. "Rosemary! Really!" He stepped forward to return it.

She waved him off. "I insist! Now go, Lawrence, before you make me cry."

"But this coin is —."

"Go, Larry! Please! Go to Mexico. Have an adventure."

She fell back in her seat and closed the window. Her car pulled away from the curb and joined the traffic exiting the terminal.

Larry stuck the coin in his pants pocket and faced the terminal with Pharaoh.

"You ever fly before?" said Pharaoh.

"Twice," said Larry. "A day trip for a conference in New York. One flight there, one flight back. You?"

"Never. If I hold your hand on the plane, don't take it personal."

"Just don't sit on my lap," said Larry.

Homer handed the men their luggage. "Don't drink the water, gentlemen and bon voyage."

CHAPTER 20

The plane shuddered repeatedly on the four hour flight, lifting and falling in the turbulent jet stream. Neither man had ever been to a foreign country. Neither of them knew Spanish. Larry sat in an aisle seat, Pharaoh next to him by the window in First Class.

Pharaoh was giddy after his fifth serving of cognac in a balloon snifter, briefing Larry on their destination from a guide book he marked with a yellow highlighter. He'd been talking non-stop since the plane hit cruising altitude. It took his mind off his initial fear of flying.

Larry listened nervously, touching the gold coin in his pants pocket at least a dozen times to make sure it was still there.

It was a special coin. A $20 dollar Saint-Gaudens Double Eagle. The coin was stamped at the Denver Mint in 1933, only a day before President Roosevelt took America off the gold standard and ordered all of the 445,000 minted coins to be melted into gold bullion for their melt value. But twenty of the coins never made it to the melting vat. A mint cashier fudged the accounting books. He knew the value of rare coins in the numismatic black market and sold all but one of the coins to a shady Philadelphia jeweler. It took the U.S. Treasury Department forty years to recover the nineteen coins. The one coin the cashier kept was never discovered. Rumors circulated that the coin was still out there in the black market.

Now it was in Larry's pocket. Its estimated value was ten million dollars. Larry's khaki pants cost sixty bucks. Not a great security vault.

Pharaoh read aloud. "P.V. is what the locals call Perto Varto."

"Puerto Vallarta," corrected Larry.

Pharaoh dangled his empty snifter in his hand. A flight attendant appeared and refilled it. "Perto Varto's a big town to cover. Two hundred and fifty thousand locals, not to mention tourists and expatriates." He pulled a paper from his pocket and studied it. "Mrs. Chumley booked us at the Sunny Siesta Resort and Spa, a short hike from the local marina. It's five-star. Good security. They don't kidnap foreign businessmen from the classy hotels."

"*Kidnap*?"

"For ransom, Larry. You're an important man from Chicago. We can't forget that. Criminals, they smell the money."

Larry leaned back in his seat. "But it's a resort town."

"And all the tourists got money to burn. We'll have to dress down. Middle class. Make it look like we won a free trip. Shorts, tee shirts and flip-flops." Pharaoh pulled an old photograph of Jack Douglas from the back of the guidebook. "So how do we find this Jack Douglas fella? What's the plan?"

"He's an artist. There's an art district near the center of the city. We'll start there."

"After I get me a pistol," said Pharaoh.

"A pistol?" said Larry.

"For your protection. Don't you worry, I won't let the cartels get you."

The captain's voice came over the loudspeaker. "Attendants prepare for landing."

Pharaoh stared out his window. "There's the Pacific Ocean! Sure is blue!"

Ten minutes later the plane coasted onto the runway at Gustavo Díaz Ordaz International Airport. Rolling hills covered in dense tropical foliage rolled away to the east of the city.

Larry and Pharaoh grabbed their bags off a luggage conveyor, showed their passports to a customs officer and headed through the glass doors of the terminal.

When they stepped outside, they felt a warm slap of hot humid air on their skin.

"It must be a hundred degrees!" Larry complained.

Pharaoh pointed at a palm tree rustling in the breeze.

"My first palm tree," he announced. "They got them in Florida, too." He led Larry to a waiting cab. "I'll handle this. You keep your eyes peeled for anything suspicious."

Larry's eyes darted from one pedestrian to the next. No one looked dangerous. They were mostly Americans and Canadians wearing big smiles and loose clothes made for the tropics.

"Where to?" said a local cabdriver.

"The Sunny Siesta," said Pharaoh. "What's the fare?"

"Twenty dollars."

"I'll give you ten."

"The standard fare is twenty."

Pharaoh patted the thick envelope in his pocket. "Can you break a hundred?"

"Si," said the driver.

Pharaoh and Larry climbed in the backseat of the cab while the cabbie loaded their luggage in the trunk.

"I thought we wanted to keep a low profile," Larry said.

"We do," said Pharaoh.

"Then why did you slap your pocket like that? It's thick with money."

"I did that on purpose," said Pharaoh. "You see, if something does go wrong, the bad guys will be comin' after me, not you. It's part of my bodyguard strategy."

CHAPTER 21

The hotel suite was painted in soft pink pastels, the smooth floor made of fine wood. A king bed faced the open window with a magnificent view of the ocean and Banderas Bay beyond.

Pharaoh was on the balcony, a can of Mexican beer in his hand from the minibar.

Larry absently counted the number of drinks his bodyguard had consumed since Chicago: a bottle of champagne, six cognacs, now a beer. The man wasn't drunk. Larry wondered how much alcohol a man Pharaoh's size could actually consume. He had a feeling he would find out.

Pharaoh called from the balcony. "Larry, you got to come outside and see the pool!"

Larry joined him. They stared down from their fourteenth floor perch at the azure pool studded with palm trees, small islands and a swim-up bar.

"Did you bring trunks?" Pharaoh asked.

"No," said Larry. "I didn't think of this as a vacation."

"Well, you can buy some at the gift shop."

Pharaoh went inside to his adjoining bedroom. He returned wearing a pair of red baggy shorts and sandals. He was thick with muscle.

"I'm gonna take a dip in the pool."

"Are you sure I'll be safe in the room alone?"

"We're in what they call *The Gringo Zon*e. Hotel's got security cameras everywhere. You'll be fine." Pharaoh counted out a thousand dollars in bills and handed them to Larry. "Here's some pocket money. Anything we buy at the hotel, we just charge to our room. Why don't you run downstairs and buy yourself some clothes. Nothin' too fancy. You want to blend in. Get some trunks and sandals, too. Middle class, remember? I'll meet you at the pool."

Larry found Pharaoh an hour later at the swim-up bar, pounding down a frosty Daiquiri. Larry adjusted his new blue trunks, waded into the pool and took a seat next to him.

A handsome Mexican bartender handed Larry a cold Daiquiri. "Welcome to Mexico, señor."

"This is Ronaldo," said Pharaoh. "He's been giving me the lay of the land."

"Hello Ronaldo," said Larry.

"I'm glad you're both in the water," said the bartender. "Mr. Pharaoh, he drinks like a fish."

"Only had me a half dozen. How's the beach here?"

"Okay. A little rocky. Too many vendors selling crap. I recommend my pool."

"How's the hotel food?"

"Best steak in town," said Ronaldo.

Pharaoh slapped Larry on the back. "Ronaldo's been giving me a local history lesson. He's going to college for it. Says people been living here since 580 B.C. according to the archaeological evidence. What did you call them? Astecs?"

"*Aztecs*," corrected Ronaldo.

"Yeah. Them. The Spanish conquistador, Cortez, he marched through Mexico five hundred years ago and destroyed the Astec empire. Beat down a native army of ten thousand Indians with his guns, armor and horses. Ronaldo, tell Larry about the pirates."

"Puerto Vallarta has a long history of pirates and smugglers. Four hundred years ago, the Manila Galleon, a fleet of Spanish ships, sailed between here and the Philippines. They brought porcelain, silk, ivory, and spices from China to get their hands on New World silver."

"Mexico ain't just tacos and burritos," said Pharaoh. "Tell Larry about the other Indians. The ones from the Caribbean."

"It is just a legend," said Ronaldo.

"A mermaid legend," added Pharaoh.

Ronaldo leaned against the bar counter. "One of my teachers at the university, he believes that at the time of Columbus, a great body of Taínos Indians left the Caribbean sea and swept across our peninsula looking for a new home. The Europeans had brought disease with them and the Taínos were dying in great numbers. Hundreds were carried across the mountains on great hammocks, their bodies wrapped in soaking garments. It is said they were the Taínos of the Sea. Merpeople. Half human, half fish. When the Aztecs discovered their crossing, they sent a great army after them and pursued them here, to Banderas Bay."

"Tell Larry about the beach."

"We have a local beach near downtown called Playa Los Muertos. Deadman's Beach. It is the most popular in Puerto Vallarta, despite the ugly name. My teacher said the Taínos, having reached the edge of the world with their backs to the sea, took a final stand there against the Aztecs in a weeklong battle. At night they buried their dead in the sand. Only a few escaped the land for the ocean in makeshift boats. It is a crazy story."

"Do you consider your teacher crazy?" said Larry.

"No, señor. He is muy intelligente. Very smart."

"Where can we find him?" said Larry.

"Professor Marquez is on vacation, following the old trail of the Taínos. Every summer he looks for artifacts to support his theory. It would be cool if he found one of the sea people's skeletons."

"That would be real cool," said Pharaoh.

Ronaldo picked up a glass and wiped it clean. "Searching for mermaids must cost a lot of money."

"Money ain't no object," said Pharaoh. "We have the corporate wealth of a major museum behind us."

"That so?" said Ronaldo.

"We didn't come to Mexico to play games," said Pharaoh.

"Well, if you need anything, come see me first," said Ronaldo. "Boats, girls, night clubs. Whatever you want."

Pharaoh pulled a twenty dollar bill out of a wad of cash and slid it across the bar to him. "For now, just keep the rum flowin'."

CHAPTER 22

After a long dinner with Pharaoh at the hotel's excellent steakhouse, Larry found a map and brochures of local attractions on a rack by the main desk. He spent an hour in his room mapping out a route of art galleries and artist studios to visit the following day. He was bound to find his missing artist or someone who knew Jack Douglas at one of them.

A quick shower at sunrise awakened Larry's senses. He slipped on khaki pants, sandals and a button down cotton shirt he had purchased the day before in the gift shop. He could hear Pharaoh rustling in his bed through the open door that separated them. Larry went outside and stood on the balcony, staring out at the deserted beach, listening to the constant roar of the forbidding ocean attacking the shoreline.

He didn't like being here, out of his element, away from his daily routine. There was no train to take him to work. No specific route to take to his office. No regularity. He stared back at his neat bed. Why had he straightened the sheets and pulled the covers tight? He had room service for that. Larry remembered his years in the orphanage. None of the boys in his dormitory were allowed to have breakfast until the beds were made.

Pharaoh joined him on the balcony, stretching his thick muscled arms over his head as he yawned.

"Sleep well?" said Larry.

"Never better." Pharaoh stared down at an attendant skimming the surface of the pool with a net. "Nice and peaceful this time of day." He stared out to sea. "What if Jack Douglas ain't here in Perto Varto? What if he's somewhere out there?"

"Maybe he is. Either way, I promised Mrs. Chumley I'd find him."

"We're both out of our element here. Strangers in a strange land. Same way I feel when I go to downtown Chicago during the day."

"How so?"

"All those tall buildings, people in suits. It's a white man's land. But at night? When the bathrooms need cleanin' and the floors need shinin'? That's when my folk get to visit. Here it ain't so bad. Color lines ain't so strong."

Pharaoh opened Larry's closet and studied the small safe mounted to an inner wall.

"How do you feel about this?" he asked Larry.

"The safe?"

"Same as the one in my room."

Larry picked up a plastic card from a side table. "We can program our own key code."

"Sure we can. But think like a professional thief for a minute. Could be a hotel employee with access to the hotel's master key card system. Doors and safes. Digital key codes. This ain't Fort Knox, Larry."

"Then we can keep the cash at the front desk with our passports. The hotel would be liable if a theft occurs."

"But then we're too visible. The locals talk to each other, tell the bad guys who's got money and who doesn't."

"Then what do you suggest?"

Pharaoh tapped his crotch. "Best safe I know is right here. Ain't nobody gettin' in my underwear without a fight."

Pharaoh went to his room and returned with the envelope of cash. He counted off a thousand dollars and handed it to Larry.

"More walkin' around money." He slid the envelope into his drawers. "You hungry?"

"Almost."

"Restaurant opens in twenty minutes. You take a walk on the beach while I get gussied up. The bad guys ain't up yet. You'll be fine."

Sandals in hand and pants rolled up, Larry walked along the shore, challenged by the unpredictable surf. He had never touched an ocean before. He bent over, scooped up a handful of seawater and tasted it. It was sweet and sour at the same time.

A few hundred yards down the beach he watched a brown-skinned fisherman launching a panga into the sea. The man was old and sturdy. He wore long baggy pants and a long-sleeved shirt. A wide brimmed hat covered his head.

Larry watched him start his engine. The man stood up in his panga and tossed a wide net behind him. It skimmed the surface, dragging behind the boat. The fisherman sat back in his boat and puttered out to sea.

A small boy appeared from nowhere and sat next to Larry.

"Do you know him?" said Larry.

"He is my grandfather," said the boy in broken English.

"Does he fish every day?"

"Si," said the boy.

"To feed his family?"

"To feed his soul," said the boy. "He loves his ocean."

CHAPTER 23

It was a ten minute ride from the hotel to Avenida Libertad in Old Town. A dozen galleries and gift shops lined the palm-fringed cobblestone street.

The first shop they visited was a commercial shop displaying indigenous Huichol art; yarn paintings, prayer bowls, beaded sculptures and handcrafted fantasy figures. Pharaoh showed the Jack Douglas photograph to the owner. She had never seen him before.

The next shop sold handcrafted jewelry. Three more shops sold tourist knickknacks. No one recognized the man in the photo.

"Let's forget the shops," said Larry. "We'll hone in on the galleries where the real artists are, including expatriates."

A few of the galleries were closed during the hot summer season. Larry found the Galeria Bandera on Avenida Aldama open.

It was on the second floor. On display were high quality paintings and sculptures by local artists.

The owner was an expatriate American from San Francisco who had lived in the town for twenty years. He recognized Jack Douglas in the photograph.

“Good old Jack in his prime. He was a handsome man back in the day. Doesn’t look anything like that now. Take off fifty pounds and add a beard.”

“You know him personally?”

“I *knew* him personally. He rented a cottage I owned in Old Town for a couple of years. Jack turned it into a studio. All the local artists were excited at first. He had a worldwide reputation. But after he settled in, he became a world class drunk. Jack never finished a single piece he started. He haunted the alleyways and dive bars, preferred the company of low life Indians. He called them ‘God’s people’. After he missed a few months’ rent, I visited his studio. None of his neighbors had seen him. He simply vanished. His studio was torn all to hell. Ripped canvases, smashed statues, none of his work was salvageable or sellable.”

“What was in his work?” said Larry.

“From what I could piece together, he had a fascination with *mermaids*.”

"Where do you think he went?"

"Everyone I talked to thinks he sailed west. His last known sighting was on the beach off the Malecon downtown. He bought a panga, a small sailing rig, from a local fisherman."

"How long ago?" said Pharaoh.

"At least three years, maybe longer."

"Can you refer us to anyone else who knew him?"

"Well, there's Maria Barajas. She owns a hoodoo shop over on Insurgentes Street. It's near the municipal flea market."

"Hoodoo? Like voodoo?"

"Yeah. When Jack went native on us she was his guide. I suggest you bring a bottle of tequila. Cuidado con las brujas!"

"What does that mean?"

"Beware the witches," said the gallery owner.

Back on the street, Pharaoh stopped in a liquor store and bought a bottle of local tequila while Larry flagged down a taxi for the flea market.

The cab ambled past rows of white-washed downtown buildings. Small pharmacies, liquor stores and gift shops lined the streets. The taxi entered the hotel zone, passing dozens of local men and women waving pamphlets at tourists on foot.

"What are they selling?" Pharaoh asked the driver.

"Condo timeshares. You want a timeshare? I have a cousin who sells them. He'll give you a free bottle of tequila."

"No," said Pharaoh. "We're here on business."

"What do you want at the flea market? Necklaces? Rings? I have a cousin who sells them."

"No thanks," said Pharaoh. "You got any gun shops here?"

The driver adjusted his mirror and studied Pharaoh. "Why do you want a gun? Are you American agents?"

Pharaoh shook his head. "No, nothing like that. I just like guns, is all."

"That is the problem with America. Everybody has a gun," complained the driver. "Here we do not like them." He pointed at a police officer standing at an intersection. He was wearing a bulletproof vest and carrying a machine gun. "Only la policia and the drug cartels have guns. The rest of us want to live in peace." The driver pulled over to the curb. "Here is your flea market. Enjoy your stay in Mexico, señores."

CHAPTER 24

Maria Barajas didn't look like a witch in her floral print dress. Her gray hair was pulled back in a bun. She wore makeup on the heavy side and her long painted nails were manicured. Her English was perfect. She carried herself with class and style.

The tiny hoodoo shop was clean and organized. Dark wooden shelves displayed bottles of bath salts and body rubs. A glass display case held perfumes and colognes. She sold a variety of spiritual waters used in religious rituals to cleanse people, objects, or dwellings of negative energy.

"I'm known for my waters; holy water, war water, peace water, blue water. Every now and then I get the crazies," said Maria. "Old hippies looking for magic mushrooms and religious fanatics looking to fill their mojo bags with spells and curses. But most of my clients just want to smell good."

Pharaoh set the bottle of tequila in front of her. "I was told you might like this," he said.

She picked up the bottle and studied the label. "Good quality," she said. "I haven't had a decent drink in months." She bent under the counter and produced three shot glasses. "Care to join me, gentlemen?"

Larry almost objected, but stopped when he felt Pharaoh's foot crushing his own.

"Glad to," said Pharaoh.

She deftly opened the bottle. After she poured she raised her glass in the air. "To Jack!" she said. "Poor romantic bastard that he was and maybe still is."

Pharaoh and Larry picked up their glasses. "To Jack."

Larry took a small sip. His eyes rolled and he grimaced. "How do people drink this stuff?"

"Very carefully," said Maria. She poured another round for Pharaoh and herself. "It's muggy in here. Let's sit on the veranda."

She grabbed the bottle and led the men out a back door to a small herb garden surrounded by a high fence of living weeping bamboo.

Maria picked a small leaf from a plant and tasted it. "These are my girls," she said. "I use them in my secret sauces."

"And your waters?" said Larry.

"Boiled tap water. I use different tea blends for the color."

They sat in chairs made from cedar splits and tanned pigskin decorated with brightly colored cushions and pillows.

"Jack left a tidy nest egg behind for me. We ran out our welcome with all the local so-called artists. Most of them are hacks anyway. It's amazing how much tourists will pay for a canvas of crap. Get your name listed in the travel books and you're a celebrity! Jack shunned them."

"The art gallery owner, he said Jack and you hung out with the local Indians. He said Jack called them 'God's people'," said Larry.

"Jack couldn't find any here. Mexico has a long tradition of savage conflicts. The Teotihuacan people, Mayans, Toltecs, then the Aztecs."

"What about the Taínos?" said Larry.

Miss Barajas smiled softly. "You know the name!"

"But very little about them. Do you think any survived?"

"Only a handful."

"Do you know a Professor Marquez?"

"Very well."

"We're told he thinks certain members of the Taínos were merpeople. Half fish, half human."

"Not a *fish*," said Maria. "Humans designed for the sea."

"Do you believe the stories? That they ever existed?"

"Yes," she said. "Let me show you something."

She took another shot of tequila and stood up, her back to them. She lifted her dress to her waist, exposing her buttocks. "I still have a great ass," she said. "But notice my lower spine? My coccyx, or tailbone, is the remnant of a lost tail." She dropped her dress and sat down. "Some Taínos swim. Some of us don't. The ocean was the last refuge for the Taínos. We heard stories of sea gypsies, outcasts in the Sea of Cortez and areas south. That's why Jack went there. To see if they are Taínos."

Larry produced a copy of the mermaid stamp and handed it to Maria. "Jack painted this."

Maria stared at it for a long time. Tears came to her eyes. "That's Jack's hand, alright. Pure genius."

Larry gave her a brief history of his research.

She studied the stamp again and smiled. "I hope he is still alive."

"I'm determined to find out," said Larry.

CHAPTER 25

Larry and Pharaoh returned to the hotel. They spent the afternoon under a large umbrella by the pool. Pharaoh liked the taste of tequila. The pool bartender kept them coming.

On Larry's insistence, Pharaoh wore a sling bag he bought in the gift shop across his chest to carry the cash. It was more appropriate than carrying money in his underwear next to his sweating testicles.

Pharaoh was getting agitated, bored with the faces of the foreign tourists at the hotel. He was in Mexico. He wanted to get out among the people, not sit with the scaredy cat tourists, hiding behind armed security guards at the hotel's front gates.

"What's our next move, Larry?"

"Tomorrow we find a charter boat. Sail to our latitude and longitude. If we're lucky it will be nothing but ocean. Then my job is done."

"And we're back in Chicago," realized Pharaoh, "back to the routine."

"Yes."

Pharaoh stood up and stretched. "I'm gonna change and take a run along the beach. As long as you stay in the hotel zone you'll be fine."

Pharaoh went to his room and took a thousand dollars out of his sling bag. He stuffed the bag inside the bottom of a zippered cushion of a chair next to his bed. He found a *Do Not Disturb* sign and hung it on the hallway door. He locked the door between his room and Larry's for added security.

Ten minutes later he appeared on the front steps of the hotel wearing a loud blue and yellow Hawaiian shirt, denim shorts and flip-flop sandals. He wouldn't be jogging today.

Pharaoh waved down a taxi. "Take me to where the women are," he instructed the driver.

"What kind of women?"

"Loose ones."

The driver smiled.

It was a long drive away from the beaches and tourists. The road led out of town east towards the mountains and turned to dirt.

“I’m not diggin’ this,” Pharaoh told the driver.

“Not to worry, señor,” smiled the driver. “We don’t have whorehouses in the city anymore. Most tourists can find girls on the Internet now. But we have social clubs. The Smiling Bandito is the best. The girls wear lingerie. They will dance with you and sit on your lap if you are a good tipper. I bring Germans there all the time.”

Ahead on the right was the club. It was a large tin shack built on stilts. Another taxi was parked outside. The driver parked next to it.

“See señor? Other tourists come here.”

Pharaoh paid his fare and went inside the club. The joint was dingy, lit with strings of lights. A large bouncer sat on a stool by the door and demanded ten dollars for a cover charge. Pharaoh paid it and walked to the bar. He studied the clientele; a pair of heavyset German men, a handful of bare-chested college frat boys wearing shorts and flip-flops and an old man in a wheelchair breathing on a respirator. Three women in worn lingerie were working the customers for drinks and tips.

Wheelchair man was receiving a lap dance from an older woman. Her face showed no emotion. Just another day at the office. One of the Germans was playfully spanking the second girl on the ass. The third woman was sitting on the edge of a dirty sofa, grabbing the attention of the college boys with her open legs, encouraging them to buy another round of tequila shots. The boys were rowdy and drunk.

A skinny female bartender greeted Pharaoh with a toothless smile. He ordered a cold bottle of beer, watching her hands to make sure she didn't slip a mickey in his drink.

He knew all about mickeys, named after Chicago bartender Michael "Mickey" Finn, who preyed on his drunken customers. There were two kinds of mickeys; the first was a laxative used to get rid of obnoxious barflies. The second was a drug, usually chloral hydrate, a soluble sedative which incapacitated customers who were taken to a backroom or an alley and robbed of their money and valuables.

There was a jukebox at the end of the bar. A giant stuffed teddy bear wearing a sombrero sat on top of it.

Pharaoh noticed the shuffle of a beaded curtain leading to a dressing room. An attractive woman came through it, wearing an ivory-colored halter dress with a plunging neckline. She moved gracefully on three-inch heels. Her hips were full, her large breasts firm. She wore a blonde wig. Pharaoh guessed her age at thirty. She swayed across the room to the jukebox and stood over it, punching in song selections.

A song started playing. A rhumba. She kept her back to the men, swiveling her hips to draw their attention. She slowly turned, her eyes burning through Pharaoh as she danced seductively across the room to him, snapping her fingers. She reached the bar and slapped the countertop with the palms of her hands.

"They call me Marilyn. Buy me a drink?"

Pharaoh motioned to the bartender. A large bottle and two shot glasses appeared on the counter.

"Fifty dollars," said the bartender.

Pharaoh paid. She took notice of the wad of money. What pocket he pulled it from, what pocket he put it back in.

"Nice outfit," Pharaoh told the dancer.

"It's a copy of the famous subway dress Marilyn Monroe wore in *The Seven Year Itch*," said the woman in decent English. She poured them a drink. "What brings you up the hill?"

"I'm looking for the real Mexico," said Pharaoh.

"It isn't here," said Marilyn Monroe. "This is an illusion."

CHAPTER 26

The sun would be setting soon. Pharaoh had been gone for hours. Larry sat poolside on a recliner, his lap covered with brochures. The endless string of fruity drinks mixed with a variety of alcohol was having an effect on him.

Ronaldo, the usual bartender, arrived with a blue cocktail.

"What's this?' said Larry.

"Agua Fresca," said Ronaldo. "Just a hint of rum."

He set the drink next to Larry and sat across from him on a recliner, watching the frolicking tourists in the pool.

"Do you like to swim?" Ronaldo asked.

"Not really," said Larry. "There was a public pool in my neighborhood. The priests used to take us there. They'd line us up and push us in the pool. 'Sink or swim,' they'd tell us."

Ronaldo shook his head. "My friend at the front desk said your friend took a taxi and left. I thought he was your bodyguard."

"He is."

"You trust him?"

"He's from my neighborhood."

"That don't mean shit, Mr. Settlebottom."

"I know."

"And you two with all that cash..."

Larry gave him a surprised look.

Ronaldo stood up and winked at him. "Your friend Pharaoh, he likes to brag."

Ronaldo pointed at a woman walking along the pool's edge towards them. "Uh-oh. There she is again. Poor widow."

Larry turned his head and stared at the woman.

A white bikini top covered her round breasts. A black sarong was wrapped around her waist. Her perfect face was obvious under a wide-brimmed straw hat.

"Her dead husband was a famous surgeon in Guadalajara," said Ronaldo. "Every day she comes to watch the sun go down. She is still young enough to attract any man, but such a lonely lady. She is very rich."

The woman stopped next to Larry. She spread a beach towel across the reclining lounge chair Ronaldo had vacated and leaned back.

"Buenas tardes," said Ronaldo.

"Buenas tardes," she said.

"Quieres una cerveza?"

"Por favor," said the woman. "Con lima."

Ronaldo went to fetch her beer from the bar.

The woman glanced at Larry. "Hola," she said.

"Hello," said Larry.

She closed her eyes, feeling the ocean's breeze against her perfect skin.

Larry noticed her pedicured toes. The young widow suddenly opened her eyes, catching Larry staring at her.

"I am Conchita. And you?"

"Lawrence," he said.

"An American?"

"Yes. From Chicago."

"Ah, Chicago! Al Capone, sí?"

"A long time ago."

"Do they still have gangsters in Chicago?"

"A different kind of gangster now."

"There are gangsters everywhere," laughed Conchita. She lifted her taut long legs off the chaise and sat up, facing him. Her face was beautiful with just a hint of age lines. She looked at the charter boat brochures on Larry's lap. "You are renting a boat?"

"Yes," said Larry.

"To go fishing?"

"No," said Larry, "I'm looking for an island far from the mainland."

"Then you want a big boat. The ocean can be dangerous."

She took the brochures from Larry, thumbed through them and tossed them aside with a slight wave. "Don't bother with any of those. I know a captain with a good boat at a fair price. When do you want to go?"

"I was hoping tomorrow," said Larry.

Ronaldo returned and handed Conchita an ice cold beer with a lime tucked in the lip of the bottle. She smiled up at him. Ronaldo smiled back at her. They seemed to know each other quite well.

"Ronaldo," she said, "call our friend Captain Ruiz. See if he is free tomorrow." She turned and looked at Larry. "He charges eight hundred dollars a day. *Cash*. Is that a problem?"

"No," said Larry.

"Bueno."

Ronaldo hurried away to make the phone call.

Conchita plucked the lime from her bottle and sucked the juice off it, catching a dribble on her chin with her pinky finger. She licked it off slowly. Her eyes narrowed, locked towards the west.

"It will be a beautiful sunset."

Larry's eyes glanced at her tanned legs, following them up towards the parted sarong, a patch of white bikini between her shapely thighs. She glanced at him again, catching his stare. Larry blushed slightly.

"Would you like my company on the boat? I have nothing else to do."

"If you'd like," said Larry.

"Anyone else going?"

"My bodyguard," said Larry.

The widow smiled and shook her head. "You do not need a bodyguard to take a boat trip," she said. "Besides, I am not dangerous."

Ronaldo returned. He knelt between their chairs. "Captain Ruiz is free tomorrow. Eight o'clock in the morning at the marina. The name of his boat is the Tigerfish."

Conchita raised her hand. "I will take Lawrence myself." She picked up Larry's fruit drink and tasted it. She gave Ronaldo a dirty look. "Why this cheap booze? Bring Lawrence a real drink, a strong Mexican beer!"

Ronaldo nodded and hurried away.

"I'm not much of a drinker," Larry admitted.

"Neither was I. Then my husband died and I learned to enjoy myself again." She took a long sip from her bottle, licked her lips seductively and placed his hand on her soft warm leg. "Now tell me all about you, Lawrence. No lies. I don't have time for lies. Lies make people crazy."

Larry smiled. "As a baby I was left on the doorstep of an orphanage. I don't know what my original name was, whether I'm Irish, Italian or German. I was adopted in my early teens by a lovely pair of sisters, Mrs. Settle and Miss Bottom."

Conchita stopped him with a flutter of her hands. "No, no, no. None of that matters! I don't want to hear about baby Lawrence or Lawrence the teenager with pimples or Lawrence the college boy. You have today and you have tomorrow. That is the reality of your life. Who you are now, not what brought you here, but why you are here. Do you know why you are here?"

"I am looking for someone."

She fluttered her hands again. "No, no, no. That is not why you are here either. Are you willing to think more deeply about yourself?"

"I have tried in the past, but it depresses me."

"You or the illusion you have about yourself?"

"Is this a therapy session?"

She laughed. "No, not at all. I just enjoy engaging people with healthy minds. Which do you prefer, pleasure or pain?"

"I would have to say 'pleasure'."

"But aren't they the same thing sometimes?"

"You got me there," said Larry.

CHAPTER 27

A sliver of sun cracked through the blinds of the dirty room. Pharaoh sat up on the floor. Where was he? How did he get here? He smelled coffee brewing. He rubbed his eyes and saw an old man in a wheelchair staring down at him. It was the old guy from the bar.

The man pulled a respirator from his mouth. "Tough night?"

"Where the hell am I?" said Pharaoh.

"Still up in the hills," said the man in perfect English.

Pharaoh felt a large bruise on his jaw. "What the hell happened?"

"Those college boys, they jumped you," said the old man.

"Why?"

"They were drunk. You were drunk. You didn't like the way they were treating the señoritas. One of them called you a nigger and it was on."

Pharaoh reached down and checked his clothes. There was blood on his Hawaiian shirt, a large gash over a pocket of his pants.

"They cut your money out," said the old man. "Rolled you."

"Sonofabitches."

The old man laughed. "You can probably find two of them at the hospital in town. You got some good licks in before they smashed your head with a bottle."

Pharaoh tapped the top of his head. There was a patch of dried blood there.

"Eight stitches," said the old man. "Don't worry. I used to be a doctor."

"And now you're here in this shithole," said Pharaoh.

"Better here than ten years in an American prison."

"What for?"

"Medical malpractice. Reconstructive surgery. An ugly woman thought I could make her beautiful. It didn't work out."

Pharaoh pulled himself to his feet and went to the window. He drew open a curtain and looked out. The dive bar was across the street.

"How did I end up here?"

"Marilyn Monroe and the bouncer carried you across the road."

"How long have I been unconscious?"

"Since last night."

Pharaoh paced back and forth. "Shit man, I got to go!"

"Relax, amigo. Have some coffee first."

"I let a friend down," said Pharaoh. "I never should have come here."

"But you did. It's human nature. We think we are better than what we really are."

"You don't understand," Pharaoh shouted "I was supposed to have my friend's back. I'm tryin' to make restitution for a wrong I committed."

"But instead you took a break to chase pussy."

Pharaoh rubbed his arms up and down his body, walking and talking. "I'm a piece of shit. Larry don't deserve this. I got to do right by him. Got to make amends."

Wheelchair man sighed. "The world is an ugly place. We are imperfect creatures. Understand this and you will find peace."

"You live across the road from a whore house."

"And I own it. A cheaper lap dance you'll never find."

"I need a gun."

"Guns cost money."

"I got money back at my hotel."

Wheelchair man rolled across the room to a dinette table. He tossed Pharaoh a key. “I used to own a sailboat. Had a few pop guns aboard. Might be in my shed out back.”

Pharaoh grabbed the key and went outside to a small tin shack surrounded by tall thick grass. He unlocked the door and opened it. The shack was piled high with junk.

Pharaoh sorted through moldy seat cushions, broken fishing poles, lobster cages, and tarps. He found a white metal box with a red first aid cross painted on the lid and opened it. Inside was a small black pistol and a small black box of acorn-shaped bullets. Pharaoh didn’t know much about guns. He guessed it to be a .22 caliber. The swing-out cylinder held eight rounds.

CHAPTER 28

Larry sat in a chair on the balcony listening to the steady crashes of surf against sand below. He was looking forward to a day at sea. What could possibly go wrong?

He had knocked three times on his bodyguard's door since dawn but there was still no reply. Pharaoh didn't close the door between their rooms the day before. Why was it closed and locked now? Pharaoh said he was going for a jog yesterday. But someone had seen him leave the hotel in a taxi. Larry felt secure at the hotel. Over dinner the night before, Conchita convinced him that many parts of Mexico were safer than most big cities in the United States.

Maybe she was right. Maybe he didn't need Pharaoh's services after all. Maybe he just wanted a temporary friend. He never made any at the orphanage. The nuns taught him not to get close to the other kids. It could only lead to his sense of abandonment when they were swept away with the promise of a real family.

Larry had taken a stroll in the moonlight with Conchita after dinner and visited the marina next door. It was a safe place, well-lit at night with armed security guards dressed in clean white uniforms. Hundreds of boats, mostly yachts, were berthed along the sturdy clean docks. Larry had only been on a boat a few times in his life; on the Chumley yacht for dinner parties while it was tied to a dock. He was surprised at himself, thinking of Conchita. She was beautiful and engaging. *Worldly*. She made him feel safe. Pharaoh wouldn't be needed today, he decided. He found a pad of paper on a side table and wrote a note for Pharaoh.

"Your services won't be needed today. Ronaldo introduced me to a very nice woman at the pool. We rented a boat for a day trip at sea. We expect to return at sunset."

Larry slipped the note under Pharaoh's door. He returned to his room and opened the wall safe, locking his wallet and credit cards inside. It was a safer repository than his pants. He counted his cash in hand. Eighteen hundred dollars. More than enough to pay the boat captain his eight hundred dollars, tip included. If he needed more cash, he could get some from Pharaoh when he turned up. Larry examined the Double Eagle gold coin. There was a small button-down pocket inside his khaki shorts. The coin would be safe there with his room card.

He studied himself in the mirror. He had gotten some sun on his face yesterday but his legs were a pale white. After dinner with Conchita he had stopped by the gift shop and picked up sundries; bug repellant, sunscreen, and a pair of sunglasses. He put on the ventilated olive Boonie hat he had bought. It provided 360° of shade and had an adjustable chin strap for strong winds. Satisfied, he headed downstairs to meet Conchita in the lobby.

Larry found her talking to Ronaldo on the steps of the hotel. She wore a sheer white sundress, the outline of a black bikini visible beneath. She turned and smiled at Larry.

"Right on time," said Conchita. She kissed him on the cheek. Her lips were warm, her breath minty sweet. She took Larry's hand in hers and led him towards the marina.

"Bon voyage!" shouted Ronaldo.

Hundreds of sailboats, yachts and fishing boats were docked in the marina. Conchita led Larry along the concrete promenade to a floating slip. He felt the rise and fall of water beneath him.

She smiled at him. "It takes a few minutes to get your sea legs."

An older double-decked fishing boat, its engine running, waited for them at the end of the dock. The Tigerfish needed a good paint job. The faded tan awning over the captain's chair had large holes in it.

On the lower blood-stained deck, a pair of young deckhands filled a large cooler with ice. They had dirty rags in their back pockets and grease stains on their tee shirts. Their eyes were bloodshot and yellowed.

Captain Ruiz was at the wheel, adjusting the throttle of the boat's twin diesel engines. He was a big surly man with long black hair and a gray beard. He nodded down at Conchita as she and Larry boarded the boat near the stern.

She shouted up to the captain in his high seat. "Hello, Captain Ruiz! This is Lawrence."

"Hello, Lawrence," he said. He spoke irritably, as if under the duress of constipation.

The two deckhands stood and smiled at their guests.

"Hola, Diego and Pablo," said Conchita.

"Hola, señora."

"This is Lawrence."

The deckhands giggled as they pronounced his name. "Buenas dias, *L-a-w-r-e-n-c-e*."

Captain Ruiz climbed down from his controls and took a beer from the cooler. He popped it open.

"To good weather!" he said. After a long drink he looked to Conchita. "You have the money?"

Conchita turned to Larry. He fumbled in the pocket of his khaki shorts and pulled out the roll of cash.

"Eight hundred. Yes?" said Larry.

"Sí," said the captain.

Larry handed him the money. All eyes were on him as he tucked the remaining cash back in his pocket.

"Free cerveza and tequila all day," said Captain Ruiz. "There is a head below if you need to piss. Or you can piss over the side if it's downwind. Diego will cook our lunch later." He pushed Pablo hard in the shoulder. "Cast off," he said. "We have a long day ahead of us." He turned and snapped a question at Diego. "The fuel tanks are full?"

"Sí," said Diego.

There was a stack of white plastic chairs tied to a pole with bungee cord. Captain Ruiz roughly yanked two of the chairs from the stack and slapped them down on the deck by the stern. He offered Larry and Conchita a seat.

"What is our destination?" the captain asked Larry.

Larry pulled a piece of paper from his pocket and handed him the coordinates from the mermaid bottle. "The first set of numbers indicates latitude, the second set —."

"I know what the hell they mean," Ruiz said sharply. The surly captain climbed up behind the wheel.

The boat pulled away from the dock. Larry leaned in towards Conchita, trying to be heard over the roar of the engines.

"Are you sure about this?" he said. "This crew - they seem a little rough."

"This is what you get for eight hundred dollars," said Conchita.

"I have more cash in my room. Perhaps a better boat..."

She patted him on the thigh. "Relax, Lawrence. I have known Captain Ruiz a very long time."

She glanced back over her shoulder. Captain Ruiz smiled down at her with an affectionate grin.

"What about life preservers?" Larry asked.

She pointed at a large metal foot locker. "In there, but you won't need one."

The boat maneuvered out of the marina into a deep channel, chugging past cruise ships unloading eager passengers for a day trip into the city.

"Every day the Americans come," said Conchita. "Some by sea, some by plane. For forty years they have come here to taste their Mexico."

The boat passed a lighthouse and entered Banderas Bay. It skipped past several smaller boats pulling parasailing tourists behind them.

"Banderas Bay is the biggest bay on the Pacific coast," Conchita shouted to Larry. "Forty miles across. It will take an hour to reach the open ocean. There the waves will change. They will be bigger."

After thirty minutes, Larry stood up and pointed off in the distance. Several boats were crowded together, tourists crowding the deck rails.

An enormous humpback whale rose out of the sea. It slapped down hard on the ocean's surface, soaking a dozen whale watchers on one of the boats.

Larry turned to Conchita. "Wow! Did you see that?"

Conchita's face was down. She was reading a Spanish romance novel in her lap. "Whales don't come here in the summer. That one is lost." She pulled a tube of sunscreen from her bag. "Put this on. You don't want to get burned by the sun."

Larry applied ample amounts of lotion to his legs, arms and face. He offered the container to Conchita. “Would you like some on your back?”

“I’m Mexican,” she said. “I have brown skin. I won’t burn.”

Conchita stood up, removed her dress and sat again. She looked stunning in a black bikini.

Larry leaned back in his chair and watched the disappearing coast. Something was wrong here. The light affections Conchita had offered earlier had faded away. She seemed cool and distant now. Whenever Larry glanced at the two crew members, they stared back at him with malicious grins. Captain Ruiz ignored his guests, honking the boat’s loud horn just to be heard as it pushed on towards the open ocean.

“The captain seems mad about something,” Larry told Conchita.

She offered a tight smile. “He’ll be happy when the day is over.”

CHAPTER 29

Pharaoh had rehearsed over and over again what he would say to Larry. He would tell him about the botched robbery and the dead fiancée. He would promise him his full-fledged allegiance and beg for forgiveness. He would show Larry that he still had most of the money and that he now had a gun to protect him from harm.

Pharaoh entered the hotel suite and slid the gun box under his bed. He replaced his torn shorts for a new pair and unlocked the door between the two bedrooms. He expected Larry to be sitting there, waiting for him. Maybe he would fire Pharaoh on the spot. Pharaoh couldn't blame him. He hadn't done his job. He hit the ground in Mexico like a loose cannon, got drunk by the swimming pool, and got even drunker at a whore house. A bad ass like him, he even got rolled by a bunch of punk college kids. There was no logical excuse for his behavior. Pharaoh had lost it. He bragged too much and let down the only real friend he had in the world.

But Larry wasn't in the room. Pharaoh ran with a panic back to his own room, to the chair where he had hidden the money in the cushion. It was still there. He pulled all the money out and stuffed most of it in his sling bag. He pulled a short stack of twenties and hundreds and stuck it in his new shorts. He noticed a note on the floor near the door jam. Pharaoh picked it up and read it.

"Your services won't be needed today. Ronaldo introduced me to a very nice woman at the pool. We rented a boat for a day trip at sea. We expect to return at sunset."

Pharaoh crushed the note in his hands and tossed it in a wastebasket.

"Damned bartender! A hustler just like me."

He hurried out of the room and went downstairs. Wheelchair man was outside the hotel, waiting in the backseat of a cab in valet parking. Pharaoh gave him two hundred dollars for the pistol.

"How's your friend?" said the disgraced doctor. "Pissed? Did he fire you?"

"He ain't here," said Pharaoh. "Went on a boat trip for the day."

"Uh-oh. That can't be good. You said he was afraid to leave the room without you."

"Something changed," Pharaoh said. "I think a woman got to him."

Wheelchair man laughed and took a long breath on his respirator to get his lungs back.

"I'll just have to ride shit out until Larry comes back," Pharaoh figured.

They shook hands.

"Good luck to you, my friend," said the doctor. "I hope things work out for you. But they probably won't. Such is life."

Pharaoh nodded. "Thanks for covering my ass last night, doc."

"No bother. Good Samaritans come in all shapes and sizes."

Pharaoh's senses were on high alert. It was time for *Ticks and Tricks*. Fight or flight responses. He walked through the lobby and headed towards the pool bar. He visualized his list of nonverbal cues for lying.

Ticks: People itched or sweated when they lied. They scratched their cheeks, hands or neck. They might bite or lick their lips or tug at an ear.

Others rubbed their sweaty hands together or got dry mouth and pursed their lips.

Deceptors shielded their mouth or eyes before answering with a lie. Some closed their eyes.

Others cleared their throat or swallowed before answering.

Groomers tidied up their immediate surroundings; a napkin out of place, move a glass. Some pulled their hair back or straightened their tie or glasses during a lie.

Eyes darting back and forth or blinking in rapid succession were psychological fight or flee gestures.

Tricks: If a right-handed person looked up to the left they were accessing their memory of an incident. If they looked up to the right they accessed their imagination to invent an answer. *A lie.* Left-handed people did the opposite.

According to Larry's note Ronaldo had hooked him up with a woman from the pool.

Pharaoh reached the pool's edge, staring down at the bartender behind the submerged bar. Ronaldo was mixing drinks for new arrivals. He was right-handed.

"Have you seen my friend Larry?" Pharaoh asked him.

Ronaldo glanced up to the left. "No, señor. Not today."

"You know anything about him going out on a boat?"

Ronaldo arranged napkins in front of him. "A boat? No. Did you check with guest services, amigo?"

"No. Say, Larry said he met a woman here yesterday. Do you know who she was?"

Ronaldo scratched his cheek. "I saw him talking to somebody, but I don't know who. I was busy."

"Am I a good tipper?" said Pharaoh.

Ronaldo smiled. "Very good."

"Then don't lie to me."

Ronaldo set drinks on a tray. "I have to take care of my new guests." He sounded upset.

"You do that, Ronaldo. But we ain't done talkin' yet."

Pharaoh went to the lobby He spoke with a polite girl in Guest Services. Mr. Settlebottom did not rent a boat through them.

"Did you see him leave the hotel with a woman this morning?"

She shook her head and answered immediately. "No sir. I just started my shift."

He almost asked to review the hotel's security video but that would raise a red flag. There was an easier way to obtain information. He pulled cash from his pocket and walked outside to the front steps of the hotel. He walked up to a friendly valet and smiled at him with a twenty between his fingers.

"You see a tall white guy leave this morning? Larry Settebottom?"

The valet took the twenty. “Si, señor. Mr. Settlebottom from Room 1408.”

“When did he leave?”

“Around eight.”

Pharaoh handed him another twenty. “Who did he leave with?”

“A black-haired woman. Very nice-looking.”

“Is she a guest in the hotel?”

“No, señor. But I see her here many times. Mostly at night.”

Pharaoh held up another twenty. “She a hustler?”

“I think so.”

“She have a name?”

“Conchita.”

Pharaoh stuffed the twenty in the valet’s shirt pocket. “How was she dressed?”

“A white sundress. Hot body.”

“She know Ronaldo? The pool bartender?”

“He works for her sometimes.”

“On commission?”

“We all work on commission,” said the valet.

“What’s the scam?”

“I don’t know.”

Pharaoh held up another twenty.

The valet licked his lips, staring at the money. "Conchita's husband has a boat in the marina. That's all I know."

"What's the name of the boat?"

"The Tigerfish."

Pharaoh gave him the twenty. "We never talked. I don't want to come back here and kick your ass. Understood?"

The valet nodded.

Built in a lagoon and surrounded by luxury hotels and high rise apartments, Marina Vallarta was sophisticated and popular. Along the marina boardwalk were numerous shops, boutiques, galleries, and cafes. Outside the marina was an aquatic artificial basin big enough for cruise ships.

Pharaoh walked up and down concrete gangways and finger docks leading to moored yachts, sailboats and fishing trawlers. He couldn't find the Tigerfish. Pharaoh found the harbor master's office and inquired about the missing boat.

An elderly clerk in a clean white uniform checked his records and gave Pharaoh the Tigerfish's slip number.

Pharaoh visited the slip next. The Tigerfish wasn't there. He saw a man mopping down the deck of his sailboat next door. The man wore baggy shorts and flip-flops. His face was brown and wrinkled from a decade in the sun.

"Any idea when the Tigerfish returns?" Pharaoh shouted up to him.

"Why? You thinking of renting it?" the man shouted back in a New York accent.

"Maybe."

"My advice? Find another boat."

"Why?" said Pharaoh.

"The Tigerfish is a piece of crap. Dirty boat. Dirty crew. I've been asking the marina manager to move me for three months but nothing has opened up yet. Goddamned trailer trash if you ask me. I hear they're late on the rent."

"You know a woman named Conchita?"

The man dipped his mop in a slop bucket, slapping clean soapy water on his deck. "I know who she is. She's married to the boat's captain."

"Did you see a tall white guy leave with them this morning?"

"Headed out to sea just after eight."

"Any idea when they'll return?"

"Don't know and I don't care," said the New Yorker. "Most of the boats come back in around sunset. Hell of a traffic jam."

Pharaoh walked back to the hotel. This much he knew; Larry was out to sea for a day trip. He was with a woman named Conchita on a crappy boat named the Tigerfish.

Maybe it was just a harmless excursion. Maybe Ronaldo was just trying to make a few extra bucks. There was nothing Pharaoh could do for now. He would return to the hotel pool and hang out with the bartender, pry more information out of him and brush up on his long apology to Larry. Pharaoh adjusted the sling bag on his chest. Everything would turn out fine. He was in the gringo zone.

Pharaoh reached the hotel. He winked at the valet and entered the lobby. The polite girl sitting at her desk at Guest Services waved at him.

"Did you find your friend?" she said.

Pharaoh smiled and waved his hands in the air. "We're good," he said. "I'll be at the swimming pool if he returns early."

Pharaoh exited the lobby and entered the pool area. His eyes fixed on Ronaldo, animatedly talking to a pair of newlyweds under a cabana. Pharaoh went to the shallow end of the pool, hiked down the steps in the warm water and took a seat at the bar. Ronaldo returned with an empty tray and stuffed a ten dollar bill into a tip jar behind him.

"I'll bet you make good money here," said Pharaoh.

Ronaldo smiled back. "All my college bills are paid."

"I'll bet they are," said Pharaoh. "Pour me a rum and coke."

"Did you find your friend?" said Ronaldo.

"Not yet, but when I do you'll be the first to know."

CHAPTER 30

Mile after mile they traveled west on the open ocean, far from the shipping lanes, away from the fishing spots. Conchita rarely looked up from her book. The two seedy crew members spent most of their time below deck in the galley listening to Mexican music, laughing and joking. Occasionally Captain Ruiz would bark a sharp order down to Diego and Pablo. Diego would disappear into a hole somewhere to check the engine. Pablo would fetch a beer out of the cooler for the captain and hurry below to check on the progress of the food he was preparing.

Lunch was served. Pablo brought up trays from the galley and set one on Larry's lap. Larry poked at a bowl of red broth, meat and vegetables with a spoon.

"What are the ingredients?" he asked Conchita.

She set her book aside to eat off her own tray. “It’s Menudo: mostly intestines, stomach, and tongue. Good for hangovers and sea sickness.”

Larry tried a small taste and set it aside. He nibbled at a tortilla instead.

Conchita slurped up her food. She wasn’t very lady-like. When she finished she belched and stood up. She sat on a bench seat at the stern, her long legs, flat stomach and ample breasts on display. She stared out to sea for a long time, occasionally turning back to stare at Larry. She seemed sad.

“What is it?” said Larry. “Why do you look at me that way?”

“You shouldn’t have come, Lawrence. You should not have told me about the cash in your room. I am sorry you are an orphan, but aren’t we all, really? You will never find your mermaid. No one ever does.”

Captain Ruiz slowed the engines. Pablo ran to the side of the boat and grabbed a long coil of rope with a small grapnel anchor attached to it.

Captain Ruiz shouted down to Larry. “We have arrived at your destination.”

Larry stood up and went to the side of the boat as the captain steered it towards a rock protruding from the sea. It was twenty feet across and three feet above the waterline.

"A sea mount," said Captain Ruiz. "We call it 'the Eye of God'."

The captain came down from his seat and took the rope and anchor from Pablo. He flung the anchor towards the rock. One of its tines grabbed hold on the far side with a loud clanging noise.

"But the coordinates. I thought there would be an island," protested Larry.

"These are not your coordinates. They are much further out. Today there is no island for you," said the captain.

He nodded to Pablo and Diego. They rushed at Larry and grabbed him from behind, pinning his arms back.

"Check his pockets," Captain Ruiz instructed Conchita.

She stepped up to Larry and pulled the money from his pockets.

"How much?" said Captain Ruiz.

Conchita counted it. "Almost a thousand dollars."

"Some of that was your tip," said Larry.

The others started laughing.

"Our tip!" said the captain.

Conchita dug further into Larry's pockets. She produced a stick of lip balm and smeared Larry's lips with it. She found his room card and waved it at the captain.

"Room 1408?" she asked Larry.

"Yes."

"What is the combination to your room safe?" said Ruiz.

Conchita's hands fluttered. "It doesn't matter. We can open it."

"Anything else?" said the captain.

Conchita reached further into Larry's shorts.

"I found something hard," she smiled. She played inside the shorts a little longer and produced the Double Eagle coin.

"What is this?" she asked Larry.

"A token. I was given it for luck," he said.

Captain Ruiz doubled over with laughter. "Don't you see? Don't you know? You have no luck gringo!"

He picked Larry up and threw him into the ocean. Larry resurfaced, gasping for air. He grabbed hold of the rope fastening the ship to the sea mount.

"Okay. Very funny. Some sort of maritime initiation, I expect. Now pull me in."

Captain Ruiz pointed at the protruding rock. "You go there."

"*That*? A rock in the middle of the ocean?"

"Go!" ordered the captain.

"Estupido gringo!" said Pablo.

Larry followed the rope to the sea mount and pulled himself up. "You aren't going to leave me here?"

Diego picked up Larry's hat and flung it at him. Larry caught it midair and tucked it on his head.

"How much money is in his room?" the captain asked Conchita.

"Ronaldo says maybe fifty thousand dollars. And credit cards."

The captain rubbed his hands together. "Good! We will take it all." He sat on the side of the boat and frowned at Larry. "What did you expect would happen? What is wrong with you? Mermaids today, unicorns tomorrow, maybe?" He pointed at Conchita. "She is a married woman. My wife! What did you want? To sleep with her? Huh? You stupid man!" Captain Ruiz pointed up at the bright sky. "The ocean, it works funny like the sun. It goes up, it goes down. Tonight is a full moon. It will raise the ocean, inch by inch. It will cover the Eye of God you are standing on and you will drown."

"I've done nothing to harm you," said Larry.

“We live in a cruel world,” said Conchita. “Did they not teach you that at the orphanage?” She stared at the golden coin in her hand and tossed it to Larry. “For you, Lawrence! For luck!”

The coin hit the surface of the rock and danced in a circle. Larry stepped on it with his sandal, picked it up and put it back in his pocket. He stared at Conchita in disbelief.

“Beneath your cotton dress, your rich dark eyes, and your smooth skin? You are a very ugly person, Conchita.”

“I know,” she shrugged, “but being bad makes me feel good. Many people are made like me.”

Captain Ruiz climbed the ladder to his seat and shifted the boat in gear. Pablo grabbed at the tethering rope, wiggled it free from the rock, and drew the anchor in.

Larry watched the Tigerfish turn and head east. He saw Conchita standing at the back of the boat, her beauty withering with the distance. He sat down on the warm rock, staring in every direction. No one would ever find him here. Larry had the plain-sighted honest resolution that he was going to die here. Always the orphan, this was an unpromising end.

CHAPTER 31

Hours slipped by. Pharaoh went down to the hotel pool towards the end of Ronaldo's shift. He ordered a few clear tequilas, the good stuff right out of the bottle. Most of it made its way into the hotel pool between Pharaoh's legs when Ronaldo wasn't looking.

Sober of mind and slurring his speech, Pharaoh played the obnoxious drunk well, shouting lewd obscenities at the girls in the swimming pool, harping up his blackness and *you know what they say about black men*. A concerned manager had stopped by Ronaldo's station twice already. Ronaldo said he had Pharaoh under control.

Pharaoh bragged about the money he had locked up in Larry's hotel safe. "Mebbe I'll buy me a schooner and sail to Tahiti."

The bartender pretended not to listen but his body language said otherwise.

When Ronaldo announced his shift was ending, Pharaoh tipped him a twenty and asked him for a good lobster restaurant downtown. Ronaldo gladly made the reservation and arranged for a taxi to meet Pharaoh at the front door at nine o'clock.

Pharaoh went to his room and slipped on a dress shirt, white slacks, and shoes. When the taxi arrived, he didn't take the one Ronaldo had ordered. He took the one behind it instead, still pretending to be drunk and promising a big tip to the driver.

He rode the taxi for a block, remembered something he had forgotten in his room and tipped the guy fifty bucks. He hurried back to the hotel on foot, avoiding the main lobby. He found a side entrance and walked up the stairwell to the fourteenth floor. The hallway was empty.

Pharaoh hurried inside his room to wait for his inevitable, unwelcome guests. He grabbed the pistol from the white metal box under the bed and opened the doors between the two bedrooms. He stuffed his large frame in a corner of Larry's closet, eyed the safe nearby and closed the door in front of him. He stared through the slits of the closet door and noticed the sun was waning off the balcony.

Any minute now.

A few minutes later, Pharaoh heard the door to Larry's room being opened. He listened to the small voices of a male and female whispering in the hallway. The female said something in Spanish about *dinero* and a wallet with credit cards. He felt the handle of the pistol tucked in his pants.

Patience now. Not yet.

Two dark figures entered the room. One of them turned on a night lamp. He smelled the sweet fragrance of a woman approaching the closet. Saw her through the slits of the closet, wearing a white cotton dress. She opened the closet door, knelt down and started working the combination to the safe.

Ronaldo came up behind her, speaking in Spanish about an override combination that opened every hotel safe. He gave her the numbers.

The woman turned the lock dials and opened the safe. "No Bueno," she said, "just a wallet and credit cards. No cash."

Pharaoh moved suddenly, bursting out of the closet, breaking off the hinges. He pushed both of them back on the bed and raised his gun.

"Looks like we have a problem," he said.

Ronaldo and the woman stared up at him, terrified by his size, the gun in his hand.

Pharaoh calmly crossed to a bedside telephone and called security. “Bring the police, too.” He hung up the phone and studied Conchita, her dress in disarray, revealing a black bikini bottom.

“You’re a looker,” he said. “At least Larry has good taste. Now, where is he?”

“Where is who?” she said.

“My friend.”

She smiled at him smugly. “We are all somewhere. Some latitude, some longitude.”

“Ronaldo?”

The bartender said he didn’t know.

Pharaoh thought about beating an answer out of them but was interrupted by a sharp knock on the door.

He spent the rest of the evening sorting out the mess with two Mexican policemen and the hotel’s head of security. From what Pharaoh could understand in the heated exchange in Spanish between the police and the perpetrators, there had been other hotel safe break-ins since Ronaldo’s employment. Conchita was Ronaldo’s aunt. Captain Ruiz was her husband.

Conchita denied taking Larry out to sea on the Tigerfish. "Where is your proof?" she repeated over and over.

Pharaoh told the police he had a witness. A man from New York who occupied the slip next to the Tigerfish.

One of the cops went to the marina and returned half an hour later. He had spoken with the New Yorker who confirmed a tall American had boarded the Tigerfish that morning. The eyewitness said the Tigerfish returned before dusk. Only Conchita had exited the boat. The crew of the Tigerfish was being held by port authorities for further questioning.

"Still no proof it was your friend on board!" Conchita argued. "There are many tall Americans."

"Then who was the man with you on the boat?" asked a policeman.

"I don't know who he was. He was from one of the cruise ships. Captain Ruiz dropped him off at the international dock before returning to the marina."

A police officer told Pharaoh the investigation would take a few days. The head of hotel security promised to provide the police with a still image of Lawrence Settlebottom captured from the hotel's security camera when he checked in. One of the cops would check in with the marina's port authority to review video surveillance of boats leaving the marina.

"As for the burglary the woman and the bartender will be charged," said the head of security.

Fingerprints were taken from the hotel safe. Ronaldo and Conchita were handcuffed and escorted to the police station. A maintenance man came in to replace the broken closet door.

One of the policemen borrowed Pharaoh's gun and inspected it. "Where did you get this?" he said.

"I found it," Pharaoh lied.

The policeman laughed and handed him back the gun. "A clever trick," he said. "Be careful how you use it in the future."

After everyone left, Pharaoh took a long cold shower, banging the walls with his fists. He started sobbing. Larry was missing. It was Pharaoh's fault. Larry had hired him for protection and Pharaoh had let him down. He remembered what Conchita had said, "We are all somewhere. Some latitude, some longitude." *Bitch.*

A clear thought entered Pharaoh's head. The Tigerfish had taken Larry out to sea and returned without him. Did they drop Larry off on an island? Did Larry find Jack Douglas?

Pharaoh toweled himself off, dressed, and went downstairs for a late dinner. Afterwards he returned to the marina and found the New Yorker on his sailboat.

"You still want to get rid of your neighbor?"

"The Tigerfish?"

"Yes."

"Come aboard, my friend."

Pharaoh climbed the short ladder to the sailboat's deck. He asked the man if he had a nautical map and if he knew how to read one. He did. Larry had shared the latitude and longitude coordinates of Jack Douglas's possible location with Pharaoh on the plane ride to Mexico. He kept them on a piece of paper in his sling bag with the money.

The New Yorker cross referenced the numbers and pointed to an exact location far out to sea. "Here it is; roughly three hundred and fifty nautical miles from here."

"It's a tiny island," said the New Yorker. "Uncharted, unclaimed and nameless. Ships avoid the area. It's dangerous to sail through at night, away from the sea lanes. It's frequented by chubascos, thunder and lightning squalls with horrific winds."

"Have you ever sailed there?" said Pharaoh.

"No, no. Hell no. Out of my comfort zone. I'm brave on the streets of New York, but the sea? That is a different beast."

"Could a boat like the Tigerfish get there and back in one day?" said Pharaoh.

"Too far out in the ocean. The Tigerfish is old. I imagine its top speed is sixteen knots. What's this all about anyway?"

Pharaoh told him about the search for the artist Jack Douglas and the attempted burglary.

The New Yorker rubbed his chin. "Sounds like your friend Larry was hijacked. Only two possibilities to consider; they tossed him in the ocean or dropped him off somewhere. Dead or alive, who knows?"

"What's the fastest way to get to this island?"

"A seaworthy sailboat if the wind is right. Otherwise, you need a big powerboat. But there is a faster way. A float plane."

"Where do I get one?"

"There's one docked in the marina by the lighthouse. Joey Grillo owns it."

"*Joey Grillo*? The lead singer from Tail Pipe, that big hair band in the 80's?"

"I hear he's a real asshole. You know how rockers are. They lose the hair, keep the ego. He owns a club here and another one up north in Cabo San Lucas. He uses the plane sometimes to commute."

"Looks like I'm taking another plane ride," said Pharaoh.

"You're just a bodyguard. The police are involved now. Why go to such extremes for this Settlebottom fellow?"

"Because he's one of those rare men in life. An innocent."

"No one is innocent," said the New Yorker. "It's impossible."

Pharaoh walked around the marina towards the lighthouse. He saw a float plane moored to a private concrete dock behind a locked fenced gate.

A young hippie-looking guy with long hair dyed blonde was sitting by the plane in a plastic chair, drinking beer in the moonlight. He wore a wife-beater tee shirt and faded jeans.

"Permission to approach," said Pharaoh.

The hippie looked up. "Joey's not here, if you want an autograph."

"I'm not here to see Joey. I'm here to see you," said Pharaoh.

The hippie rocked himself to a standing position. He walked up the gangway and stared at Pharaoh through the fence.

"You from the States?"

"Chicago," said Pharaoh.

"Do I owe you money? Drugs? This about a girlfriend? What?"

"That plane behind you. Can you fly it?"

The hippie took a swig from his beer bottle. "*Of course I can fly it.*"

"What kind of plane is it?"

"A 1973 Cessna 185 Skywagon. Only forty-four hundred were ever made. Long-range fuel bladders, a 300 horsepower, Continental engine. I just got done overhauling the props. Purrs like a kitten now."

"What's it worth?"

"A hundred and fifty grand. Joey won it in a poker game."

"How fast does it fly?"

"Average cruising speed? 136 knots."

"Joey pay you good?"

"Hell no, but the job comes with perks. Booze, weed, coke. Plenty of broads."

"Joey's leftovers."

The insulted hippie turned to leave. "Kiss my ass, man."

"I need a pilot and a seaplane. Pay is ten grand for a day's work."

The hippie turned around.

"Did Joey ever pay you ten grand for a day's work?" said Pharaoh.

The hippie smiled at Pharaoh. "Cash?"

Pharaoh thumped his sling bag. "In fist."

The hippie unlocked the gate. Pharaoh followed him down the gangplank to the plane,

The hippie turned talkative. "Joey's in L.A. for a couple of weeks. Says he's finishing a new album, but that's bullshit. His voice is shot. Hell, he hasn't even toured in five years. Last one was a Monsters of Rock gig. Bunch of old men in spandex. He was the opening act, lowest face on the totem pole."

"How do you know Joey?" asked Pharaoh.

"I'm his nephew. When he decides to tour again, he promised me a roadie gig. *With pay.* Meanwhile he keeps me down here in Mexico; polishing the plane, guarding the plane, sleeping in the plane. This is bullshit, man. I've been needle-free for two years now."

"What was your drug of choice?" said Pharaoh.

"Heroin. Cocaine. Meth."

"But you're clean now."

"Just alcohol and weed, man. I swear."

"How'd you learn aeronautic mechanics?"

"Manuals and hands-on experience. It ain't rocket science. Flying a plane is like driving a go-cart."

Pharaoh studied the floating plane. Even in the moonlight he could see the custom paint job. The plane was white with red-tipped wings. Joey Grillo's enlarged cartoon face looked down at Pharaoh, sneering. The rocker's curly hair swept away, crawling over the rest of the plane in a confused spider web.

"What's the range on this bad boy?"

"With the new gas tanks? Maybe eight hundred nautical miles."

"Is that good?"

"You got regular miles, kilometers and nautical miles. Nautical is the longest."

The hippie pulled an electric lantern from one of the plane's storage bins and turned it on. He set it on a cheap table next to his chair.

"So what's the mission, man?"

Pharaoh pulled the coordinates from his pocket. "Fly out to an island, pick up a friend if he's there, and return. I have these coordinates. The latitude is 19.761...."

"Save it, man. All I have to do is type it into the plane's GPS. It knows where to go from there."

"When can we leave?"

"First light. I'm too drunk to fly now and the gas pumps don't open 'til dawn. You wanna pay me now?"

"I'll pay you when this baby is in the air."

"What? You don't trust me?"

"I don't trust anybody."

The hippie laughed. "Yeah, you're from Chi town, alright. See you in the a.m."

"You got a name?" said Pharaoh.

"People call me Slick."

"See you in the morning, *Slick*."

"Don't forget my cash, dude."

Pharaoh returned to the hotel. When he unlocked the door to the suite he prayed he'd find Larry sleeping in his bed.

But the room was empty.

CHAPTER 32

The sun had set hours ago. Larry sat patiently, his knees drawn together, held in a tight vice by his locked arms. He thought he was staring west. It was the last direction he remembered watching when the sun went down. He could still feel the memory of the fading sun's heat on his face.

The water was still rising around him.

He measured his options. He could swim away from the rock in the swollen sea, make it two or three miles to nowhere and perish. It wasn't a public swimming pool. There were sea monsters out there; sharks and eels and barracudas.

He could stay on the rock and hope or pray that a boat might pass by and see him. Maybe the pirates were wrong. Maybe the rock wouldn't be swallowed up completely.

He had a hat to protect his face. If it rained he could use it to catch falling water and prolong his inevitable death.

He felt the coin in his pocket. No longer a coin, but a utensil perhaps. The edge of the coin might cut through soft flesh. He might catch a flying fish.

There was a strange whistle in the wind, odd heavy sounds of waves slapping into each other like discordant music in the distance. Jazz in nature.

As a boy, he used to climb to the top floor of the orphanage. There was a window box in the hallway facing west towards Exchange Street. He would sit in that seat every Sunday at sunset, his face pressed against the warm glass in summer, the cold glass in winter. From his perch he could see a handsome arched limestone gate; the Union Stock Yard gate, the only reminder of Chicago's former preeminence as the center of the American meatpacking industry and the "Hog Butcher for the World".

Larry had seen old photographs of the yards; stock pens stretching as far as the eye could see. There was still a pungent iron smell of blood in the air; the odor of dung from the long-gone yards still permeated the brick and mortar of the neighborhood.

Thousands of men had worked beyond that infamous white gate in the meatpacking industry until the 1970's. How many millions of gallons of blood had been spilled there? How many animals had been slaughtered in the long century? Such an odd monument, the stand-alone gate.

From his private window seat, Larry had concocted blues music out of the stockyard's history; an intangible cacophony of suffering, blending the high-pitched squeals of pigs at slaughter, the staccato bleats of screaming sheep, the bellow bass of herded cattle being rushed down the wooden planks from arriving trains into pens to be fed, then butchered.

He imagined the shift whistle's blow; the slogging percussion of irregular footsteps of long-gone men. They came out under the arches of the gate, immersed in entrails, internal organs and decomposing animal flesh, their clothes caked in blood, leather boots wet with vermilion stains.

He heard cymbal crashes from breaking fingers and human flesh ripped open from wild knives. He heard the low crunch-crunch-crunch of axe against bone, the high zip-zip-zip of saw blades carving carcasses on the killing floor. He saw the long narrow canals on the concrete killing floor, flushed with water towards Bubbly Creek and from there the Chicago River. Bubbles of air pop-popped in the rush, as if bashed by small wooden mallets against Lionel Hampton's metal-keyed vibraphone.

Larry laughed at himself. “Here I am about to die and all I can think about is music!”

But there was a metaphor to his thinking. The railroad-fed stockyards ceased when refrigerated trucks and the interstate highway system made them obsolete.

“Am I obsolete?” Larry said aloud. “Was I ever really here or just a foot soldier marching in step to the rhythm of an unimportant life? A pollen-gathering bee returning to its hive to feed the queen it will never meet?”

He wished Pharaoh was with him now. Pharaoh would have a field day analyzing Larry’s predicament.

Larry stood up and turned in circles. “Seriously now. What am I to do?”

His eye caught something high up in the sky. An airplane? A shooting star or comet? He raised his hand and waved to it.

Larry felt his legs; stiff from sitting too long. Maybe if he kept moving he might live longer. He remembered a whimsical piece of light music: “The Syncopated Clock” by composer Leroy Anderson. The piece was in 4/4 time. Temple blocks tapped together made the ticking sound of a clock. Larry clapped his hands together instead and marched in place. He remembered the lyrics to the song and sang aloud.

"There was a man like you and me,

As simple as a man could ever be;

And he was happy as a king,

Except for one peculiar thing.

He had a clock that worked all right,

It worked all right, but not exactly quite;

Instead of going tick, tock, tick,

The crazy clock went tock, tick, tock.

The poor old man just raved and raved,

Because nobody could say

Why his silly clock behaved

That hickory dickory way!"

He sat back down on the rock and realized he was laughing.

"If Mrs. Chumley could see me now! Larry the introvert? I don't think so! I sing, I dance, I have jokes!"

He cupped his face in his hands and cried uncontrollably. Long after his crying jag had ended, when there was nothing left but to be in the moment, he lay on his back and stared up at the sky.

There were stars everywhere; so many stars he could read a book by them. Some blinked and danced. Others disappeared and reappeared. He had never paid much attention to the night sky. The illumination of Chicago street lights and smog had always obliterated them from view. Larry stood up again.

"Sorry about that! I apologize for ignoring you all these years!"

He stared out at the loud sea; white tufts of foam, the crests of small waves skirting the surface. Every now and then, strange sea creatures, breaking free from their habitat, leapt out of the ocean, their slender silver bodies illuminated by the moon. Larry had lost his sense of perception. Were they small fish close by or large fish far away?

Something enormous rose from the ocean to his right. It cleared the surface, large fins like wings spread wide. The mottled creature slapped down on the surface and sent a wash of spray across Larry. He stumbled backwards and almost lost his balance.

Another giant breached the surface of the sea in front of him and splashed down on the surface with a loud boom.

Humpback whales appeared from everywhere now, breaching and splashing as they circled the sea mount. Some of them were singing! One sounded like an oboe, another had a higher range of a flute. A third was definitely a bassoon.

Something new crossed Larry's mind. The sea mount was a train station! A gathering place! He looked down and saw the reflection of stars against the body of a diving whale. He hadn't noticed the bright fluorescent light circling the sea mount before. What caused it? Fish? Plankton? What?

The chorale music of the whales lasted an hour before they finally swam away; a cavalry in pursuit of something new.

Larry clapped his hands together. "Well done! Bravo!"

Maybe an hour passed.

Larry heard a strange noise behind him. It reminded him of someone splashing a rubber boot in a puddle of water. He turned around slowly and stared into the face of an enormous sea turtle.

It stared back at him. The black and grey creature had a kind, almost sad face. Its leathery eye lids were large and droopy. It seemed to be having trouble seeing Larry in the dark.

"I'm sorry," said Larry. "Is this your rock?"

The big turtle stretched its large front fins forward and pulled itself further up the rock. Larry guessed it to be six feet long.

"I'm not sure there's room for two here," said Larry.

The turtle pulled the weight of its body forward again and Larry stepped to the very edge of the remaining mount. The creature extended its long leathery neck forward and raised its head. It seemed to be studying him.

"I know what you're thinking," said Larry. "What is a human doing out here in the middle of nowhere on such a beautiful night? Well, truth must be told, I was high-jacked, left here to die, actually. So if you don't mind sharing...."

The turtle pulled its head back inside its shell, turned slightly and tucked up its fins. It let out a long winded sigh and seemed to have fallen asleep.

Larry felt the swish of water against his feet. There was nowhere else to go but the inconvenient turtle's lid. He tapped at the turtle's shell. It was more leather-like than hard, with small hard bumps running along its ridges. It seemed sturdy enough. Larry sat on its back.

The creature didn't seem to mind.

Hours passed. Larry felt himself nodding off. He shook his head to stay awake. The sea turtle reached out with its giant flippers and embraced the submerged rock.

The sea rose another foot. The turtle raised its head above water and took deep breaths of air. Larry could feel its body expand under him. He had never felt the power of self-preservation before.

He reached out with his arms and held firmly to its back, feeling the gentle sway of seawater against his legs as he dozed off.

More time passed. Larry felt a hot breath of wind against his face. He opened his eyes and saw that the sun was coming up. A small patch of seamount was under them. The ocean was receding! The high tides delivered by the moon had waned.

The turtle spread its flippers and stuck out its beaked face, staring back at Larry with black opal eyes. *It's time to go*, it seemed to say.

Larry slipped off its back and watched the sea turtle crawl into the sea. There was dry rock beneath Larry's feet, enough to stand or sit on. He watched the turtle swim away, skimming the surface with powerful strokes of its fins. It never looked back.

CHAPTER 33

Pharaoh sat in the front passenger seat of the Skywagon, watching through his window as the pilot unlashed the plane from its mooring and pushed off from the dock.

Slick climbed up the short ladder and fell into the plane's driver's seat. His long hair was tucked under a white baseball cap with a Tail Pipe logo on the lid.

"You want a hat?" said Slick as he fired up the engine. "There's a whole box of them in back."

"No. I'm good," said Pharaoh.

"Suit yourself. For the record? Fuel tanks are full. Everything checked out in my pre-flight inspection," Slick shouted over the loud noise of the idling plane's engine. "Did you know water weighs eight pounds a gallon? I pumped twenty gallons out of the straight floats this morning. That's a hundred and sixty pounds."

There were two steering columns in the cockpit. Pharaoh studied the one in front of him. "Why are there two wheels?"

"It ain't a wheel, it's a yoke. If I pass out or have a stroke, then you get to fly the plane."

Pharaoh watched Slick as he pushed and pulled on red, green and blue knobs on the dashboard panel between them. The plane's propeller started spinning.

"Same as driving a car but with more buttons," shouted Slick. "The blue knob adjusts the rotary. The red one adjusts air flow. This one's for the flaps, I think."

"*You think*?"

Slick handed Pharaoh an Owner's Manual. "Any idiot can fly one of these. Everything you need to know is in that book." Slick tapped on the foot pedals. "These are for the rudders."

As the boat floated away from the dock, Slick turned the plane and faced west. "We got a no-wake zone in the marina. Have to sort of drift out before we make a run for it." He tugged on a knob, pushed another. The propeller blade turned faster. "Throttling up," Slick shouted.

The plane entered the deep channel outside the marina.

"I almost forgot. You got my cash?" asked Slick.

Pharaoh handed him his fee.

Slick smelled the money, smiled and tucked it in his pants. "Strap in for takeoff," he ordered. "I got a blind spot on the right side. Forward visibility is limited over the nose."

The men buckled themselves in their seats.

"Let's make a run for it," Slick announced. He pulled and pushed more buttons. The plane sounded like a high-pitched buzz saw as it picked up speed.

Pharaoh looked ahead. "You got boats crossing in front of you."

Slick craned his head up over the nose of the plane. "They can kiss my ass."

The plane leaped ahead as Slick accelerated. Pharaoh heard angry crackling voices coming through the plane's intercom. "Who's that?"

"The harbor tower. They want me to slow down. This is a plane, goddamnit, not a boat. How do they expect me to get lift-off without speed? Besides I got chop ahead. If I don't jump it I'll flip Joey's plane!"

The plane pushed ahead, faster and faster, banging against the water's surface. Slick pulled and pushed knobs, feet pumping.

Pharaoh felt the throbbing vibrations of the plane under his seat. He saw the right wing of the Cessna as it passed a yacht, missing it by a few feet. "You sure you got a pilot's license?"

"Never said I did," Slick shouted. "But I can fly the shit out of this plane. And for the record? Joey Grillo can kiss my ass!"

Pharaoh saw a sailboat in the plane's path ahead. Slick pulled back on the yoke violently. The plane started to climb, skimming over the topmast of the boat, missing it by inches.

Slick shouted as the shaking Cessna continued its rough ascent. "Take-offs are the second trickiest part of flying on these tail draggers."

"What's the hardest part?" asked Pharaoh.

"*Landing*."

The plane climbed for a few minutes before leveling out at cruising altitude. Slick put the plane on autopilot.

"You got those coordinates?" he asked Pharaoh.

Pharaoh reached behind him and brought up a rupsack. He had packed a few clothes, all the money and the gun box. He rummaged through it and handed Slick a piece of paper.

Slick studied the panel in front of him. "Goddamned planes have too many gadgets, you ask me; radar altimeters, barometers, engine monitors, warning systems. Too much shit to pay attention to." Slick tapped a rectangular screen. "That's our navigation screen." He had to refer to an instruction booklet to program in their destination.

Pharaoh pointed at another screen. “What’s this?”

“Shows the weather. Not a cloud in the sky. Should be smooth sailing.”

“How fast are we flying?” said Pharaoh.

“A steady hundred and fifty miles an hour. We’ll be at your destination in no time.”

“And then you’ll have to land this thing.”

“Trickiest part of flying,” Slick reminded him.

CHAPTER 34

Hours passed. They were flying below the clouds. Pharaoh stared down at the rough ocean's surface. No boats below, no islands. He saw what looked like a handful of shadows on the water's surface.

"Probably a school of bottle-nosed dolphins," said Slick. "They travel together to protect themselves against sharks and killer whales."

"You know much about the sea?" said Pharaoh.

"I don't know shit about it and don't care to learn. This money you're paying me? It'll get me back to the desert. Las Vegas, baby. Whores and slots, here I come!"

"And Joey Grillo can kiss your ass?"

"You got it."

Pharaoh pointed at the navigation screen. In the middle of the blue screen was a small white object. "Looks like an island ahead!"

Slick studied it. "Sure as shit. Looks like we have arrived."

Pharaoh smiled. "I'm comin', Larry. Just like I promised. Can you see me up here?"

"Sonofabitch!" Slick screamed.

A flock of seabirds suddenly appeared. Slick grabbed the yoke and turned sharply to the right. But he was too late. Birds crashed against the front and sides of the plane. Bodies were chewed and spit out in the propeller. Blood, heads, guts and feathers covered the windshield and side windows.

Slick pulled back hard on the yoke. The plane started a steep climb. Pharaoh heard a warning buzzer ringing.

"What's happen —."

The engine stalled. Cross winds bucked the plane.

Pharaoh looked at Slick. The pilot was terrified. He was punching buttons and pulling levers, trying to restart the plane, trying to steer. Slick turned on the windshield wipers. Streaks of blood and water turned to a thick paste.

"What now?" Pharaoh said.

Slick worked the foot pedals and pushed in the yoke. "Engine's fouled. I'm gliding for now, but we're losing altitude. Goddamned birds." He tried starting the engine again. He nodded at a button. "Keep working on the windshield wipers. We got to see."

Pharaoh kept spraying the windshield.

"We can't land on choppy open water. I should be able to make that island ahead," said Slick.

The plane floated through the sky. The windshield had cleared enough to see through a small area.

"I can see the island!" Pharaoh shouted.

Slick saw the island too. "It's just a speck!" He kept the island on his left side and circled it.

"What are you looking for?" said Pharaoh.

"Goddamned island has cliffs on all sides. There's no beach!" Slick noticed a huddle of forlorn shacks. He saw people working stripes of land. Some kind of field. Above the field was a long patch of mostly flat earth. "I think I can make it there."

"But we don't have wheels," said Pharaoh.

Slick was in a panic. "I know that! But what else we got?"

"You ever land one of these on land?"

"Shit, man. I never even flew one of these before."

Pharaoh threw his hands in the air. "Anyone can fly one of these. Just like driving a car."

"If I can ease into the flare maybe I can milk out a nice soft landing."

"What does that mean?"

"Pilot's talk."

"*Pilot's talk*! You don't know shit about flyin', man!"

"Come on, dude. Give me a break. I needed the money to go to Las Vegas."

"Okay, okay," said Pharaoh. "Think logically. How do you land this thing?"

"I have to pick an aiming point off the nose. Work the flaps to dissipate air speed. Hit the ground too hard and we'll bounce the wings. They could snap. We're in a steel cage. If we flip on our back we might be okay."

The plane was losing more altitude.

"I can't make another pass," said Slick. "We have to go in now!"

He flew south of the island, turned the plane around and faced it.

"Got my aiming point. Wish it was flatter, though." Slick worked the floor pedals. The flaps of the plane turned. The plane kept dropping. "Don't want to overshoot," Slick said nervously. "Gonna be a real tail dragger."

Pharaoh noticed Slick's hands fastened to the yoke. His knuckles were white.

Seconds before the plane touched the ground, Slick announced, "Stewardess, prepare for landing!"

Pharaoh braced his hands against the dashboard. He closed his eyes. He heard the sharp shredding thumps of the plane's pontoons tearing away from under him against the earth, heard the screech of rocks, the bounce and snap of the wings and struts. He felt a swimming sensation in his head as the plane's nose dug into the earth and flipped over. He heard something snap and break away like a whistling shot as glass shattered. Chunks of dirt and gravel spit into the cabin as the plane slid on its roof and came to a dead stop.

Pharaoh opened his eyes. He was upside down. He looked at the pilot. Or what was left of him. The plane's snapped propeller had come through the window and removed half his head. Pharaoh smelled something burning. Airplane fuel. He reached for his seatbelt and unhooked himself. He fell out of it and stared at his shattered side window, flames licking at it. It was his only way out. Pharaoh shut his eyes and belly crawled forward. He felt his face and arms heat up as he shimmied out of the plane into the open air. He kept crawling, the heat still on him. He rolled over and over, putting out the flames, the smell of burning flesh in his lungs as he gasped for air. He felt hands on him, dragging him away from the wreckage. He heard voices talking over him. He was afraid to open his eyes. What if he didn't have eyes?

And then he passed out.

CHAPTER 35

There was no comfortable position on the rock. Larry had been flat on his back for hours now, listening to the hum of air entering and exiting his lungs.

He saw swimming things under his eyelids as they changed shapes. The objects morphed into fantastic hallucinations. A whole library of stamp images appeared, one after the other in quick succession like a flip book. The fire of a dragon's breath blasted towards him in one, a wax figure melted in another, a ship sank, a rocket blasted into the sky.

He seemed to be flying over something now, freed from his body. His bird's eye view showed him the rooftops of the orphanage during his childhood captivity.

He saw a small boy in the school playground teaching himself how to operate a swing. He watched the boy climb the steps to a slide. But the boy didn't go down the slide. There was no one to play with.

He saw the boy grow a few years older, saw him walking towards the brick entrance of a high school, saw the boy exit, older still, as he crossed the street to a much larger building, a brownstone on a university campus. The boy became a young man as he left the building and walked towards a fancy car. The young man paused and stared at the car a long time, took a stack of books in his hand and flung them in the air.

Larry saw his mothers, Mrs. Settle and Miss Bottom, standing with Mr. and Mrs. Chumley. They were yelling after him to return to the car, to his planned future, but Larry wouldn't listen, refused to listen as he ran down a long path, away from the university to a long pier. He ran to the end of it and dove into a lake, fully clothed.

What he could have done, what he should have done.

Larry's eyes opened, half-blinded from the glaring sun above. His body was drenched, not in water, but in sweat.

He was back on the rock.

"A good dream?" he heard from a voice nearby.

Larry sat up and stared in front of him.

A small old man, almost elfin, his skin browned and leathered by the elements, was staring at him. He was standing on the forward deck of an oddly constructed catamaran made from sheets of wood, fiberglass and aluminum. The mast was a hodgepodge of metal and plastic poles tightly twined together and tied with leather straps. The rigging of the main sail was made of checkered shirts, cotton pants, denim coats and plastic tarpaulins stitched together with sturdy threads.

Behind the man, a pair of attractive young women in shabby bikinis made of animal skins stood at the mast, holding a bundled sail in their arms.

At the stern was a third beauty, crouched over a small pot. She was cooking something.

"Why are you here?" the man said to Larry in imperfect English.

"I was left here to die," said Larry. "Why are you here?"

The strange man pointed at a string of fish hanging from a pole. "The sea mount is a good place for fish."

"How long have you been here?"

"A few hours," said the small man. "We didn't want to wake you. We thought maybe you wanted to be alone."

"I don't," said Larry.

"You are an American?"

"Yes."

"What is your name?"

"Lawrence Settlebottom."

"A strange name."

"Most people call me *Larry*."

"That is easier. Would you like some water?"

"If you don't mind."

The old man tossed him a plastic jug. "It is rain water," said the old man. "The best kind. Drink it slowly."

Larry drank from the jug. He had never tasted water so delicious.

"Do you need to be rescued or do you want us to leave you here?"

"I would prefer a rescue," said Larry.

"For what reason?"

"So I can live."

"To do what? Sit on more sea mounts?"

Larry tossed the jug back to the man. "To understand the meaning of life."

The old man laughed. "To do that, you must die. But by then it will be too late to know."

He spoke rapidly to the women in a sort of Spanglish. The women laughed with the old man. He gazed again at Larry. "I am Dario." He gestured towards the women. "This is my tribe. With our rescue comes a price. Are you willing to pay it?"

"You want money?"

Dario laughed. "No, no money. We need a hero. A giant slayer. Are you willing to face a giant?"

"I don't know," said Larry. "No one has ever asked me to."

Dario laughed. "Stand up, please."

Larry stood.

Dario smiled. "You are tall enough. But your arms are thin, your legs skinny. You are quick on your feet?"

"I walk every day. Never bump into pedestrians."

Dario grabbed a long pole and extended one end to Larry. "Pull us up and board. But only if you are willing to slay a giant."

"What kind of giant?"

"A very bad one."

Larry gripped the pole and pulled the boat to the rock's edge. "It looks like I don't have much of a choice. I either stay here and die or go with you."

"And maybe die then. You can always run away from us when you know the truth of things. Men make easy promises, often broken when they are challenged."

"I have run away from things my entire life," realized Larry. "I don't want to do it anymore."

He released his grip on the pole and jumped the short distance between the rock and boat, landing on the bow's wooden platform.

Dario grabbed him and steadied him. "He will make a fine hero!" he told the women. "Good balance!"

The two women holding the sail released it and came forward. They rubbed their hands up and down Larry's arms and legs.

"I think you were put on this rock for a reason," Dario told Larry. "For you to be found and for us to find you! Maybe like us, you are meant to be a gypsy of the sea. Come. Eat with us. Then we will set sail together on a great and noble adventure!"

CHAPTER 36

Ismelda and the old women had removed their dresses and tied them together for a hammock. They carried the large black man towards the small village.

El Gordo was waiting for them on the narrow path, a machete in his hand. The women set their hammock on the ground. Gordo looked down at Pharaoh's burned body.

"Why did you bring him down? He is half dead already. Step aside and I will kill him now."

"You are afraid then?" said Ismelda.

"I am afraid of nothing!" Gordo growled.

"Then we will bring him back to life. When he is healthy enough to fight you maybe then you can kill him. Or he will kill you."

El Gordo laughed. "This is what you feeble people have been praying for? This is your next miracle? I see you out there on the cliffs, longing to be rescued." He kicked at Pharaoh. "And this is what you find? A half dead man with burns on his body! Ha! I am bored. I will let you play this game with me!" The pig brushed past the women and headed towards the burned wreckage of the plane.

"There is nothing left up there," said Ismelda.

"I will see for myself," said Gordo. "Now go! Put your man in the cage. Heal his wounds. When he can pick up a rock to fight with, then I will kill him."

The women lifted the hammock and carried Pharaoh back to the village. El Gordo strutted up the hill, swinging his machete in the air like a boy on a lark.

CHAPTER 37

Larry sat next to Dario by the mast. The sail had been raised and it was filled with wind. One of the women sat behind them at the stern, leaning on the steering rudder. The other two women lay before them on the platform of the bow, half-naked, their bodies smeared with coconut oil.

"You are their father?" Larry said to Dario.

"Their uncle. I keep them and they keep me. We are the last of our tribe, maybe."

"A tribe. Where do you come from?"

"Here for now, somewhere else tomorrow, from across the oceans and mountains before."

"Do the women have names?" Larry asked.

"Everything has a name," said Dario. He pointed at the women one by one. "They call themselves Nina, Pinta and Santa Maria, named after the ships of Christopher Columbus. Nina is the fire-haired one. Pinta's hair is black like the bottom of the sea. Santa Maria's hair is made of golden angel dust. Someday they will change their names again. But for now, they wear the names to remind them of the great horrors."

"Horrors?"

"Besides a handful of others, we are the last of our kind. If you do not slay the giant for us, we will remain sea gypsies until our kind disappears from the earth."

Larry studied the objects on the boat. A few nets, large plastic containers probably containing clothing and utensils. Not much else.

"Tell me more about this tribe of yours," said Larry.

Dario took the lid off a coffee can. He pulled a pipe and tobacco from it. "It is a troubled story marked with death." He stuffed his pipe with tobacco and lit it.

"Anything to do with mermaids?" said Larry.

Dario lowered his pipe. His questioning eyes studied Larry. "What do you know about mermaids?"

"In Puerto Vallarta I was told of a lost tribe also known as '*God's people*'. The Taínos. I was sent to Mexico to find a man who was searching for them. Do you know of such a man? His name is Jack Douglas."

"I know him."

"Do you know where he is?"

"I know where he is."

"Can you bring me to him?"

"Yes. When it is time to slay the giant."

"Tell me more about this giant," said Larry.

"He is only a man. His name is El Gordo. He murders and rapes. He has tossed children from cliffs into the sea. When you see him you will shake with terror."

"And probably run away."

"Only you can decide when the time comes. When your terror subsides, maybe you will do the right thing and kill him."

"When is killing a man 'the right thing'?"

"When it is right." Dario pointed ahead at the rolling sea. "But we must make a stop first. There is a ship ahead somewhere. We trade things with them."

Nina stood up on the platform of the bow and stretched. Larry noticed her long tailbone. Was it a remnant of a lost tail?

"Nina," Larry said. "Do you think you are a mermaid?"

Nina blushed and sat back down. "Not me," she said, "but my cousin is."

Larry looked at Pinta. "You're the mermaid?"

"Another cousin," said Pinta.

Larry turned and stared at Santa Maria steering the boat.

"Not me," said Santa Maria, "I am a cousin, too."

Dario put his arm on Larry's. "Patience, Larry. If there is a giant, then there is a mermaid. That is all you need to believe for now."

"Is she with Jack Douglas?"

"Maybe. Maybe not. Maybe they are alive, maybe both dead, maybe one dead. We don't know. But we will see."

The gypsy catamaran sailed through the night, the women taking turns at the rudder. After nightfall Larry was prepared a swinging hammock. He watched the meandering stars above until his head nodded and his eyes closed. He fell into a deep sleep, too tired to dream this time.

When he woke in the morning he found Nina and Pinta on either side of the sailing catamaran, arms bent in the moving water.

"What are they doing?" he asked Dario.

"Catching breakfast."

A few minutes later, Pinta snagged a large fish by hand and yanked it on the deck.

"She has caught a yellow fin tuna for us," smiled Dario. "It is a good fish." The old man found a knife, severed the head of the fish, then gutted and cleaned the body.

"Have you ever lived on the land?" Larry asked Dario.

"Here and there along the coast. Too many people. Too many rules. Too many small minds. We found a small island to hide for now, but Gordo has ruined it for us."

"Sailing the open ocean - you don't find this monotonous? Boring?"

"If we find a storm, a chubasco in the days ahead, you will wish for this day again. But when the giant is gone, we will have a home on dry land."

"He's just a man. Why not go to the authorities and have him arrested for whatever it is he has done?"

"Through our history, we have been chased and killed. Now with so few of us left, we must protect ourselves in the best way we can. There is no higher authority to us."

Larry thought about Rosemary Chumley. She and her husband scrapped their way to success. These people were scrapping to survive.

Dario continued. "So we live on the sea, a small island here and there. One of two things can happen: Our extermination or our survival."

After breakfast, the catamaran dropped anchor off a tiny uninhabited island.

The gypsy women dove off the side of the boat, returning with lobsters in their hands. They collected them for an hour, throwing them in large tubs of water.

Dario showed one of the lobsters to Larry. "A small creature, but if you are not careful he will take your finger."

CHAPTER 38

Pharaoh woke up from the feel of a sturdy hand lifting his head. Something dry and bitter was forced between his lips. Aspirin perhaps. He tasted water next, eagerly taking a small sip and swallowing. *At least he could swallow.*

A wet cloth covered his eyes. He sensed bodies around him, felt their fingers picking away at small pieces of rock embedded in his flesh. It stung like hell.

Pharaoh tried to speak. "I'm looking for my friend Larry. Is he here?" But nothing came out of his parched throat.

He felt reassuring fingers touching his lips, lathering them with ointment.

"Shush," said a feminine voice. "You are badly burned; your face, your hands, your feet and neck. Try not to move for now."

She started humming, soft and sweet; a younger woman's voice, tired but reassuring.

He felt a sheet being placed over him.

"There is nothing more we can do for now," the pleasant woman whispered to Pharaoh. "We must keep your skin moist, keep your wounds clean and feed you aspirina for fever. Try not to move. It will pop the blisters. They will infect you and maybe kill you."

Pharaoh heard an old woman's voice. "Tsk, tsk, tsk," she sighed.

He remembered when he was a boy, his mother had sounded the same when he caught the Mumps virus. He was in bed for a week with a fever and muscle pains. But this was different. The younger woman said he was badly burned.

Pharaoh wanted to stand up. He needed to find Larry. He couldn't speak. He could barely breathe. He tried wiggling his toes and fingers but the pain was so great he tensed up and screamed silently. Pharaoh felt the younger woman's calm hand touching him gently as she continued to sing the lullaby.

He wondered if he was already dead, parked in limbo, waiting for his judgment day.

CHAPTER 39

For two days and nights the sea gypsies sailed west. A summer storm passed over them on the second night, delivering precious rain for drinking water. Dario aimed the catamaran downwind, dropped the sails and took to the rudder to ride out the gentle storm.

The women and Larry lathered up with soap and showered in the rain, holding on to the mast for balance. Pinta and Santa Maria pushed their bosoms against Larry and rubbed their long legs against his.

"You have good sea legs," Nina told Larry.

"Must have been the tennis lessons in college," said Larry. "My instructor said I was well-balanced."

He broke into a giddy uncontained laugh. If Mrs. Chumley could see him now; standing in the rain with three half-naked women! If the kids from the orphanage could see him; Larry the loser, the quiet kid, the last boy left in the orphanage for adoption covered in soap bubbles.

He shouted up at the storm clouds, “I’m having an adventure, Rosemary!”

Dario asked, “Who is Rosemary?”

“The reason I’m here,” said Larry.

“Your wife?”

“My crazy best friend, full of mischief.”

Dario nodded and smiled.

On the afternoon of the third day the catamaran sailed up to a large yellow ship anchored at sea. The name *Felicity* was stenciled on the ship’s bow.

“It’s a research ship,” said Dario. “We visit every now and then.”

There were three cranes on the deck. An oblong vessel with four metallic arms was chained to the deck near the stern. It looked like a large orange crab.

“What is that thing?” said Larry.

“A baby submarine,” said Dario.

Several men in orange jump suits came to the ship’s rail and waved below to the sea gypsies.

A heavyset bearded man in his fifties appeared from the bridge. He was dressed in the white uniform of a ship's captain. He wore a holstered gun around his waist. The captain called down to Dario. "It's been four months. We thought maybe you won your island back!"

"Permission to come aboard, Captain Grey! We brought lobsters!"

"Permission granted," shouted back the captain. He walked down the metal stairs to the main deck.

Nina tossed a line to a deckhand. The catamaran dropped its colorful sail and was tethered to the side of the ship next to an iron ladder. One by one, barefooted Nina, Pinta and Santa Maria climbed to the ship's deck, sarongs wrapped around their tanned waists. A deckhand pulled them up the last rung, grabbing their asses as they passed.

1980's Rock 'n Roll music started blaring over the ship's public announcement system. The gypsy women danced with a handful of the crew members.

"Up you go," Dario told Larry. "We will spend a few days here."

Larry climbed the ladder, Dario behind him. He grabbed a handle of the metal bulwark and pulled himself to the deck. It was sturdy and solid, almost like being on dry land again.

The captain hugged Dario. They were old friends.

"Anything new in the ocean?" Dario asked the captain.

"A fish here, a fish there." The captain looked at Larry and addressed Dario again. "Found a stray, did you?"

Dario smiled and nodded. "This is Larry. He is going to kill my giant."

"That's what you said about the last guy." The captain pumped Larry's hand. "Welcome to the Felicity. I'm Captain Grey."

"He's the sheriff here, too," added Dario. "See the gun?"

"For pirates," said the captain, slapping the holster.

"I live in this ocean. There are no pirates out there," said Dario.

"Then to protect the weak ones on this ship," said the captain.

"That I believe," said Dario.

The captain stepped back and sized up Larry. He shook his head, staring at Dario. "You've got your work cut out with this one. He looks like a pencil pusher, if you ask me."

A handful of deckhands snickered.

Dario shrugged. "I take what the sea gives me. If you give me your gun I will kill the giant myself."

Captain Grey laughed. "And I would be tossed overboard by my black-hearted crew." The captain slapped Larry on the back with a powerful hand. "Enjoy your stay, Larry. Eat, drink and be merry while it lasts."

The captain joined the others dancing with the gypsy women. He raised his hands in the air and spun around in circles with gyrating Pinta.

Dario tugged at Larry's arm. "Come on," he said. "Let us find a soft bed."

They went down two flights of stairs and entered a hallway with sleeping berths on either side. Dario found an empty berth with a bunk bed, a small closet and a metal cabinet next to it.

"Top or bottom bunk?" he asked Larry.

"Either is fine."

"You get the top then, you're taller." Dario opened a metal locker and inspected the contents. "Towels, soap, shampoo and razors," he said.

"Where will the women sleep?" asked Larry.

"Wherever they want."

"What exactly are you trading?"

"Besides the lobsters? Nina, Pinta and Santa Maria decide for themselves. They offer the sailors simple pleasures. In turn, the men on the ship give us supplies to survive. Everyone is happy. The touch of kind flesh is a powerful thing, a healing thing. Come, let us find food."

Dario led Larry up a flight of stairs to the dining mess. It was a large room with seating for thirty.

The ship's cook, a big busty blonde-haired woman wearing a white apron, came out of the kitchen and swallowed Dario up in her arms. She spoke with a thick Danish accent.

"Ah! My little woodpecker is back! What did you bring us dis time?"

"Lobsters."

"Ugh. So much work for me!" Her eyes met Larry's. "What do we have here?"

"This is Larry, Helga. He is going to slay my giant."

"Of course he is!" Helga released Dario and locked her arms around Larry's waist. She lifted him off his feet. "You need meat on your bones. And more muscle. I can get you into shape." She turned to Dario. "You won't get jealous?"

"I am already jealous," he smiled.

Helga sat Larry down on a bench seat at one of the long galley tables. "We have Sauerbraten cooking for dinner wit roasted sirloin of beef, sweet and sour gravy and real potatoes." She went into the kitchen and returned with a freshly baked loaf of bread, a bowl of butter and grape j am. "Eat dis for now." She patted him on the head and returned to the kitchen.

Larry broke off a piece of bread and smeared it with butter. It was good. He broke off a second piece and offered it to Dario. Together they ate the whole loaf.

A tall man in his late fifties with long grayish blonde hair tucked under a baseball cap with a Brisbane Bandits logo appeared in the mess. He pulled three cans of beer from a cooler.

"Welcome back," he said to Dario with an Australian accent. "You found another stray, I see?"

"This is Larry," said Dario. "My new giant slayer."

The man nodded at Larry. "Where did Dario find you?"

"I was stranded on a sea mount."

"Sounds like a long story, mate."

"It is."

"They call me Wild Bill. Not like your American gunfighter Wild Bill Hickock. I'm named after an Aussie jackaroo and horse thief named Wild Bill Sullivan. When you have some free time, visit with me. Maybe we'll have an enlightening conversation."

Wild Bill left with his cans of beer.

A few others came and went for coffee or sodas. They were a friendly bunch, a mix of academics, scientists and ship laborers.

Larry returned to his berth after a long hot shower. Dario was sleeping on the lower bunk, snoring peacefully. There was an open philosophy book on the floor next to him. *The Birth of Tragedy* by the German philosopher Friedrich Nietzsche.

Larry heard a series of booming noises outside and left the room to explore the source.

When he reached the open deck he witnessed a handful of crew members running out long strings of cable off metal grids mounted on either side of the ship. At the ends of the cables were orange cylinders. He approached the closest deckhand, a younger man wearing an orange jumpsuit and a hardhat.

"What are you doing?" Larry asked.

"Seismic tests."

Larry saw the water erupt with a loud clapping noise at several locations a few hundred yards out.

The deckhand started singing. "Happy birthday to me, happy birthday to me...."

Captain Grey appeared next to Larry. "I'm short a spotter. Do you mind?" He handed him a pair of binoculars and a red flag.

"What am I looking for?"

"Whales, dolphins, schools of fish. If you see any, raise the flag and yell 'ho' so we can stop the airguns."

Larry followed the captain up a set of steps. They positioned themselves near the rail and studied the ocean through their binoculars.

"What are you testing for?" Larry asked.

"There's a rift of canyons under us. They run from Alaska to the equator. We're measuring the sea floor, making a topographical map."

"What are you using out there? Dynamite?"

Captain Grey shook his head. "Charges of compressed air. Sure as hell acts like dynamite, though. This is our last day blowing shit up. Tomorrow we start planting."

Wild Bill appeared at the base of the steps and yelled up to the captain. "I thought you were done blasting!"

Captain Grey lowered his binoculars. "Last day, Bill. Just doing what I'm paid for."

Wild Bill ripped off his baseball cap and smacked it against the ship's metal hull. "Shit show energy companies! Data mining, my ass! They're just a bunch of money hungry whores." He went below deck.

"Wild Bill seems upset," Larry said to the captain.

"Him and all the other environmentalists. Besides, he's an Aussie. They're peculiar" The captain raised his binoculars again, studying the horizon. He was nonchalant. "Some scientists say the airguns are extremely bad on the environment. Whales and dolphins go deaf, lose their sonar. Fish stop laying their eggs. Who the hell knows? The oil drilling companies already got kicked out of the Atlantic Ocean over airgun testing. After they caused a few oil spills, everyone with a beach house ran to the lawyers. We'll be banned in the Pacific by next year. But when the fossil fuels run out on land? The energy companies will come back to the oceans for large-scale drilling of oil and gas."

"Just a matter of time," Larry realized.

"As soon as people run out of gas at the pump. I'd rather job my boat out to marine archaeologists looking for the lost city of Atlantis, but that won't happen. I'm stuck on this ship of fools, sometimes with six different companies at the same time, all with a different mission and goal. A week doesn't pass without a fist fight between one of the marine biologists and one of the energy boys over some newly discovered pink lobster." Captain Grey spotted something in his binoculars. He raised a red flag in the air and yelled, "Ho!"

On either side of the ship, crew members stepped away from detonator panels.

"What is it?" Larry asked.

"Off the bow about five hundred yards. See that whale breaching?"

Larry turned his binoculars towards the bow. He didn't see anything. Just a flat sea meeting the sky.

"You missed it," said Captain Grey. "She went under."

The sturdy crew waited half an hour with no new signs of the distant whale before the tests resumed. The captain took back his binoculars from Larry.

"Go take a tour below deck," ordered Captain Grey. "Looks like NASA launching a satellite down there with all the equipment my science geeks brought along."

Larry took his offer and went below. He stood in a narrow metal hallway and adjusted his eyes to the fluorescent lighting overhead. There were small rooms on either side. He stuck his head in one.

Two men were staring at monitors, watching waves of crashing data on their screens. One of the men turned his head and waved at Larry.

"Looks like you're studying the stock market," said Larry.

The man laughed. "Just a simple hydrographic survey. We're turning our bathymetric data into 3D models."

"What causes all those bouncing lines?"

"Swaths of sonar sound waves, multibeam echoes. I take it you're not a scientist?"

"No," said Larry. "Far from it."

The second man turned and looked at Larry. "What brings you to the good ship Lollipop then?"

"I'm with the sea gypsies."

The men smiled at each other and offered high-fives.

"Let the good times roll!" one of them said.

Larry ducked out of the room and inspected other offices along the corridor. He felt like he was back in Chicago, at one of the museums, staring at strange machines with unknown functions measuring, weighing and scaling the world to a tangible result.

He found Wild Bill in the last room on the right. Wild Bill had his feet up on a desk. He was sipping a beer. There was a rack of labeled vials to his right containing mixtures of sand and water.

Video footage of the ocean floor was playing on a large screen overhead. A lumbering crab came into view.

"Mind if I join you?" said Larry.

Wild Bill waved him inside. "Grab a seat, mate."

Larry took a chair next to him. "What are you watching?"

"A crab walking like a drunk. A few hundred feet below us there are currents created by differences in densities of masses of water. When they collide, the water moves, gets agitated like the wind. The crab is caught in it."

"What's your occupation?" Larry asked innocently.

"You saw that big metal thing parked near the stern?"

"The submersible."

"Her name is Sweetie Pie. I'm the operator. One of the telecomm giants wants to run a cross-continental cable under us to transfer information between China and Mexico. Or so they say. I'm the guy who sets the markers on the sea floor." He took a sip of beer. "Oi, the things I have seen. It's one thing to watch an ocean special on the GEO channel for an hour. It's a whole other thing to be down under day after day, months at a time. And by down under, I mean down below. You see things. Start to connect the dots. Humanity doesn't have a clue what it's doing."

Larry pointed at the vials. "An experiment?"

"Sediment samples from the sea floor." He picked up a vial and showed it to Larry. "Geological DNA. With the proper analysis it can tell you past climates, what sea creatures existed when, and any catastrophic ocean events."

"How does that tie in with a cross-continental cable?"

"It doesn't. I think the fossil fuel industry is secretly funding the project. Why would a cable company want to know what's *under* the ocean floor? Serves no purpose to them. But who the hell knows? I have a mortgage, three kids in college, and a golf widow with a country club appetite."

Larry looked up at the video playing overhead. A strange-looking brown fish with an enormous head swam up to the camera's lens. It opened its crescent-shaped mouth revealing sharp fang-like teeth. Larry leaned back in his chair expecting the fish to leap through the screen at him.

Wild Bill laughed. "That's an Angler fish. Voted one of the top ten ugliest fishes on earth. It lives in the lonely and lightless depths of the sea." He picked up a pen and pointed at a long filament above the fish's mouth. "I call it a fishing pole. The tip of the filament glows in the dark to attract prey. This one is a female. Her mouth is so flexible she can swallow anything twice her size."

"How big is she?"

"About three feet long."

"Sure is ugly."

"You like ugly? I have more." Wild Bill typed on a keyboard and brought up a new video image. It was a fish with a black body, white tail and a transparent head showing its glowing endoskeleton and organs inside the casket of a soft skull. "This is a Spook fish. It also lives in the bottom trenches of the ocean. Its head looks like the cockpit of a plane with all those moving parts. Notice the eyes? They're inside the head to protect it against the pressure of the deep sea. We could sit here all day staring at all the strange shit in this sea."

"What about mermaids?" Larry said. "Did you ever see one of them swimming past your cameras?"

Wild Bill narrowed his eyes and studied Larry thoughtfully. "Dario told you his story?"

"Yes."

"It's a whopper."

"Yes."

"And fascinating as hell. If there is any truth to it. On his last two visits, Dario lured a couple of washed-up guys off this ship to help him. They never returned. Maybe it was the gypsy gals they was after. Or maybe what Dario says is true. You can find evil just about anywhere. Giants I'm not so sure about." Wild Bill took a swig of beer and wiped his mouth with the back of his hand. "And now it's your turn, mate. Come on now, what the hell were you doing on a sea mount in the middle of this god-forsaken ocean?"

"It's a long story."

"I got all day."

Larry gave Wild Bill a brief rundown of his exploits. The man listened with intrigue.

"So what do you make of it?" said Larry.

Wild Bill pointed at the strange fish on the overhead screen. "The world is still a strange place. We didn't think any of these fish existed twenty years ago. But there they are. As for mermaids? Did they ever exist? It's plausible, if you study the human chain of evolution. Life came from the sea and evolved to the land. Was there a humanoid creature that stayed in the water? There is the aquatic ape theory. I don't know. Whales and porpoises, certainly. It makes for good reading."

Wild Bill froze the image on the screen. He stood up and fished through a couple of boxes, pulling out a leather-bound book. "I spent a couple of years diving in the Caribbean for treasure. I found this old diary in a Puerto Rican book shop. Do you read Spanish?"

"No," said Larry.

Wild Bill sat next to Larry and thumbed through the marked pages. "This diary was written by a Spanish sailor who sailed with Columbus. He mentions the Taíno islanders of the Caribbean and how the Spanish tried to enslave them. The sailor claims the Indians in the coastal villages believed in a mermaid entity named Aycayia. One night under a full moon he observed hundreds of merpeople swimming up to the beach in a small bay. They were greeted as family by the shoreline villagers, exchanged fish and crabs for fruits and vegetables. There were a dozen boats offshore manned by legged Taínos who traveled with the merpeople. The sailor reported the rendezvous to higher authorities. When the merpeople returned a month later, Spanish ships blockaded the bay with nets and bombarded the waters, killing everyone in the sea. Sailors were ordered to drag the dead bodies to the beach where they were cremated in an enormous bonfire."

"A similar story to the fate of the Taínos on the beach at Puerto Vallarta," said Larry.

"A second documented incident happened aboard one of Columbus's ships. A captain and his crew chased a pod of mermaids and mermen in the open ocean, caught them in nets and hung them from the ship's rigging until they perished. Their bodies were ground to pieces and tossed overboard."

"Extermination."

"Of a limited aquatic humanoid species. I've read other stories. The Haitians believed in '*La Sirene*, the mermaid,' quite the Sheila still popular in voodoo myths. Columbus himself mentioned seeing three mermaids in one of his log books. Blackbeard, the English pirate, recorded in one of *his* logs that he had encountered merpeople on several occasions. One of his marked maps still exists, highlighting charted waters of the Caribbean infested with merpeople. He thought they wanted to steal his gold."

"So the conundrum remains – fact or fallacy?" Larry concluded.

"Maybe you'll be the bloke with the conclusive evidence."

"Sure. After I face a *giant*. Maybe I'll find a unicorn to ride on this adventure, too."

"Don't be so short-sighted mate," said Wild Bill. "Seventy percent of the earth is covered in water. The Age of Discovery lasted from the 1500's to the 1800's. It would make sense that humanoids evolved in the water like other mammals such as dolphins and whales. A limited population, living in a limited tropical warm water environment might have a slim chance of survival without detection. If there ever was a mermaid or merman they would have to be coastal dwellers. Air-breathers living in a very narrow environment between land and sea. They may have been hunted to extinction for human exploitation and domination. The oceans still contain mysterious creatures. There are still sea serpents we know nothing about. Once we touched the bottom of the sea, we discovered new life forms far beyond our imagination. They will survive mankind for the next great epoch of evolution."

The men stared up at the frozen image of the strange fish on the monitor.

"Seen enough?"

"For now," said Larry.

Wild Bill turned off the screen. "Spending too much time below changes a man," he admitted. "I can never go home again intact with the past, back to the house on the hill and the noise of humanity. My golf game is totally lost. What about you?"

"My life has been unexceptional until now. Much of it is my own fault. I never really stepped out in the world."

"Most people die all at once. Some of us die in pieces."

"May I confess something to you?"

"Sure."

"I have a record collection, mostly jazz and the blues. No one knows about it. I close the windows and doors when I listen."

Wild Bill shook his head. "That's it? That's your big secret, mate?"

"Yes."

Wild Bill smiled at him. "You're like my sea creatures. Nobody knows anything about them either."

"Even I don't understand me," said Larry. "I never bothered to take the time."

"Afraid of what you might find?"

"I didn't want to be singled out from the herd."

Wild Bill reached over and shook Larry by the shoulders. "Screw the herd. There is no herd. Most of what we learn in life is mythical bullshit. We're sold a story since the first day we're born and most of us spend the rest of our lives trying to fit in to *it*. But what is *it*? It's a cultural mirage. There is no *it*. It's only you and what happens to you today and all the tomorrows that follow. Don't spend even a little time looking over your shoulder at yesterday or you'll get sucked right back into the *it*."

The sound of a clanging bell rang from a loudspeaker.

"Dinner is being served in the mess," said Wild Bill. "Time for the herd to eat. Our cook, she's a good one. Meat with every meal."

Larry stood. “Thank you for the enlightening conversation.”

Wild Bill stared at Larry, a long hard look sizing him up. He smiled. “Forget space, the ocean is the last frontier in our lifetime. When mankind implodes, and we will, we’ll need to be equipped to life in the oceans when the land goes sour. Will you be ready?”

“I doubt it,” said Larry.

Wild Bill laughed. “Neither will I. What are you doing tomorrow?”

“No plans. I’m sort of stuck here at the discretion of my gypsy friends.”

“I have an extra seat on the Sweetie Pie. Want to take a pleasure trip?”

“To the ocean floor?”

“Why not? We’ll play some Duke Ellington for the little fishies.”

“I’d like that very much,” said Larry.

“Be on the main deck after breakfast tomorrow,” said Wild Bill.

On the way back to his berth, Larry saw Pinta in the hallway. Her hair was wet and she was wrapped in a towel. A hand reached out from one of the sleeping berths, pulled her in and closed the door. As Larry passed, he heard her happy laughter at the end of someone's joke. She was so wild, so free.

Larry found his berth, Dario was sitting on the lower bunk smoking a cigar and flipping through the pages of a men's magazine.

"Ah! You're back!" Dario announced. "Let's go eat."

"In a minute, please." Larry stood over Dario. "There is something I need to ask you."

Dario tossed the magazine aside. "Go ahead, Larry."

"This giant-slaying business. How do I prepare for it?"

"There is no real training. When you see what El Gordo is and what he has done, if you are a just man you will find a great anger inside you. Then you will decide his fate or yours."

"One more thing. You introduced me as your *new* giant slayer. What happened to the ones before me?"

Dario shrugged his shoulders. "The giant killed them."

CHAPTER 40

With the arrival of the sea gypsies over sixty people were crowded together on the ship. The kitchen staff fed the crew in two dinner shifts.

Captain Grey always ate on the first shift. He sat at the head of the center table, visible to all, but more perceptively, able to see everyone else.

Tables were covered with white table cloths. Loaves of freshly-baked bread and open bottles of red and white wine crowded the centerpieces of the tables. Wine glasses were at each setting.

Guests at the captain's table were by invitation only. Larry was surprised to be offered a seat on the captain's right with Dario at the captain's left.

There was no pecking order at the other tables. It was first come first seat. Scientists sat with sailors. The gypsy women shared a table with Wild Bill and four frisky male researchers. Wild Bill had three cans of beer stacked in front of him.

Helga's daughter, a pretty girl with whitish blonde hair, brought piping hot bowls of food out from the kitchen, proudly delivering them to the tables. She knew how to slap away happy stray hands venturing too close to her firm buttocks.

The captain poured himself, Dario and Larry glasses of chilled white wine. He raised a glass and offered a toast. "To the deep blue sea and the real sailors among us."

Dario and all the sailors rose from their seats. "Here, here!" they adjoined.

The chilled wine tasted delicious in Larry's mouth. Fruity with a hint of apple.

"How long have you been at sea?" he asked the captain.

"A year this time. Too long, I'm afraid. An anxious crew and unhappy guests causes friction on a parked ship. All the lifeboats are padlocked against mutiny." He changed the subject. "Are you a married man, Larry?"

"No."

"I thought as much." The captain pointed a shiny fork at a few of the men in the room. "You can always tell the married ones. Their faces are sallow, ticks in the eyes. They lose interest in their mission here, feel a sense of helplessness for what they can't do back home. It took me four wives to learn my lesson."

"What lesson was that?" said Larry.

"Don't get married again. Too much heartbreak. Given time, all women cheat on a man away at sea. I'm numb to it now. The Felicity is a faithful wife."

Larry observed the mingling scientists and sailors. "You have quite the mix of personalities here."

"Enough so that I carry a gun," said the captain. "PhD or GED, it doesn't matter what the man's education. We all take turns going crazy when we're trapped together at sea. So I play god. Sometimes I play judge and jury. Sometimes I'm even the town drunk. The best way to flare up an argument here is with a belief, an opinion or an attitude. We don't talk politics here. We don't talk football. Your supposed free will on this ship is determined by the latitude of my tolerance on any given day."

"A benign dictatorship."

"It's human nature to argue, to disagree, but someone has to control things. I care about each and every person on this ship as long as they're here. The minute I land in port and I see their asses walking down the gangway, my job is over. That is, until the next batch boards my boat and the madness begins again."

"And the man with the gun rules again?"

"It takes an oasis like this ship in the ocean to show us what we're all about," said the captain. "The strong control the weak. Which category do you fit in?"

Larry thought a moment to find an answer. "I don't think I fall into either category, Captain."

"That's bullshit. You only say that because you've never been tested." Captain Grey picked up a fork and pointed it at Larry while he spoke directly to Dario. "What are you going to do with this one? He has no conviction! Look at his hands. They're weak." The captain set down his fork and leaned back in his seat with his glass of wine. "No offense, Larry, but the last two guys Dario took off this ship, they had something." He nudged Dario. "The first guy you took? Calhoun. What was he? Special Forces?"

"A Green Beret," said Dario. "Retired. He had a bad knee."

"And he couldn't kill your giant. The second guy. My deckhand Kendricks. What was he?"

"He used to be a professional wrestler."

"And he couldn't kill your giant."

"He knew how to fight but he didn't know how to kill."

Captain Grey turned to Larry. "What is your background if you don't mind my asking?"

"I manage a stamp and coin museum in Chicago."

The captain laughed. He took a large swig of wine to clear his throat before continuing his casual but persistent interrogation. "I can't even begin to imagine how it is that you're here." He raised his hands in the air. "Now the good news is, once a month a tender ship out of San Diego delivers supplies to us. You'll be wanting a ride back to the States, I suppose?"

"I made a promise to Dario."

"His problem is bigger than any solution you can provide. You're not what I would call a man of muscle, Larry. Maybe you're smart, but I never met a skinny kid with straight A's who kicked the shit out of a four hundred pound gorilla on the school wrestling team. Isn't that right, Dario?"

"Give me a gun and I won't hold Larry to his promise," said Dario.

"There you go again with your gun talk. Just contact the Mexican navy to visit that island of yours. If what you say is true they'll send in their marines and problem solved. No more giant."

"And the end of my people," said Dario.

"There are seven billion people on this planet! You can always find people."

"Not like us," said Dario.

"Oh hell," said Captain Grey. "I've been blowing up this damned ocean for years. Dragged nets across it, harpooned it. Not once did I find anything, *anything at all* that even closely resembles a mermaid."

"Because we are at the edge of extinction," said Dario.

Captain Grey stared down at his untouched plate of food, his mind racing. His eyes dimmed with moisture. He looked over to Larry and his shoulders sagged as if having witnessed a great tragedy. "Are you a godly man, Larry?"

"I think to be alive is a beautiful thing. I didn't always feel that way."

"What changed your thinking?"

"Sitting on a sea mount waiting to die."

The captain guffawed with laughter. "That might bend my soul spiritually. It certainly got your mind bending." Captain Grey nudged Dario. "Is this why you picked Larry to fight your battle? Brains over brawn?"

"Larry was available," said Dario. "What he does or doesn't do only he can say."

The captain turned on Larry again. "Maybe sometimes life is a beautiful thing, but we only get it in very small portions. There is great misery in this world, much of it created by malicious men.

And then there is a higher degree of misery created by pure evil. Facing evil is the greatest test any man can face. Most of us just melt or shit our pants when we are confronted by it." The captain picked up his fork and rang it against the rim of a wine glass. "A moment, please! Let us say a prayer over our meal."

People set down their forks. The diners fell silent.

Captain Grey stood and bowed his head. "A prayer for lost causes! In your hands, O Lord, we humbly entrust Larry to you. Deliver him from the pain and suffering caused by the evil he shall face and bid him an eternal peaceful rest when he fails. Welcome him into paradise where there will be no sorrow, no weeping or pain, but fullness of peace and joy with you, your Son and the Holy Spirit forever and ever. Amen."

"Amen," small voices around the room repeated.

People reached for the silverware but the captain wasn't done with his speech just yet. His eyes moved from one diner to the next.

"No one ever writes the history of lost causes. On land you are men, able-bodied and planted on the hard ground, but here? The water will not let you escape. Turn in any direction and all you will find is a horizon. There are no mountains beyond, no pleasant break of trees, no huddle of houses with the smoke of chimneys to console us. We are alone here. Utterly alone. Man is powerless and useless against the sea. It is a merciless phantom circling the earth. Do not trust it. Amen again."

The captain sat down. "I'm sorry, Larry," he said apologetically. "It's the best I can do given your life-threatening circumstance." Satisfied, the captain ate his dinner.

During the meal Larry picked at the food on his plate, studying the people in the room. They were from all walks of life. Members of the master species that controlled the planet. Some were maddened by the ocean. Others, like Larry, were simply adrift.

Towards the end of the meal, Helga came out from the kitchen, a large sheet cake topped with burning pink candles between her hands. Everyone started singing a birthday song as the cake was placed in front of the young crew member Larry had met on deck earlier.

"Happy crew, happy life," the captain mentioned to Larry.

"And if they aren't happy?"

"Then they put up with me until their contract ends. Society isn't that complicated, Larry. The man with the gun makes the rules."

CHAPTER 41

The sleeping berth was hot as a sauna, the air stifling. Larry tossed and turned in his bunk, unable to sleep. On the other side of his closed door spilled the loud noise of happy debauchery. He slid off his bunk and stuck his head out the door.

Dario was sitting in a metal folding chair at the far end of the hall, commanding a boom box on his lap playing loud dance music.

The gypsy women, Helga and her daughter were dancing and carousing with every man available. Female hips swayed and jiggled. Thick-bodied sailors and rail-thin engineers jumped and flailed like fraternity boys. The steam of body heat rose in the air and wafted like a fog.

Larry joined Dario and sat on the floor next to him, observing, saying nothing. He had never been to an orgy. He had never even visited a strip club. Larry's timid sexual nature had never been tapped.

One at a time, a gypsy girl disappeared to one of the berths with an eager male participant, appearing a few minutes later, having abandoned their exhausted prey to a fitful night of drunken sleep.

The gypsy women always returned with a gift in their hands: cans of Spam, green beans, corn, peas, carrots, evaporated milk. Nutrients and flavors not found in the sea.

Nina had a new knife from a deckhand.

Pinta had received a stack of tee shirts from a drunken biologist guilt-ridden over his wife who lived in Omaha.

Santa Maria proudly displayed a metal box of fishing tackle given to her by the drunken birthday boy. Dario removed the sailor's groping hands from her ass and sent him to bed.

Dario set the gifts in a pile next to him.

Helga came to him and sat on his lap, whispering something naughty in his ear. She gave him a long kiss on the lips, rose up and walked down the empty hallway to her berth, tossing heated glances back at him.

Dario stopped the music on the boom box and set it on the floor. He picked up a duffel bag and handed it to the barefooted gypsy girls, their bodies glistening with sweat. They dropped on their knees and carefully gathered their collected goodies in the large bag.

"Come," Dario said to Larry, "time to kiss the sea."

He pulled him to his feet and led Larry up the iron steps to the open deck.

The ship's deck was bright from strings of white lights. The sea, illuminated by the moon, looked like black rolls of wet asphalt. There was a steady sound of distant waves folding and churning.

Larry and Dario stood at the ship's rail, watching the sky. Dario filled his pipe and lit it with a stick match.

"We have done well tonight," decided Dario. "Good provisions to last us through the weeks ahead."

Flashes of heat lightning struck the air in the distance, sending showers of light dancing across the face of the sky, bouncing between the high dark clouds.

Dario spoke softly. "So often we seem to be alone in this great universe. But we are never really alone."

The gypsy girls appeared from below deck hauling the heavy duffel bag between them. They helped each other store it aboard the catamaran. When they finished, the gypsy girls climbed the ship's ladder and joined the men at the ship rail. Pinta and Santa Maria pressed their warm bodies against Larry, hugging him, holding him.

Nina reached out towards the dancing light of the sky above with a bare arm, her long tousled hair blown back from a soft breeze.

"What is she doing?" Larry asked Dario.

"Kissing God goodnight."

"This dark ocean," Larry mused. "Even with my eyes open, it's like a dream, waking something always in me but never exposed."

Dario smiled. "See what happens when you escape the rat race? Back there you were nothing more than a shaved monkey dancing."

CHAPTER 42

The sun broke on the horizon, bringing with it a relentless stinging heat.

Pharaoh woke to the pungent stench of something organic burning in the air. It smelled like vinegar. He struggled to pull himself up on the cot on one elbow. The pain of charred skin rubbing against the cot made him scream with delirium. It choked his throat, still rough and swollen. Barely audible.

He took several short breaths to calm his insides. Would he be able to see today? He carefully reached for the wet patch covering one of his eyes and lifted it. He blinked twice to clear the foggy glaze of moisture.

Things slowly came into focus. He saw that he was in some kind of makeshift cage. There was a blue tarp overhead, blocking the sun's harsh rays.

Pharaoh pulled the wet patch off his second eye, blinked a few times and brought his new world into wide focus.

A few ramshackle shacks stood in a crooked row, built from scraps. Garbage was strewn in piles near a much larger open-faced lean-to with a sloping roof and three makeshift walls. Like his cage, its high ceiling was made of tarps.

Pharaoh saw moving bodies at work. A couple of old men and women with bandanas covering their mouths were plunging long sticks into a large stone-lined fire pit of roasting plants, turning them slowly.

An old man pulled one of the roasted plants from the ashes with a thick stick and rolled it to a small pile of other cooked plants outside the open-faced shed. They looked like big brown pineapples.

Next to the cooling plants stood a dozen large wooden barrels; the kind used to make wine or whiskey.

Pharaoh saw the outline of a younger woman approaching the work area. Like the other workers, she covered her mouth. He could tell she was younger by the way she moved. Her shoulders were back, her step sure. She slowly came into focus. Long black hair trickled off her shoulders. Cool steel eyes committed to the work at hand revealed a certain and absolute beauty. She carried a stack of wood in her arms and dropped it next to the fire pit. Her head turned suddenly. She stared across the work yard directly at Pharaoh in the cage.

Pharaoh raised a hand and gave her a weak wave.

The woman looked in several directions, wiping her hands against a dirty sun dress. She pulled the protective scarf off her mouth and hurried up to Pharaoh's cage, dropping to her knees, a finger to her lips, warning Pharaoh not to speak.

She spoke rapidly, her eyes cautiously darting away. "You are badly burned. Do not try to speak just yet. You have come to a very bad place. There is a very bad man here who wants to kill you when you are able to stand. He is a pig. The longer you stay still, the longer you will live. Do you understand me? Comprende?"

Pharaoh nodded.

She offered a brief smile. "I am Ismelda."

He nodded again, taking in her soft brown eyes. He tried to speak, his voice too soft to be heard. She leaned in to listen but could not hear the words.

"You are the mermaid," he said.

Pharaoh pointed a finger towards the workers busy in plant production.

Ismelda understood his small gesture. "We are making mescal for Gordo, the pig. It is like tequila."

She stood suddenly, her head shaking at the sight of someone on the other side of the cage.

Pharaoh tilted his head slowly, the pain burning from his neck to his brain. His eyes met those of Gordo, staring back at him, a grotesque open smile of broken, rotting teeth and puffy blood red lips.

Pharaoh had never seen a bigger face - such an ugly face. He closed his eyes and kept them closed, hoping he was in some kind of bad dream and that when he awoke the giant would be gone and only the woman remained.

Pharaoh felt the twisting rattle of the cage. The giant spoke in a low voice, his voice was deep and full of rocks. "You can see now. When you can stand, we will fight to the death. I am chief here."

The pig laughed and walked towards the lean-to, troll-like and heavy of foot, swinging a machete in his hand. It caught the morning sun and sent slivers of light in his path. He shouted for Ismelda to return to work.

Pharaoh looked back at the woman.

Before she turned to leave, she said, "I prayed for someone to come and rescue us. I am sorry it was you."

She covered her mouth with the scarf and returned to work.

CHAPTER 43

The morning sea was calm, the blue of its horizon matching the cloudless sky. The bright sun's reflection burned against the steel deck.

Larry stood at the rail with the submarine pilot. They both wore tee shirts and khaki shorts.

"We'll only get our feet wet," said Wild Bill. He pointed at the orange submersible. "Sweetie Pie is thirteen feet long, eleven feet wide, and seven feet tall. She holds two passengers. See the big clear bubble? That's our cabin, a spherical pressure hull made of clear transparent acrylic nine inches thick. Optically perfect with a 360 degree view. Up, down, left, right. She only takes one man to operate. While I work, you get to enjoy the show, mate."

"Is she safe?"

Wild Bill laughed and pointed at the gypsy raft tied to the ship. "Safer than that. Safer than a race car at the Indie 500. Safer than the Hindenburg. Think of it as an underwater glider."

"That's reassuring. How deep can it go?"

"Two miles."

"Expensive to build?"

"Two million dollars."

Larry felt the coin in his pocket. If he sold it, he could own his own Sweetie Pie someday.

Sailors in orange overalls and hardhats were using Velcro straps to secure four metal boxes to a pair of freeboards, two on each side of the submersible.

"Besides us, she can carry a payload of five hundred pounds. That's a heap," said Wild Bill.

"What are in those boxes?"

"Sensors."

Finished loading, one of the sailors nodded to Wild Bill. "She's ready."

"Let's put her in the soup," ordered Wild Bill.

A second sailor went to a control panel and operated the controls of a crane. A thick metal arm hovered over the submersible. A pair of pincers fixed to thick cables was lowered to the steel sides of the sub. The crane lifted it off the deck, turned it out to sea and lowered the Sweetie Pie into the ocean next to a ship's ladder.

Wild Bill patted Larry on the shoulder. "Let's go visit the blackety black, shall we?"

They climbed down the ship's ladder and stood on one of the submersible's freeboards. Wild Bill pointed to a short ladder at the back of the submersible's cabin.

"Guests first," he ordered.

Larry shimmied up the ladder and dropped into the cabin. The cabin looked like the cockpit of a lunar module. To his left were a dozen analog gauges in two neat rows; pressure gauges, oxygen gauges, depth gauges, oil level indicators, two clinometers, even a clock. Larry was surprised that he could stand erect on the flat-bottomed floor.

"Take the front seat," Wild Bill hollered through the clear bubble.

Larry took a few short steps past the control console and settled in a comfortable leather swivel seat facing ahead. There was a small refrigerator to his left and a basket of snacks to his right. Wild Bill dropped into the cabin behind him, reached overhead and closed the portal. He turned a large round wheel and locked the cabin.

"We're airtight," he said.

He flicked a few switches. Larry heard the slight purr of a small electric engine.

"I'm building up our cabin pressure," said the pilot. "Only takes a minute." He flicked another switch and aimed his voice towards an intercom. "Systems check," he said.

Larry heard Captain Grey reply, "Copy."

Wild Bill pulled a pair of monitors in from the sides and positioned them above his lap. "This little ship of ours is driven with electronic touch screens." He pressed one of the screens. "AC on."

Larry felt a chilly breeze against his bare legs. He swiveled in his chair and watched Wild Bill tapping circular analog gauges. Behind the pilot a small propeller started spinning in its wheelhouse with two smaller turbines spinning on either side of the submersible.

"Thrusters on. Ready for release," said Wild Bill.

Larry looked above and saw the pincers retracting. The Sweetie Pie was free. Wild Bill touched a screen and the Sweetie Pie crept forward, slowly sinking into the sea as water crept up and over the cabin bubble. Now underwater, the noise of the spinning electric turbines was reduced to a gentle hum.

Larry leaned back and watched a digital depth gauge as numbers ticked higher and higher: twenty, thirty, forty, fifty and climbing.

"We're at a hundred feet," said Wild Bill, "deepest a human being can dive without oxygen."

Larry watched a school of silver and blue fish dart past the sub. The rays of the sun danced against their scales, sending shards of light in all directions like a burning sparkler. They reminded him of the Rock Island rail station, busy bodies bumping against each other, all in a hurry for another work day.

The Sweetie Pie continued its descent. The light of the sun was dimming.

"We're approaching seven hundred feet. Lights out from above and the threshold for scuba tanks." There was calm serenity in Wild Bill's voice.

Now the light was gone. The Sweetie Pie dropped down, down, down in complete darkness.

Larry looked at one of the screens. A scanning sonar showed the outlines of underwater objects in a topographical display of green, red and blue outlines below them.

Larry looked out, seeing long gray shadows swimming past against the blackness.

"Just three Manta Rays chasing a female," said Wild Bill.

The Sweetie Pie kept sinking.

It was an eerie place to be. Larry was spellbound. The warm interior lights of the cabin must have appeared like a Christmas ornament to the fish outside. Wild Bill pressed a button and music came on. "The Grand Canyon Suite," a soothing orchestral piece by Ferde Grofé.

Wild Bill flicked on a bank of switches. Bright headlights illuminated the darkness as the sub moved forward and down, waltzing with the peaceful swelling music's rhythm.

"We're entering a trench," said Wild Bill.

Larry stared to his left. Barely visible in the distance was the peak of a tall gray wall. "How deep are we?" he asked.

"Just under a mile," said the pilot.

Larry sat back and stared ahead, feeling the music in his bones against the stark gray sea. "I expected more color," he said. He looked between his legs, able to make out the flat bottom of the seafloor.

The Sweetie Pie seemed to be following a trail, moving along like a slowpoke mule. There was movement below - brown and white spotted slithering things hurrying in and out of holes in the sand on the seafloor.

"Sea snakes," said Wild Bill. "The same behavior you find in a burrowing colony of prairie dogs on the plains of America." He pointed to his left. "Now that's something you don't see every day!"

Larry turned and watched a brown prickly shark with black points on its fins. It was as long as the sub. The shark's green eyes shone brightly as it swam alongside.

"What is it doing?"

"He's just curious," said Wild Bill. "Wouldn't you be?"

The Sweetie Pie crawled half a mile before Wild Bill stalled the engines and parked it on the seabed.

"We reached our first position," he announced.

The voice of a crewman from the ship replied, "Copy."

Wild Bill pushed the monitors to the side and picked up a handheld device with a toggle switch.

"Time to plant some sensors," he told Larry. "Hand me a grog out of that cooler, will you?"

Larry opened the cooler by his feet and handed him a can of beer.

He watched Wild Bill maneuvering a pair of mechanical arms outside the bubble. They detached a large gray metal box from one of the running boards. It had a long V-shaped iron anchor welded to its base. The mechanical arms raised the box above the seabed and drove it into the sand.

"That should hold," decided Wild Bill. He aimed his voice towards an intercom. "Number One is locked to the floor. Please confirm position and signal."

It took thirty seconds for a reply from the ship. "Confirmed. We have the signal and position."

Wild Bill retracted the metal arms, guided them to the sides of the ship and drove on towards his next destination. "What do you think so far?"

"Peaceful. Almost cerebral," said Larry

"So it seems." Wild Bill turned off the intercom system to the surface. "This is a hostile environment. Outside, the water is just above freezing. These deep ocean fish have adapted to living in extremely high pressure with low light conditions. No mermaids down here."

He toggled a controller, sweeping the headlights from side to side, revealing a strange fish shaped in a ball with spikes protruding from all sides, its open mouth revealing rows of fang-like teeth.

"Look familiar? That's the Hairy Angler fish I showed you on the video yesterday. Seems different up close and personal. Black as night with photophores light organs created by bioluminescence, a chemical process to attract prey." He moved the light again. It fell on another fish species. "That one there, it doesn't have any pigment at all. You can see right through it. Find a land creature like that!" He moved the light again. It shone on a hideous-looking deep sea monster. "The Gulper eel. It has a hinged skull that rotates upward to swallow large prey."

Wild Bill moved the light again. It revealed a brown Viperfish, a wicked thing with enlarged eyes to better see in the dark, long teeth and a deformed monster's head.

"This is the planet we live on, Giant Slayer. Hidden dragons and monsters. The things of nightmares. Adaption and survival by any means possible. Vicious, cold and cruel. Is this a planet built by a god? There is no god down here. These fish are cannibals, living in a low energy environment of slow-standing water, unaffected by winds or waves. They adapt to a low food supply, eat scraps from above, eat each other. There is no plant life this far down. The pressure down here influenced their weird anatomies. Their soft cartilage and low-density flesh would look like a blob of pudding on the surface. Here is proof that the world teems with life, even in the most inhospitable corners. Now I ask you, Giant Slayer. What mermaid could live, would want to live in this shit of an ocean?"

Wild Bill reached over and turned off the exterior lights. Outside was total darkness, blacker than any night. He pulled a screen towards him and killed the interior lights. Larry listened to the scientist's heavy labored breathing, heard him sipping from the can of beer.

"So much for cerebral," said Wild Bill. "Spend enough time like this and you'll go mad. I wonder sometimes, is this what it must be like inside the human brain? The human soul, should it exist? Our decisions, our dreams, made in darkness? But these creatures down here, they don't kill in anger or meanness. They only kill to survive. Certain humans are capable of the same when driven to it."

"Why are you telling me this?" Larry asked.

"If you ever find your mermaid and your evil giant, what then? What new boundaries can you live with? If Dario and his gypsy women are to be believed, you're headed towards a real shit storm of *kill or be killed*. You aren't made for it, mate. I can tell by your demeanor. You seem to be a bloke destined to a calamitous casualty. No offense."

Larry's thoughts traveled back in time. He was a boy again, kneeling inside the dim confessional of a Catholic church. He saw the gray outline of a priest on the other side of a screen, his head bowed, waiting for an innocent boy's reply. Larry thought of answering with the standard "Bless me Father, for I have sinned." Instead he replied, "Forgive me Father, for I do not know who I am."

Wild Bill interrupted his chain of thought. "Then again, maybe this freeing experience is your destiny changer."

Larry heard his own surprising voice. "Who better to slay the giant than the least expected man? At least I can take a strike at it. If I run away, I run."

"Before or after you shit your pants?"

"Before, I hope."

"Don't make too much of it," said Wild Bill. "Our lives are just a blip on the map of human existence. As you get older, you realize your insignificance more and more." He rapped on his skull with a finger. "The human compass we carry here in our heads? One day we realize it points to nothing. North is just north. It doesn't mean anything."

"But killing a man..."

"It's a natural instinct, given the right circumstances," said Wild Bill.

CHAPTER 44

The scent of sweat and vinegar permeated the air. Pharaoh lay in his cage, his head propped up on a soiled pillow, watching Ismelda and the old people at work. He counted nine in all.

Inside the lean-to was some kind of recessed round pit. An old man and two old women walked like mules in a circle, pushing a long thick handle inserted through the eye of a large stone grinding wheel. They were crushing some of the roasted pineapple-sized plants that had been stacked outside the shed. Every ten minutes they stopped their round walk and waited for two other old people to clear the smashed plants from the pit with shovels. They carried the crushed syrupy plants outside and dumped them in one of the twelve wooden barrels.

The beautiful woman Ismelda pulled a large iron kettle of boiling water off an open fire and poured the water over the plant mash in the barrel. When she finished she covered the barrel with a lid and placed a rock on top to hold it down.

More old ones, their hands covered with worn gloves or wrapped in bandages were poking through the hot smoldering coals of the outdoor fire pit with narrow spades, pulling out charred plants to be crushed by the milling wheel. It was exhausting work, better suited to a man half their age.

Ismelda chastised the other workers. "Cover your nose and mouth. Try to protect your eyes! The wood we burn is bad. It will make you sick!"

She wiped her hands as clean as she could on a smeared towel, picked up a small bag and came to Pharaoh's cage, unlatching the door to enter. Pharaoh was still unable to walk. The pig had not locked him in yet.

Ismelda knelt by Pharaoh and started changing his bandages.

Pharaoh practiced speaking, his voice a soft whisper. "It is hard work."

Ismelda looked at him, surprised. "You can talk!" She dipped her fingers in a clay jar and pulled out a sticky salve. She carefully rubbed it on Pharaoh's burns. "This is aloe. With time, it will heal you."

"Those plants you cook. What are they?"

“Piñas, the hearts of the agave plant. First we bake them, then we crush them. We put them in the barrels with hot water and cover them to ferment. In a week or more, the pig will start drinking the mescal blanco, a cheap pulque.”

“And the rest of you?”

“Even if we were allowed, we would not drink it. There are no trees on this island. The wood we burn came from boats and furniture. Much of it is painted or varnished. We used gasoline and motor oil to start the fires. It sours the mescal.”

“Then why manufacture it?”

“We hope to poison our captor.”

“What brought you to this island?”

“We needed a new home. But El Gordo changed things.”

“El Gordo. The pig man?”

“Yes. All in one day, he killed the stronger men with his machete. Next came the young women. We are his slaves now. Me and the old people.”

“Why didn’t he kill you?”

“He wanted a pet.”

“That ain’t right.”

“We are too weak against him now. Gordo, he is too smart for us. There are no guns here. No sharp things. Gordo makes sure.”

Pharaoh turned his head and looked at the shack where El Gordo was sleeping. "Have you tried burning him in his house?"

"Yes."

"Surrounding him as a group? Beating at him with the shovels?"

"Once. He killed two of the old ones with his machete. We will not try again."

Pharaoh shook his head. "Maybe when I get better...."

Ismelda shrugged, sympathy in her eyes. "He will kill you before you are well enough to even try."

"If I can stand and hold a shovel, I can fight," he said.

Ismelda gently touched his face with salve. "I see you are brave. This will end someday."

"But not today," said Pharaoh.

"Not today," said Ismelda.

The old woman Calista came from the fire pit. She carried a fish roasted on a stick and passed it into the cage for Ismelda.

"You are very weak. You must try to eat," Ismelda told Pharaoh.

She tore off a piece of fish and placed it to his lips. He took it in his mouth and chewed.

"It's good," he said.

"It is all we have for now," she said. "The pig, he locks up what little food there is."

She pulled a plastic water bottle from her bag and he drank from it.

Pharaoh's eyes studied the bottle. "Where did this come from?"

"Sometimes people visit the island by boat. The pig kills them. He makes the old ones strip the boats and sinks them."

"Geezuz," Pharaoh said. "This ain't right. This is madness."

She fed Pharaoh more fish, gave him a long drink and packed up her things.

"This is not your problem," she said. "I am sorry you landed here."

"But I was supposed to come here," he said, "with my boss Larry. We came to find Jack Douglas. Larry found his message in a bottle. Is Larry here?"

"There is no Larry here."

"What about Jack Douglas?"

"He is here. He is alive," she reassured him.

"Where?"

"Another time," she promised. She glanced at the pig's shack. "I must get back to work. He will be awake soon." Ismelda backed out of the cage. She turned and looked at Pharaoh. "Was your boss man Larry in the plane with you?"

"No," said Pharaoh. "I don't know where he is."

"But he knows of this place?"

"Yes."

"Maybe he still comes," she said.

"I'm not worth finding. He thought I was his friend but I betrayed him."

"Why is Jack Douglas worth finding?"

"Larry says he's special."

"He is. But he can't help us anymore."

"Why not?"

"He is mad in the head. What is your name?"

"Pharaoh. Pharaoh Williams."

"A pharaoh is like a king?"

"Believe me, I ain't no king. Anything but."

Pharaoh watched her return to the others. She was telling them something. A few of the old people glanced back at Pharaoh in his cage. They looked hopeful.

Pharaoh looked over at the closed shack where the pig was sleeping, a serial killer who slaughtered innocents on a whim.

Pharaoh didn't want to die. Praying was the only option at the moment. But pray for what? That he wouldn't die? That God would give him permission to kill just this one time? Pharaoh tried to remember prayers from his childhood, when his mother dragged him to church. But no prayer came to mind. His childhood was gone. He would probably be dead soon. He wanted to see a palm tree now, to remind him of his impossible dream. He looked down at the small beach by the uneven dock; pictured his family there, sitting on a Florida beach building a sand castle.

CHAPTER 45

The Sweetie Pie returned to the surface in the late afternoon. Larry watched the crew return the metal crab to the deck. He looked for Wild Bill, to thank him for the experience, but Wild Bill was already at the bow of the ship, an eager participant in an outdoor barbecue hosted by Helga and the sea gypsies.

Men wore straw hats and plastic leis around their necks. Someone had found some grass skirts. The gypsy girls wore them around their waists, dancing a primitive hula to a shipmate's tinny ukulele.

Dario found Larry and handed him a drink in a plastic cup. "Welcome to the luau. Did you enjoy your trip?"

"It was highly informative," said Larry.

"But no mermaids?" said Dario.

"Not today," said Larry.

"You want to see a mermaid that bad?"

"It would help me embrace your cause," said Larry.

"Then tonight you will see mermaids," decided Dario. "But until then? We must celebrate life. Come, come. Pinta wants to dance with you."

Larry tasted his drink. He almost coughed it up. "What is this?"

"Tequila on the rocks," said Dario. "It will put hair on your balls."

Larry heard a loud grinding noise – metal against metal. The Felicity was taking up its anchor. They were moving to a new location, the gypsy boat in tow.

Pinta ran up to Larry and pulled him aside to dance. Larry took another sip from his cup. He would need lots and lots of hair for what was ahead.

The ship traveled fifty miles in the night and anchored.

Dario shook Larry awake in his bunk. "It is time," he whispered. "Come with me."

Larry followed him to the rear of the ship's deck, behind the crab-shaped submersible. A work light swung overhead in the breeze. He was surprised to see Helga standing there.

She hunched her shoulders. "What? You tink I am a cook my whole life? Before den, I was a hard hat diver."

Next to a work bench was a vintage deep sea diving suit. It looked like it was made of heavy gray seal skin. Next to it was a large spherical helmet. It reminded Larry of an outer space helmet from a 1950's movie.

"Dis is my old underwater dress," said Helga. "A high pressure suit. No leaks or tears. Sit down."

Larry sat on the bench.

Helga kneeled in front of him and placed the suit fabric under his feet. She pulled it up to his waist. "Dis has two layers. Da inside layer is a bib to trap water if da dress leaks. When we're done da suit will be heavy; 170 pounds. But once you get in da water and have buoyancy it will be easy for you to move. Stand up."

Larry stood. She wrestled the bulky suit up his waist and wormed his arms inside the sleeves. She bent down and placed a heavy pair of lead shoes over the enclosed suit, lacing up the leg straps to his calves and wrapping Velcro straps over them for extra protection. A padded rubber horse collar was placed over the dress and tucked into the suit at the shoulders. She wrapped Velcro wristbands around his wrists.

"Wit da ankle straps, dey prevent your suit from overinflating. Too much air in da suit and you blow up like a balloon. Your hands will be useless. We don't want dat." She raised a metal breastplate over his head and rested it on the rubber collar of the suit. “Dis connects da metal helmet to da suit wit wingnuts. Airtight.” She pointed at two long coils by the ship’s ladder while she dressed him. “You have two hoses. Dey are your umbilical cords. One is oxygen for breathing; da other is your safety line.”

She pointed at a yellow waterproof box. “Dat’s our communication system. Microphones and speakers at both ends hardwired tru da umbilical cord. You can talk to us and we can talk to you in your helmet. Use short sentences. Dario will be feeding you da safety line. If for any reason our communications system fails, you have a Plan B.”

Dario raised a section of umbilical in his hands for a demonstration. “Let’s make this simple,” he said. “If you feel me pull once, I am asking if you are okay. If you pull once back, you are saying okay. If I pull three times, it means I am pulling you to the surface. If you pull three times you are asking me to pull you up. Now if you pull four times, you are saying STOP or STAND BY. Okay?”

“Okay,” said Larry.

Helga laughed. “Most deep sea divers get two weeks training before a first dive. You got two minutes. You sure you want to do dis?”

"I'm sure," said Larry.

Dario smiled at Helga. "You see, Helga? I told you he is braver than he seems."

"Or he's stupid," she replied.

Dario picked up the helmet. Helga showed Larry a pair of knobs on the front. "Da knob on da left is your air control valve. Turn right to open for more air, left to close. You feel dizzy? Open the air. We will be listening to your breathing. If we say ADD AIR, you turn the knob to the right. Show me how it is done."

Larry demonstrated for her.

"Good," she said. "If we tink you have too much air, and say LESS AIR, what will you do?"

"Turn the knob to the left," said Larry.

"Congratulations!" Dario told Larry. "You are officially a deep sea diver."

"The knob on the right is your communications and lifeline. Don't touch it. Okay?"

Larry nodded.

Helga and Dario placed the helmet over Larry's head. There was a round open glass face plate in front. "Can you hear me?" asked Helga.

"Yes," said Larry.

"Good. Now, when you are in da water, you'll see air bubbles coming up from da back of the suit. Don't worry. It's just dispensed air." Helga continued the lesson. "I will strap you in good and tight and button you up now. We are above a coral reef. Maybe tree hundred feet below us. We will lower you to da bottom for one hour. No longer, no less."

Dario put something in Larry's mouth. "Chew on this and swallow. It will give you energy."

Larry bit into it. It tasted bitter.

Dario held a water bottle to Larry's mouth and he washed it down.

Helga punched Dario in the arm. "Why did you give him dat? He's new at dis."

Dario raised his hands defensively. "He wants to see mermaids. I gave him a cactus button. I am just trying to help."

"Is something wrong?" said Larry.

"You'll be fine," Helga reassured him.

Together, Helga and Dario picked up a heavy belt weighted with iron. "It weighs eighty pounds," said Helga.

They secured the belt around Larry's waist. Dario tied straps around his thighs to the belt. Helga pulled a harness over his shoulders and attached it to the belt, front and back.

"Good and tight?" she asked Larry.

"It's heavy," he said.

"It's supposed to be heavy. We don't want you to float away!" She picked up a wrenching tool and tightened the wingnuts around the helmet.

Dario started a compressor. Larry tasted cool oxygen in his suit.

"You ready?" asked Helga.

"Yes," said Larry.

Helga strapped a large flashlight to his left wrist. "Don't turn it on until I tell you. Just press the big button." She picked up a green stick and tucked it in his belt. "An underwater sparkler. Crack it with both hands for illumination."

Larry nodded. "Like a flare?"

She nodded. "It is a flare. I like sparkler better. Any last words?"

"None I can think of," smiled Larry.

"Good! Let's button you up."

Helga closed the glass face plate and locked it in. She and Dario held Larry by the arms and led him to the ship's ladder. He turned around to face the ship. He found the rails of the ladder and stepped down, one step at a time. It was hard going with the added weight of the suit. Helga backed away and started feeding the umbilical cord as Larry disappeared under the surface. He let go of the ladder.

Dario put on a headset and spoke into a microphone. "Can you hear me?"

Larry's voice came through the headset. "Loud and clear."

Larry felt himself sinking slowly. He heard Helga in the background of the helmet speaker chastising Dario. "Dat was no cactus button. Dat was peyote!"

"To help him open the door to perception," said Dario.

Larry could move his arms and legs freely in the water. He stuck an arm out and saw the flashlight strapped to it. He tilted his head up. Only a dim work light from the ship was visible. He kept watching it until it faded away. He turned his head left and right.

A dirty yellow smog seemed to engulf him. As he continued dropping, the yellow turned to a dusty green.

"One hundred feet. Don't be afraid of the dark," Said Dario.

Larry raised his arms. He felt only a faint resistance of water against his suit.

He recalled a novel he had read as a boy; *Twenty Thousand Leagues under the Sea* by Jules Verne. He remembered the giant squid, the fantastic submarine and the eccentric Captain Nemo, a man without a country. Was he an outlaw, a bad man or a visionary?

What's the plot, Larry? What's the plot?

"Two hundred feet," said Dario.

Larry was in complete darkness now. Another story popped in his mind; *Moby Dick*. A giant whale, another eccentric captain, the obsessive quest of Ahab.

Why did he hate the whale?

He thought of Huckleberry Finn, drifting down a long river on a journey of personal discovery. Innocence lost. A great adventure. Larry smiled. He had forgotten about all the books he had read as a boy, sitting by the window in the orphanage.

What happened to me? Where was my adventure? Wait! I am having one now! A little late getting started but here I am in the blackety black about to sit on the bottom of the sea!

Larry stared ahead at nothing. No distance ahead, a pure black paint against the faceplate glass inches from his nose.

"How are you feeling?" asked Dario.

"Splendid," said Larry.

"Good. You are almost at the bottom."

Larry heard Helga in his ear. "Turn on da flashlight when I tell you," she said. "Don't be surprised by what you see. Primary colors disappear da deeper you go. It's a law of physics. Red is da first to go, den yellow, den green. All dat is left at 300 feet is a dirty blue. Okay?"

"Okay," said Larry.

"Now turn on da flashlight," said Helga.

Larry fumbled for the flashlight strapped to his wrist. He pressed the large button. A wide stream of white light pierced the darkness. There were pale blue particles in the water like floating dust mites.

"I'm dropping you slower," said Dario. "Let me know when you touch down."

Larry found that he could bend at the waist. He shined the light below.

"I see sand," he said. Larry touched down. "I'm at the bottom."

He could no longer feel the tension of the umbilical cord. Larry aimed the flashlight above his head and saw its light floating effortlessly, weaving in the water like a long endless snake until it reached a wall of darkness.

"What do you see?" said Dario.

Larry turned in all directions, shining the light around him. "There's a long pockmarked wall behind me. Looks like concrete."

"That's the reef," said Dario.

“Other than that, everything is flat.”

“Okay,” said Dario. “You can walk around and explore if you like. How are you feeling?”

“Wide awake. The cactus button works fast!”

“See you in an hour. Remember the signals?”

“One pull and we’re okay. Three pulls means take me up. Four pulls means wait.”

“Remember, Larry. You are not alone.”

Larry stood planted in the sand. How long had he been here? A minute? Ten? He had no sense of time. The light was steady in his hand, focused on the reef ledge in front of him. He guessed it to be about ten feet high. There was no movement on the reef. No fish of any kind coming or going. It was dead.

He turned away from the reef and saw a curious sea horse facing him. Larry had no sense of depth perception. It could have been an inch tall or a foot. Its tiny black eyes stared at him. He stared back. A pair of small dorsal fins behind its eyes fluttered like butterfly wings. The sea horse swam away zigzagging into the mouth of a gray hammerhead shark. Larry had no idea how big it was or how far away. Its odd eyes were positioned on either side of its flat hammer head. It came up to him, its wide face distorted, studying him, wondering what he was.

Larry's breathing accelerated but he wasn't afraid. The shark didn't seem real with its cartoonish features. How did the shark manage to just float there? The bottom of the sea was as foreign to Larry as outer space.

The hammerhead jerked its head suddenly, its body half bent as it stared back at a force of motion, like rocks dropping from above. It moved its tail and vanished in the darkness as quickly as it had arrived, replaced by three descending objects surrounded by blinding swirls of sand rising from the sea floor.

Stinging pellets of rock and sand tapped against Larry's deep sea suit. The flashlight in his hand went dead and he was immersed in the black ink of the sea bottom.

The stinging stopped. He heard odd sounds, like baby talk. Whatever was out there was moving towards him from above. He stayed motionless, waiting to be grabbed or bitten in half. He heard voices, garbled and high-pitched; one to the left, one to the right, one in front of him. He could not die in a panic against the unknown.

He remembered the flare tucked in his belt. He pulled it loose. What did Helga say? Just break it in half? He placed his hands on either side of the long stick and snapped it in two.

A bright green effervescent light leapt from the stick flare. Sparks tapped against Larry's face window. He raised the flare in front of him, catching the glistening rainbow-colored tail of what he thought was an apparition hovering like a blonde-haired angel in front of him.

A mermaid!

Larry's eyes blinked rapidly. Was she real or imagined?

He looked to the left. A second mermaid stared down at him from above, a fan of long red hair sweeping away from her face, rising towards the surface. Her arms moved in small motions, acting like buoys to keep her erect.

The third mermaid, the one on his right, drifted down towards him, her hands gently paddling up and down. Small bubbles trickled away from her nostrils and rose towards the black ceiling. She looked like a dark-haired saint pulled from a mosaic of glass in a church window.

Were the gypsies playing tricks on him? Was it Nina the redhead? Pinta the brunette? Santa Maria the blonde? How could they dive so deep? He saw their eyes; imploring eyes like those of saints trapped in canvas portraits, eyes begging for mercy, sad eyes witnessing a crucifixion, tired eyes from lost hopes.

The mermaids hovered there, trapped together in the long moment with Larry, none able to break the spell of the encounter.

His mind started to unravel in spectacular bliss. He could hear the hum of the ship's engines above, a steady symphony of rumbling, sweeping sounds in musical concert. A thick school of fish raced behind the mermaids like a marching band dressed in twinkling neon until they disappeared.

The mermaids started to swim circles around Larry, the reflections from their tails turning to long ribbons until he was surrounded in a rainbow of color.

The mermaids came to a stop in front of him. The colors fell away like raindrops, swallowed up by the sea floor turned gold.

The dark-haired mermaid came up close to Larry's face plate. He saw fine whiskers on her face, thin as angel hair. Her worried eyes locked on his and she seemed to speak:

Loorince.

The blonde-haired mermaid added, *Settle.*

The red-haired mermaid whispered *Bottom.*

They repeated the words over and over until it was a steady choir of lilting sound.

Loorince Settle Bottom Loorince Settle Bottom Loorince Settle Bottom....

The flare in Larry's hand started to sputter. He remembered a boy at the orphanage who stood by a light switch by the dormitory door, flicking the switch on and off, on and off, white to black and back again as a new boy cried with fright.

The mermaids came together, side by side. They stopped singing, one final long stare from their eyes to his until they backpedaled and floated up, up and away towards the surface and out of his vision.

The flare died and he released it.

Once again Larry was trapped in total darkness; his chest pounding, his breathing irregular, ears ringing from the high-pitched scraping sound of steel wheels burning against steel rails. He was in Chicago again, a passenger on a crowded train pulling into a station. He saw himself climbing off the train, blending into a crowd of people until he was swallowed up in a rushing stream of humanity carried forward to an inhospitable manmade reef of brick and steel.

Larry heard words in his head, repeated again and again. "Lawrence Settlebottom. I am Lawrence Settlebottom! I live with purpose, I am alive!" He realized his lips were moving, that he was saying them. "I am free! Finally free!"

He felt something tugging at him. It pulled again and again.

He heard a voice in his helmet. "Add more air, Larry. Add more air."

He found the air valve attached to his helmet and turned it, tasting a rush of new oxygen to clear his head.

He sensed his feet being plucked from the sand he had been embedded in. He was going up, up, up. He spent his arms wide, pressed his legs together. He sensed a resurrection as his body rose from the womb of the sea.

He tilted his head back and saw the lights of the ship coming into focus. His helmet clanged against the steel ladder of the ship and clarity returned. He pulled himself up, step by step, regaining the weight of the deep sea suit no longer submerged.

He grinned at the smiling faces of Dario and Helga, smeared and distorted in the helmet glass. They pulled him on deck.

Dario knocked on Larry's helmet. "Everything okay in there?"

Larry gave him a thumbs-up.

"Good! Good!" said Dario.

Larry was led to a bench and sat. Helga unharnessed him and removed the helmet with Dario.

Larry tasted the fresh salty air of the sea and breathed deeply. When he was removed from the suit he pulled Dario to him and spoke in his ear. “I saw mermaids. They sang to me.”

Dario nodded. “They like to sing when they are free.”

“This is a hard world, up and down,” realized Larry. “If I can contribute to a greater good, perhaps I will find a better way to live.”

Dario agreed. “Justice is a hard practice until one finds a moral compass to steer by.”

Larry held an open palm before Dario. “I have a compass in my hand now. Can you see it?”

Dario stared at Larry’s empty palm. “Yes, I see it. It is a good compass. Where does it point?”

“Your mermaid island and Jack Douglas.”

“We should leave now,” said Dario. “Time has a way of weakening a man’s resolve. If you are ready to finish your journey, we are ready.”

Larry noticed the gypsy boat tied to the stern. Nina, Pinta and Santa Maria were unfurling the sails.

Helga pulled Dario to her and buried his head in her bosom. “I will miss you, little man.”

Dario smiled up at her. “Maybe I will be back, maybe I won’t. It all depends on Larry.”

CHAPTER 46

A furnace of blasted heat settled on the island before noon, intensified by a slow steady wind dusted with burning sand.

Pharaoh lay in his cage. Whips of air came from nowhere and danced around his body like pesky flies. He looked out through the cage wire, watching his newfound enemy, moving like a troll among the old people, inspecting the barrels of ripening alcohol.

In a few days the pig man would start drinking the poisoned hooch. Maybe he would be sloppy with his machete when the time came. Pharaoh would have an advantage there.

When Pharaoh was a boy he used to visit a local boxing club. His mama, she thought taking up boxing might be a good way to release the anger of growing up in poverty and keep him off the streets where trouble was a daily occurrence.

Pharaoh enjoyed boxing for a little while. He was taller and heavier than other boys his age. He could take a hit to the body and knew how to deliver a strike of his own.

He raised his hands wrapped in moist rags. Could he jab, cross and hook with them now? If it came to fisticuffs he might outlast the moping pig and wear him down. There would be no rounds, no corner for rest.

But the machete - Pharaoh never faced a man swinging a giant blade before.

Pharaoh was too badly burned to jump a rope or even shadow box. Raising his arms sent lightning strikes of pain to his brain. But his feet were healing. He knew he could walk when the time came. His meager diet of fish and occasional water did not supply him the nutrients a boxer needed to go the distance, but when the time came to fight the big slob of a man he would muster up his courage and mentally block his pain. That or he would surely die.

His eyes studied the lay of the land. He might be able to get his hands on a shovel or a long piece of rebar when he was freed from his prison. If he could get the pig near one of the shacks he might be able to tear loose a piece of metal siding or roof to use as a shield.

Pharaoh felt a little hope inside. It faded when he realized the size of the pig's hands. They were like enormous ham hocks. Getting slapped in the head by a hard left or a right would surely rock Pharaoh. He recalled a beating he took from a bigger boxer who knew how to stand and bring it. All it took was three punches to lay Pharaoh out. He quit boxing after that, saying he didn't care for the sport, didn't like the hoodlums at the gym selling crack and other dope in the alley. It was a straight-faced lie but his mama bought it.

Judgment day was coming soon for Pharaoh. The day he stood up on his own two feet would be the day he died. He remembered what brought him to the island.

Jack Douglas.

According to the coordinates he was somewhere on the island. Ismelda had confirmed it. But where? Douglas wasn't among the workers in this forsaken place. Was he a part of this madness or already a victim to the pig man's machete?

Too late, Pharaoh realized the giant pig was outside his shack, staring at him, smiling. The pig came towards him in a lopsided charge, huffing and puffing, brandishing the machete. When he reached the cage he dragged the machete across the steel mesh, releasing a high pitched scream worse than any out-of-tune violin.

The pig slid the machete in a sheath, grabbed the cage with his hands and rattled it, shaking the foundation as he let out an enormous blood-curdling scream, his yellow eyes rolling around in his head. As suddenly as he had begun, he calmly stopped his recreation, picked up his machete and lumbered away without saying a word.

Pharaoh reached down and felt the soiled sheet covering him. He had wet himself with fear, just as any man would when sheer rage and insanity provoked the intelligent mind.

CHAPTER 47

A cloudless sky above, the sun had reached its pinnacle, unleashing its full force. The gypsy catamaran laden with fresh food, canned provisions and supplies sliced through the calm waters of the open sea towards a new destination. Dario sat by the rudder, a firm hand guiding the boat.

Larry was at the bow, eyes closed; feeling the heat of the sun and the wind against his bare chest. Already his skin had turned light bronze in color. In his head he listened to Charlie Parker's "Bird Gets the Worm".

The gypsy girls leaned against the full mainsail behind Larry, studying him. *Was he the one? This tall, thin, gentle man? Why him*?

Dario drew smoke from his pipe and waved the girls close to his side at the rudder. They knelt before him. He spoke softly, barely above a whisper.

"I know what you three are thinking," he said. "Why did the sea gods give us Larry on the rock that day? The other men who faced the giant were bigger and stronger. They were trained fighters. Now kind-hearted Larry, he comes along, raised to believe in angels and demons. Do we not have a demon on la isla? Larry will see him and will strike him down. And why? Because Larry has finally reached his age of responsibility and with it he is ready to release his manhood."

"And after the giant dies?" asked Pinta. "What for Larry then?"

"Larry will decide."

"I hope he stays with us," said Nina.

"Why wouldn't he stay?" said Santa Maria.

"Even without the pig, our lives are hard," said Nina.

"I would like to have Larry," said Pinta.

"He is a good dancer," said Santa Maria.

"Do not fight over Larry just yet," said Dario. "It takes time to become a hero, to find a purpose and meaning to one's life. Imagine what is going on inside his head right now?"

The girls turned to watch Larry standing at the bow.

"Fear?" said Nina.

"No, not fear. Larry never sought this. It was thrust upon him. How does a man plan for a future he cannot see? What horror does he imagine lay ahead? Only he knows. We must go about our work quietly now. Do not interfere with his mindfulness. Speak softly. Give no advice. Let Larry work things out in his mind so he will be ready to face evil when the time comes."

"And while he thinks?" said Nina.

"We will make him things."

Dario opened a wooden box by his feet. He reached inside it and handed Pinta baggy cotton shirts and large pieces of animal hide.

"Stitch these together. Soak it all as one in brine to make it strong and stiff when it dries. This will be Larry's armor."

He pulled out plates of bone and a palette of bright feathers for Santa Maria.

"He will need a Cuacalati. Use these bones of eagle and jaguar to fashion a helmet to cover his head and jaw. Decorate the crown with dull feathers so that Larry will blend in with the land like a thin tree."

He handed Nina pieces of wood, a patch of leather and a bungee cord.

"Nina, you will make Larry a slingshot to catapult small rocks."

Dario reached deep into the box and withdrew a long black piece of obsidian rock. "I will fashion a spear with a glass edge sharp as razor so he can poke his enemy." He opened a deck board and lifted out a large olive green turtle shell. "This will be his shield." He shushed the women away with a gentle wave. "Off to work, now! Go, go, go!"

The women found the tools necessary to complete their tasks. They scattered themselves on the deck and began their work.

Dario tied the rudder off to a beam, picked up the turtle shell and carried it up to Larry. He set the shell down next to him and returned to his station at the stern.

Larry glanced down at the large shell, picked it up and studied it, turning it over and over in his hands. He raised the shell high in the air to block the sun.

Here, on the open sea, the essence of who Larry Settlebottom had once been had scattered like the waves of the sea, rolling by in constant motion, swallowed up in turmoil, ground and separated in wet beads only to form a new wave and begin as something else; still a wave, but a different wave. Like jazz, the sea was music. It was free. Larry was free, finally and fully alive, his future uncharted.

"When do we reach the island?" he asked Dario excitedly.

"Maybe tomorrow, the wind in our favor."

Larry pointed. "There is something up ahead of us, as far as the eye can see."

The catamaran sailed into an enormous garbage patch floating on the surface.

"It is a vortex," said Dario. "The ocean currents meet here and trap things."

The wind in the sail was barely alive. The catamaran skimmed through the choking flotsam, a collection of plastic bottles, chemical sludge, Styrofoam cups, and gnarled fishing nets.

The gypsy women passed out knives and went to the bow. A half dozen seals were trapped in the abandoned nets, the stink of dead fish around them. The women set about freeing them from the toxic soup and pulled the seals up on the boat. The mammals just lay there, exhausted. Larry found a knife and joined in freeing the helpless creatures of the sea.

The boat inched forward. A dolphin was cut loose, then another, diving under the waste to swim for freedom under the choking surface. Dozens of sea birds had their feet removed from nets and flew away.

"Who is responsible for this garbage?" asked Larry.

"Just read the labels," said Dario. "China, Japan, the U.S., Mexico. But no one claims it."

CHAPTER 48

Ismelda clung to the side of the cliff, guided by moonlight, taking each step carefully until she reached the rope attached to the metal stake secured in the rock above. She flung the canvas bag over her shoulder and lowered herself to the big smooth rock polished by sea tides. A gentle wave capped with white foam rolled up and tickled her feet.

She studied the entrance to the cave. A low arch of small boulders had been built to make the entrance smaller, blocking out the outdoor heat and occasional winds. She stepped to the mouth of the lava cave and listened. There was the flicker of light far back inside the lava tube, in sync with the tapping of a frantic chisel.

"Jack!" she called out in a half whisper. "It is Ismelda."

A beam of light turned toward her. A man's muffled, hoarse voice called out, "Are you wearing sandals?"

"Yes," said Ismelda.

"Watch out for shrapnel."

Ismelda lowered her head and entered, pausing long enough to adjust her vision. It wasn't a typical cave. There were no stalactites or stalagmites. No flowstones, no soda straws. The long cave opened up to her in width and height. At least twenty feet high and twenty feet wide it had been formed by flowing basaltic lava, now a cooled and hardened smooth surface. Scaffolding lined one of the walls far into the cave.

Closest to the entrance were solid flat oxidized walls of bright blood red, as if painted. Beyond, the red walls drizzled into a spattering of dripping chocolate fudge, peanut butter, butterscotch and cherry. "Ice cream toppings," Jack once said.

The light from within revealed outrageous kaleidoscope colors of white, yellow, green, purple, red and orange in the mineral deposits of the rock walls, ceiling and floor. Jack once described it as a jar of glass jellybeans.

But the cave was more than pretty colors. It was a sacred site for Jack. A present from God for him to create his final unfettered masterpiece, away from the prying eyes of the public. Art for art's sake. Pure.

Ismelda set the canvas bag on one of the three raised alcoves carved in the rock. It served as a bare bones kitchen, with a handful of old encyclopedias and a pile of sticks used for fuel next to a small pit shaped like a bowl.

Ismelda used to love reading books. They had taught her Spanish, English and some French. She especially loved the encyclopedias that gave her a glimpse to an outside faraway world. But now, with the pig in control of her life, all but the books in the cave had been burned to make the pig's liquor.

A second alcove held Jack's carving tools; an odd assortment of chisels, hammers, axes, rasps, files, dremels and sandpaper. There was a box full of dead batteries, another box of makeshift candles, and a small crate filled with saltpeter Jack had contrived from soaking bat guano in water. Separated, the white saltpeter contained potassium nitrate. Jack called it "Chinese snow" and used it to create small explosions in the rock surface of the cave to shape his art.

The third alcove was a makeshift bed, softened with dried moss. It was a minimalist existence, here in the cave. How long had it been since Jack had enjoyed the sunshine? He had come to la isla over three years ago, just before El Gordo went insane and started killing. The pig thought Jack had escaped the island on a makeshift float, but having found the cave and nature's perfect canvas, Jack Douglas had found a bigger purpose to pursue in life.

Ismelda looked at the string of untouched dried fish hanging over the bed. There were no bones on the floor. She emptied the canvas bag and called out to Jack. “I brought you cans of peaches and tomato sauce.”

A bobbing light came towards her, mounted on a strap wrapped around Jack Douglas’s skull. He wore a filthy brown leather poncho. His long gray hair and beard was matted and filthy. A large bandana was tied to his neck, used occasionally to cover his mouth and nose when he chiseled away, creating flying dust and chips of rock debris. A pair of clear goggles hung on his chest, held by a string around his neck. Beneath his baggy clothes he seemed skinny and frail, but there was still power in his arms to chisel and shape his latest creation.

She put her hands on her hips and studied his gaunt face. “You are forgetting to eat again,” she scolded.

“No time, no time,” said Jack dismissively.

Ismelda picked up a small chisel and poked a hole in the can of tomato sauce. She handed the can to him.

“Drink,” she said.

He hesitated, glancing back at his work in progress deep in the cave.

Ismelda wagged a finger at him, "You cannot finish your life's work if you are dead. If you don't take nourishment your mind will wander and you will ruin things. Is that what you want?"

"Of course not," Douglas smiled. Half his teeth were missing.

"So drink," she said like a stern mother.

He removed his work gloves, took the can from her and drank. His long thin fingers were covered in dried blood and colored rock dust.

Ismelda turned to the kitchen alcove. She found a half-filled gourd under a slow drip of water from the roof of the alcove. "Why do you forget to drink the water?" she chastised.

"My mouth is a hollow of rot. Anything I put in it tastes like blood now."

Ismelda huffed. "What am I to do with you Jack? Why are you so stubborn?"

"All consumed men are stubborn."

"Especially the dead ones," Ismelda teased.

Jack finished off the contents of the tomato can and tossed it towards the entrance.

"You are as bad as El Gordo! Such a pig!" said Ismelda.

"No one is as bad as Gordo," said Jack. "Later, when I have a mind to, I'll toss the can into the sea and my house will be clean again."

She handed him the water gourd. "Drink."

Jack cupped the gourd in his hands and drank.

"I have news," said Ismelda. "A small plane has crashed on the island."

Jack Douglas looked up at her, a bright twinkle in his aged blue eyes. "Oh?"

"There is a survivor. He is a black man from the States. Very big, but burned badly. His name is Pharaoh. He says he was sent to find *you*. The pig has put him in a cage. When the man can walk, El Gordo promises to kill him."

Douglas nodded. "Then he should stay off his feet."

"The prisoner says there may be another man coming to find you as well. Maybe he will bring men with guns."

"We can only hope."

Ismelda glanced towards the rear of the cave. "You are almost finished?"

Jack turned his head towards the darkness. The light strapped to his forehead revealed a length of intricate colorful carvings on the walls.

"The rock will tell me when I'm done," said Jack.

Ismelda smiled. She reached into an alcove and plucked a dried fish from a string. She offered it to Jack. "Eat," she ordered.

Jack set down the gourd and absently plucked at the flesh of the fish. "What I really want is a thick steak. Medium rare with a baked potato and a cold beer."

"What you need next is a good dip in the sea," said Ismelda. "You stink of sweat."

"Good sweat," said Douglas. "Just like Michelangelo's when he worked on his back to paint the Sistine Chapel." He picked up the gourd and raised it to her lips. "Now it is your turn, little flower. Drink."

Ismelda drank down the last of the water. A few beads rested on her dry cracked lips.

"How are you holding up?" asked Jack.

"Like you, I still have purpose."

"Good," said Jack. "Purpose feeds the heart, the mind and the soul. Without it we are not truly alive."

Ismelda leaned against his shoulder, burying her head. "Am I still alive, Jack?"

He pulled a clean rag from a back pocket and wiped at her dirty face. “You are very much alive! With time all things change. You must remain patient.”

“Last week, above you on the cliffs, I wanted to kill myself,” she admitted.

“What stopped you from jumping?”

Ismelda shook her head. “Regret for those I would leave behind. They have no one else but me.”

Jack put his hands on her shoulders and tilted her back from him. The bright light of his headlamp shined down on her, revealing a beauty that could not be smeared by time or trouble.

“You are our strength, Ismelda. You are this island, not El Gordo. You can outlast him.”

She nodded. “The pulque is almost ready. If we are lucky, he will die from the poison.”

Douglas laughed softly. “That’s my little flower talking! Now off you go, not to be missed. Can’t you see I’m working?”

Ismelda smiled as she backed away towards the entrance, the spring of a young woman in her step.

Douglas bent over and scooped up a handful of rock dust from the floor. “Take these fairies to protect you on your journey.”

He tossed the dust in the air towards Ismelda. It fluttered in a cascade of colors, flecks falling on her hair and shoulders.

Ismelda pointed at the cave behind him. "When do I get to see it?"

"When it is done."

"What if the pig kills me first?"

"He won't," said Douglas.

"How do you know?"

"Because you are a woman and he is a man with piggish desires."

"Are all men brutes?"

"Most, when we are in our prime."

She turned to leave, again asking, "But if he should decide to kill me first?"

"Then I will bury you down here in the world's brightest catacomb."

CHAPTER 49

The night sky dazzled as the catamaran approached a chalky block of rock ahead with sheer cliffs a hundred feet high.

Dario pointed. "There it is: la isla. The village is just around the bend. It is past midnight. Everyone is asleep. No one will notice us."

A few minutes later the catamaran passed the ramshackle shacks.

"Not much to look at," said Larry.

"It is all we have left," shrugged Dario. "See the dock? It is the only landing place for boats on the island."

"And Gordo is there in one of the shacks?"

"Sleeping now, but he is there. When you kill the pig, hang a white sheet on the dock and we will come in from the sea."

"And Jack Douglas?"

"Patience, Larry."

Nina fastened a large canvas bag containing food, water, armor and weapons to a plastic buoy. She placed the canvas bag next to Larry and set the plastic buoy in his lap.

"It will help you float," she said.

Dario pointed ahead. "See there, Larry? Along the cliffs? A narrow trail leads down to the sea. There is a cave there, hidden from view by the rocks. The pig cannot reach it. You must swim hard towards it or the surf will drag you under and you will drown. Are you ready?"

Larry moved to the catamaran's port side and sat with his legs in the water, staring at the island looming closer.

"Wait for the wave," said Dario.

Larry squeezed the bag, staring ahead. "The villagers know I am coming?"

"Only one believes in rescue anymore. Ismelda."

"How will I recognize her?"

"There is only one Ismelda," said Dario.

Larry nodded, a sad blues song playing in his head. *The Sky is Crying* by Elmore James.

"Get ready. On the count of one, two, *three*!"

The girls launched Larry into the sea towards the eye of the cave ahead.

"Swim, Larry, swim!"

Larry flailed at the water. A foaming wave rose under him and pushed him forward in a tangle of bag and buoy.

"Kick, Larry, kick!" shouted the gypsies.

Larry kicked away. The wave carried him past the outcrop of rocks. He found a broad platform of rock at the water's edge and tossed the canvas bag on it. He pulled himself up and stared at the passing catamaran as the sea forced it south and away from the island.

The sea gypsies waved to him. He waved back. The boat rounded a bend and disappeared from sight.

He was alone now; a bag of tricks at his feet, a man alone sent to save one small piece of the world.

Larry faced the cliff wall. Even in the darkness he could see the narrow steps etched in its side. He unfastened the canvas bag from the float and pulled out the short razor sharp spear. He stepped up to the cave entrance, poking his head inside.

There was the flicker of light inside. A candle perhaps? Not enough to illuminate so much as a room, but enough to see the silhouette standing before him.

It was a man dressed in rags; tall and thin with crazy hair, a long dirty beard and the tired eyes of Jack Douglas. Douglas was holding a large stone over his head, poised to strike.

Larry set the spear on the floor of the cave and held his hands up in surrender. "Hello, Mr. Douglas. My name is Larry. I'm from Chicago. I was sent to find you. You're famous again. The mermaid stamp?"

After a spell, Douglas lowered the rock and stepped back, examining Larry from top to bottom. He scratched his head, trying to remember things. Douglas closed his eyes to think. When they opened, his irises had turned his eyes from a dull grey to sparkling blue. Color filed the features of his thin face and he smiled sweetly.

"It isn't a stamp. It's a portrait." He turned and started towards his sleeping nook carved in the wall. "If you don't mind? Sleep would be best at the moment." He climbed into the nook, turned towards the wall and seemed to have fallen asleep.

Was this it then? Such a quiet ending to his search. Larry pictured the widow Chumley reading his boring prose letter in the breakfast nook of her mansion. Would she be disappointed?

He would have to breathe life into the letter; mention the sea gypsies, the black widow and her crew that left him to die, the ship of fools, his chatty bodyguard Pharaoh. What had become of him? *And the mermaids at the bottom of the sea…*

The story was still unfolding. There was more to Jack Douglas than the emaciated hermit sleeping in the nook. The morning light might shed more answers.

The woman Dario mentioned – Ismelda. Perhaps she had a story to tell as well. And then there was the giant. Larry still had to face the giant.

He peered down the dim hall of the cave. There were carvings on the walls and ceiling. He ventured outside, retrieved his bag and returned. He sat by the entrance, making himself comfortable, the spear across his lap.

The cave offered Larry serenity. He listened to his heartbeat. Was it echoing in the cave? He closed his eyes to find a small think point of black. He focused on the point until colors emerged under his eyes, his brain and mind connected, his body removed from gravity. There was nowhere else he had to be but here, right now, in this cave, living in the moment.

CHAPTER 50

The startled pig woke up in a dripping sweat. He did not like the sound of the wind in the darkness rattling the shack's walls. It was a reminder of the time the people of his tribe tried to burn it down while he slept inside.

Gordo felt the rope of the machete tied to his wrist. It was an extension of his hand now. The blade glistened off the sliver of moonlight trickling in from the small opening overhead that served as a window and brought in the breeze.

He saw the sleeping outline of Ismelda under the window. How could she sleep like that? Covered up, her face turned away from him like a mouse hiding.

He was safe with her here. No one thought to attack him again since he kept her close by in the vulnerable hours of sleep. She was here for any pleasure; maid, whore, conversation, it didn't matter.

Some day she would produce a proper baby for him, a normal child to prove he belonged.

He unlatched the door and stepped outside, the rushing wind blowing back the matted hair from his face. The warm breeze lifting off the sea reminded him of his boyhood when he slept outside to fight the tormenting sting of his growing flesh and bones before he was a man.

Gordo walked the perimeter of the small village, looking for things out of place. The black man was asleep in his cage. The restless snores of the old people in their shacks were steady.

He checked one of the pulque barrels, lifting a lid to take a smell. It was harsh to the nose, still fermenting.

"Soon," he smiled, "very soon."

He went to the metal locker by his shack and unlocked it with the key around his neck. He found a can of sardines and carried it to his favorite rock to stare at the sea. A strip of moonbeam wiggled on its surface like a giant snake in front of him.

He fumbled to open the sardine can's pop top with his fat fingers. Unsuccessful, the pig used the tip of his machete to pry it open. He drank off the oily juice, licking his lips to savor the flavor before devouring the neatly packed rows of tiny fish. The flesh was rich and dense. He tossed away the empty can. Where it landed he did not care.

Something on the horizon caught his eye. What was it? A ship? No, not a ship. It was smaller. *A sailboat maybe*? He ambled to his shack and found the binoculars hanging inside by the door. He stepped outside and held them up to his fat face, studying the distant object again.

Yes, it was a sailboat. A catamaran made of slop. The sea gypsies were back again. *Bringing another champion, no doubt.*

Gordo lowered the binoculars and spit on the ground. He lumbered to the sleeping shacks, raking the machete along their sides.

"Te despiertas!" he yelled. "Wake up. Your friends are back."

One by one, sleepy-eyed residents appeared and looked out to sea. Ismelda came out of the pig's shack wrapped in a blanket and joined them.

"I see nothing," she said to the pig without alarm.

The pig raised the binoculars in front of her. "I saw them with my own eyes. They are out there, hidden by the clouds now!"

Ismelda calmly sat on the pig's rock, pulling in the blanket to ward off the wind. "They are there. They are not there. Why does it matter to you? You have your machete."

Gordo crossed to Pharaoh's cage. He could see the whites of his eyes inside. Like the rest, Pharaoh was studying the horizon.

"Maybe it comes for you," laughed the pig. "No navy, no coast guard. Just a crazy old man I let escape." Gordo brandished his machete and turned to Ismelda. "Maybe I kill this one now."

Ismelda stood and flew to them, stepping between the pig and Pharaoh. "You are not so brave then? To kill a man locked in a cage?"

"One less problem," said the pig.

"Because you are afraid," spat Ismelda.

"I fear nothing," said the pig.

"You lie," said Ismelda. "You are a coward."

"Do not call me that!"

"You are afraid of me. You fear these starving old people. You killed your mother and father because you were afraid of them."

With surprising swiftness the pig swatted her in the face, knocking her to the ground.

"They made me ugly!" screamed El Gordo.

Ismelda looked up at him and laughed. "You do not hurt me. I am dead inside."

The pig reached down and lifted her by the hair. "We will see how dead you are."

He dragged her inside his shack, slamming the flimsy door shut behind them.

Pharaoh struggled to stand. He grabbed the bars of his cage, rattling them, listening to the sounds of the pig's beating. "Come back, big man. It's me you want!"

The old woman, Calista, came to him and placed her hands on his. "There is nothing you can do for now," she pleaded, "You must rest."

Pharaoh pressed his face against the bars, yelling at the others. "You have to do something! You can't let him do this!"

Calista stepped away from him. "We have tried, señor. Many times. But look at us. We are old and spent." She paused, listening to a new sound coming from the pig's shack. Calista smiled at Pharaoh. "Do you hear that señor? She is laughing at him. Ismelda is strong. When the sun comes up, you will see her again."

Pharaoh fell back on his cot and covered his eyes with a bandaged arm.

"This ain't real," he whispered.

He felt tears running down his damaged face. They stung his flesh but he didn't care. God was punishing him. He was a helpless sinner hiding behind a thin veneer of burned flesh exposing a heart of fear. If he could walk, would he have gone to the woman's rescue?

Probably not, he told himself. *I ain't ready.*

Will I ever be ready?

Probably not.

CHAPTER 51

Larry felt a prodding foot in his side.

"Hey, you. Larry from Chicago. Wake up."

He opened his eyes and sat up. His spear had been removed from his hands and was leaning by the entrance. Jack Douglas was admiring Larry's Cuacalati helmet.

"You ran into my old friend Dario, no doubt. The crown feathers are a nice touch."

Larry rubbed his eyes. "He and his female crew saved my life and in exchange, I promised to slay the giant."

"You better rephrase that, Larry from Chicago. Something more in tune with 'I promised to *face* the giant and died an ugly but noble death'."

"You're not the first to mention that."

Douglas crouched down next to him, emptying the contents of the canvas bag.

"Help yourself," said Larry.

"I am," said Douglas. He found a can of Spam, a pair of potatoes and an onion to go with it, and carried them to his kitchen alcove. "You talk. I'll cook."

Larry pulled himself to his feet. "I was initially sent to Mexico to find *you* but along the way something else happened."

He watched as Douglas deftly prepared breakfast with his gnarled hands, using a flint to spark a small stack of wood chips in a stone pit.

"How are Dario and the ladies?"

"Surviving at sea."

"He's been trying for a thousand days to convince strangers to come here and kill that bastard Gordo. Two came. Both lost. Now you. Anyway, so you found me. Who cares?"

"Rosemary Chumley, my benefactor."

"*Chumley*? Chumley's Chews? The gum lady?"

"Yes."

Douglas added more fuel to the small flame. As it grew he pulled a sharp knife from the wall and chopped the onion and potatoes into a skillet.

"You don't have any Chumley Chews with you?"

"No sir."

"Too bad. I haven't had gum in ages. Now why did you bother looking for me?"

"I work for a museum in Chicago. Your miniature mermaid painting - no one has ever seen anything like it, Jack. Such detail, so alive."

"A house painter with the right brush could have done as well."

"Nonsense. At first it was thought to be some kind of stamp."

"Truth is, it was just my feeble attempt at being noble. I gave the locals some bullshit story one day about messages in a bottle rescuing sailors. Back in my prime, maybe I would have done something about the situation here. But I'm just a non-partisan historian with a chisel now. The people upstairs..."

"Upstairs?"

"Living on the island, what's left of them. A sorry bunch now. I used to live upstairs until Gordo went bat shit crazy three years ago. Now I stay down here, out of harm's way working."

Larry stared into the dim cave. "Sculpting?"

"Something like that." Douglas stirred the food in the pan. "Any more questions while I'm holding this sharp knife in my hand?"

"The model you used for the mermaid... was she real or imagined?"

Douglas smiled to himself. "Oh, she's real, alright."

"Is she still here? On the island?"

"She was alive yesterday."

"Upstairs?"

"Yes. You can't miss her. Ismelda is the only one still alive under sixty."

"*Ismelda*... Her eyes... they're haunting."

"Besides the perfect symmetry, what you see in them is pure kindness," said Douglas.

Larry hesitated. "And the mermaid's tail?"

Douglas picked up on it. "Does Ismelda have one? I guess you'll have to see for yourself, should you live long enough."

The men rinsed their plates at the water's edge outside the cave. In the morning light Jack Douglas looked ghostly white. His blotched skin had taken a beating over the years. His face gaunt, arms thin, but still strong enough to strike a hammer.

"You want a tour I suppose?" said Douglas.

"It would be an honor."

Douglas led him back inside. He lit a pair of torches and handed one to Larry.

"Follow me."

Larry followed him down the passageway, listening intently as they weaved their way past loose scaffolds and rubbles of rock. There was no echo here, just a flat sound absorbed by the stone.

"There are a few smaller limestone caves on this island. I leave them for the bats. This is a dry cave made of colored lava," said Douglas. "The only water that enters the cave percolates from the surface by the entrance to provide me a few cups of fresh water every now and then. In here nature has provided me a perfect palette, a rainbow of colors two hundred feet long on the sides and the ceiling. Six hundred feet to spin a yarn."

"What's the theme?"

"A soon-to-be-lost culture done in relief. There have been hundreds of lost tribes over the centuries, but only one society with tails."

"Mermaids."

"In modern times myths and legends are viewed as works of fiction, fantasy, even superstition. But some fairy tales have been proven as fact through archeology. In pre-history a malignant mistrust of any life form that might compete with legged humans for dominance emerged. All across the world Mer cultures were blamed for floods, storms, shipwrecks, and plagues. Homer called them evil sirens in his Odyssey. They were misrepresented in

Etrurian sculptures, all the Greek epics, the Annals of the Four Masters, the Book of Invasions and in bas-reliefs in Roman tombs."

"Propaganda to discredit a competitive species?" said Larry.

"Touché. It took me three months to scrape down the cave, another six months to outline my figures, scenes and sequences in charcoal. I wanted a three-dimensional quality to suggest movement by incising, etching, and working the rock. I wanted interaction, conflict from one generation to the next, engravings and painted surfaces to show the history of a distinct people with a muddy past, driven extinct not just on one continent but the entire earth."

"You never talked about your art before," said Larry. "Why now?"

"Guess I'm bored talking to myself for three years."

They came to a facing wall at the far end.

Larry raised his torch. Bright colors drizzled down in a vertical rock fall from the ceiling.

Douglas spoke softly, with reverence for his work. "The Bible has the origin story of Adam and Eve. The Mer legend begins in ancient Assyria with the Phoenician goddess Atargatis and her consort Hadad. My work started here. What I call Rainbow Falls."

Larry's eyes fell on a sunken relief of a life-like mermaid sitting on a protruding rock at the top of the waterfall, her long golden tail resting in the falling waters. The mermaid's tail seemed alive as it reached outside the relief to rest at the top of the waterfall.

"The goddess Atargatis?" said Larry.

"Yes."

Larry lowered his torch. There was a figure in the falls behind a veil of shimmering blue water made of stone.

"*Hadad*?"

"Mer images first appeared in caves thirty thousand years ago in the late Paleolithic, the Stone Age, when land dwellers began to sail the seas. You've heard of the Chauvet Cave in southern France?"

"Hieroglyphics, as I recall."

"It contains wall paintings of lions, woolly rhinoceroses, deer, panthers, even bears. Know what it doesn't contain?"

"What?"

"Humans with legs. But there are dozens of Mer depictions, a tribe of river-dwellers. All kept hush-hush in the press and the scientific journals. Since the cave's discovery in 1994, it has been closed to the public. No one wants to talk about an alternative humanoid species this late in the game of human dominance of the planet."

"You make it sound diabolical, Jack."

"The peaceful Mers were mentioned in the early parts of the Old Testament, but they were carefully written out of it in subsequent translations during the Dark Ages. You might say they were the first mass genocide in human history."

Douglas led Larry along the length of the cave. There were hundreds of figures either painted in murals or carved in the surface of a moving never-ending hectic sea. The kaleidoscope of colors was magnificent with impeccable detail.

Larry's eyes scanned the surfaces as he listened to the man's rambling, a certain madness mixed with absolute truths. Each section of the cave produced a new diorama. Larry's senses were stimulated by sensations of silence, darkness, temperature, humidity and acoustics, carefully crafted.

His hands skimmed the surfaces, touching a thousand Mers swimming past Gibraltar to the Atlantic. His hands traced the massacres of Mers in the Caribbean and on Muerto Beach. He followed pursued Mers into the mountains and hills of the Aztec empire where they were burned, dismembered, or hung. Some colors were warm to the touch like fresh blood. Other colors were cool; Mers frozen to death on ice floes, Mers harpooned by whalers.

On the ceiling; rumbles in the stone, always the sky with constellations, clouds, fingers of lightning, matching thunder and deluges of rain.

Douglas was a magnificent storyteller. Despite his emaciation he still had his wits. "In pre-recorded history the Mers first spread across the Mediterranean to Greece and Rome. Over time they scattered and settled along the sea coasts of Europe outside the Mediterranean. In Ireland you find the Merrows with membranes in their hands. In Spain there is the famous legend of Sirenuca. The Scots called them *Ceasg*, the 'maid of waves.'' Douglas pointed at a great city under the sea. "The lost city of Atlantis. Fact or fiction? It was populated by Mers."

Douglas crossed to the opposite wall. "It took a thousand years for the Mers to populate most of the sea coasts of the planet. The Jengu of Cameroon, the Iara of Brazil. Ancient Chinese tales described them as wonderful, skilled and versatile beings, whose tears became pearls."

Douglas pointed to a series of island and coastal images. "Vietnam, Japan, Indonesia, South America, the Philippines, everywhere you look you'll find remnants of Mer cultures." His torch fell upon a great underwater land mass. "This is the lost empire of Mu. A tropical paradise in the Pacific destroyed by submerged volcanoes. It was second only to Atlantis in size."

Larry followed the volcano's eruption for several feet. Mer bodies swept away, burned alive or melted by a juggernaut of volcanic lava and ash.

"The Mers, like men, survived natural calamities. But they could not survive the barbarian blood lust of land strangers unable to live in the two worlds of sea and land."

"Including the Caribbean," said Larry.

"Some Mers survived for a while alongside the natives of the New World until the Europeans came. And the rest, as they say, is history."

Larry looked at a length of wall leading towards the entrance. It was a blank canvas.

"What I carve next remains to be seen," said Douglas. "It may just end with El Gordo slaughtering the last survivors."

"And all is lost?"

"The Mers are already extinct, Larry. A dried up DNA pool, no more tails. It's just a matter of time to acknowledge their extermination."

"So this is it? The world's largest tombstone?"

"Just the busy play of a lost soul biding his time before death comes knocking."

Larry admired the man. His work was a foil against madness. Jack Douglas had realigned himself with the universe and put away a million distractions to stay still and pay attention to the now. This was his last great work. He would die in here, fine-tuning, eventually grieved that his human clock had worked against him, that he would never achieve the final perfection he so desired.

Was Larry so different? He had a private cave as well. A converted bedroom overrun with plates of music. But did *that* Larry truly exist anymore? Had he gained a new identity? Not quite, but one was forming. How many men found themselves thrust on an empty stage, left to fill it with actors and actions of their own doing? Those many long nights he had brooded, spending his isolated time listening not to the blending unity of sounds but the isolated percussions, the lonesome riff of the saxophone, pulled apart from the whole.

What was a man really? A lonely instrument, longing to join the orchestra?

He wanted to embrace life, share it, feel it, live it, love it, cherish it, laugh with it, sing by it, dance, make funny faces, swim naked in the sea, do jumping jacks, meditate and levitate, bounce, bounce,

bounce for pure joy at the opportunity of having been born, to at least have had the chance to be alive. *Alive*! Is this what the widow Chumley had wished for him? To go on a great adventure and maybe be reborn?

The deprivation provided by the cave had created new patterns in Douglas's brain; made him see what no one else could see in the rock. He had constructed it as a man possessed, a man having a conversation with God as he chipped away so precisely these many days with a focus, coordination and undisturbed concentration. Now the cave was in motion. It was alive with an altered sense of reality. At different angles the objects were constantly changing shape and size.

Like Douglas, Larry had chanced upon fantastical thinking born of isolation and sensory deprivation and found kindred spirit.

They stood at the entrance to the cave.

"There you have it, Larry. Small proof that I am still alive. Go now, meet the devil above. Prove that you too are a living man. I have no use for you down here."

Larry picked up his canvas bag by the door. "Today I wish to explore. Spy the land. Gather my facts."

"And delay the inevitable."

"It is how I operate, Mr. Douglas."

"If you are to win the day you must find a stupid, spontaneous courage. Now off with you. Play hero in your head. Have a randy day. And oh, yes, I just remembered. There is another visitor to the island. A black fellow kept in a cage for now. He's badly burned. His plane crashed here."

"*Pharaoh*? He knew the coordinates from your message in a bottle."

"That's him, alright. Not much good he'll do you, I'm afraid."

Larry exited the cave and stood outside. He dressed himself with the armor, weapons and feathered helmet provided by the sea gypsies. He found the narrow steps leading to the surface of the island. There was a rope next to them. He used the rope as a balance and began his ascent.

CHAPTER 52

Larry's untrained eyes took in the island. Like the bottom of the sea, it was a strange new world for him.

A low backboned rocky ridge ran the length of the island like the steeples on a dinosaur's back. The hint of a trail led north from where Larry stood. A half mile away he could make out the haphazard rooftops of the village. Larry assumed Pharaoh Williams was in a cage there, injured and kept like an animal.

The enemy camp. *El Gordo's lair.*

A slant of hill above the camp revealed worked rows of agriculture. *Mescal for the pig*, according to Dario.

Larry had never seen anything like the sparse green forest that presented itself before him. Tall and lanky Boojum trees, some as high as fifty feet stood like giant brown candles topped with clusters of yellow flowers. A few of the trees had bent back towards the earth creating natural arches.

Scrappy elephant trees resembled giant chunks of ginger covered with spikes and red flowers. Coconut palms ten meters tall with razor sharp palm fronds lived closest to the rock piles, rooting for underground water in dry creek beds. Lonesome barrel cacti were scattered about, parked like stubborn bulldogs.

Birds were everywhere, feeding on plants and insects or nesting in rocks, especially along the cliffs. He had never seen birds like these. Blue-footed boobies, swallows and frigates poked around tree trunks siphoning seeds. Long-beaked hummingbirds used their tongues to sift for sugary nectar in the red flowers of cacti. A laughing seagull sailed the sky overhead, its throat emitting a heckling sound as it studied the dry island for a breakfast of rabbit or mouse. It was a wild untamed place Larry was unable to put to words.

Mistaking Larry for a tree, a hummingbird appeared at his shoulder, its wings beating a hundred miles an hour as it studied his ear contemplating nectar inside.

Larry raised his arm slowly and the bird flew off. Now Larry felt something crawl across his sandals on the desert floor; a beetle. It reminded him of a frantic commuter bobbing through human traffic to catch a departing train. A hairy tarantula raced up to the beetle, caught it in its fangs and marched away to inject its venom at a private breakfast nook.

Haphazard piles of rocks dotted the land to the south providing hiding places and pockets of shade from the burning heat of day. Larry picked up his spear and headed there to explore. It was easy going through the twisted sparse forest. There was no worn path. The dry washes were narrow and shallow.

He reached a cluster of rocks. There were footprints here. He followed them through a small opening that revealed an open-aired chamber maybe thirty feet wide. Three small mounds were at its center marked with flat rocks. Too small to be adult graves. Names were written on the rocks; Mateo. Jadzia. Taina.

Beyond the graves was a hanging ledge that provided ample shade. Earth had been dug away from the wall below and removed. Larry crawled up to it and reached inside. The soil was damp. He plied deeper and discovered a small pool of water. He tasted it with his fingers. It was cool and sweet. He cupped his hands and drank what he could until he was satisfied.

Larry leaned against the wall to think. Why was the graveyard so far removed from the village? Why were there only three small graves? Who was visiting here? There were no clothes, bedding or fire pits. Was the water supply a secret? From what the gypsies had told him, El Gordo always stayed close to home. Using his spear, Larry measured the sandal tracks in and out of the secret circle. They all belonged to one owner. A smaller imprint, most likely a woman's.

He left the secret circle and hiked through the low scrub to the southern end of the island. Sheer cliffs ran its length. Hundreds of seabirds were in the air, making acrobatic dives into the sea for small fish. He heard the uneven singing of hungry chicks in their cliffside nests below.

Larry turned east and followed the edge of the island. No footprints. No signs of human activity. Creosote and elephant trees clung to life alongside a low forest of twisted ironwoods decorated with blue-flowered desert mallows and prickly cholla cactus. He spotted a small jackrabbit. Its nervous nose sniffed the earth, ready for snake attacks. Its head bobbed up towards the sky, alert to the death threats of large birds with savage claws dropping down from above. Everything here was food. Even Larry.

Larry turned north along the harsh coast and turned inland following the spiny back of the island towards the village as he looked for the remains of a plane. When at last he laid eyes on it he realized it was only a quarter of a mile from the village, but being on the opposite slope it was hidden from view.

The plane was a pile of metallic skeletal remains caked in black soot. The nose was crushed, wings and body collapsed and melted away, debris scattered. A human corpse burned beyond recognition and impaled by a propeller blade sat in the pilot's seat clutching what was left of a steering wheel.

Larry found a scattering of footprints near the wreck. Was it here that Pharaoh had been lifted away and carried to the village?

He found the remains of the small fanny pack Pharaoh had worn in Puerto Vallarta. Inside were several thousand dollars, their edges burnt. There was a man's wallet still intact. Larry sifted through it. It contained melted ID cards, the remains of a folded Chicago Tribune newspaper article, a punch card from a Chicago convenience store. Two more punches and Pharaoh was entitled to a free cup of coffee.

Larry followed the foot tracks leading away from the plane. They led downhill towards the village, clearly visible below rows of recently harvested plants. He found a large cactus and sat by it, blending in with his surroundings. The feathers of his helmet attracted flying insects that came and went.

He caught glimpses of a handful of people working under the awning of a tin lean-to. Some hurried back and forth to a fire pit. Even at a distance he could tell they were old. Their bodies were bent and they moved slowly. Their mouths were covered, faces hidden under straw hats. But there was one in their mix, a woman, moving with sprightly agility, her long hair moved by the wind. She paused in her task and stared up the hill towards him, raising a hand over her eyes as if adjusting an image. One of her arms came up and she seemed to be offering a small wave towards Larry.

Larry shrank back against the cactus. Was she saying hello?

Just as quickly, she returned to her busy work.

After a spell, Larry saw the frame of an enormous bare-chested man in a loin cloth coming out of a shack. The man took a few steps, his swaying body like that of a foraging bear, his face a dark scowl of grimness. When the man stood upright, Larry could see that he was indeed a giant, thick and sturdy as a tree, his enormous head nestled like a giant ball on shoulders of stone. A glint of sunlight danced across the blade of a machete in the giant's hand.

El Gordo, realized Larry. He felt a sickening rumble in his stomach.

The pig moved away from the shack to a mound of what appeared to be garbage, lifted up his loin cloth and relieved himself with a long stream of steady piss. When the giant was finished he waddled to a covered cage and raked the blade of his machete across the bars. The man shouted something, arrogance and impatience in his tone.

Larry eyed the cage. There was no movement inside. Was this where Pharaoh was being held? Larry studied the sweating giant again as he crossed to a row of barrels and inspected them. The big man picked up a gourd and dipped it in one of the barrels, tasting its contents.

The giant's mocking belly laugh carried up the hill. "Un dia mas! One more day before we celebrate!" he shouted to the workers.

The giant lumbered towards the lean-to where the workers were gathered. He grabbed an old man by the neck, lifted him high in the air and shook him like a rag doll.

"Soon I will have no use for you, old man!" The giant flung the old man away, pitching him to the earth,

El Gordo seemed invincible. *But what was he really*? Larry thought. *Just a murderous bully*. Captain Grey, on his ship, he wore a gun to maintain order and democracy in a diverse population, but the pistol never left its holster. This malicious man, El Gordo, he carried a machete, using his strength and threats to intimidate a helpless handful of people for his own gain. But the giant was alone, one man against the many. Remove the giant and the tribe could survive, Larry rationalized.

Larry suspected the giant had his own reasons for becoming a bully. He was obviously an anti-social misfit, acting out his rage at having been born a freak. It had made him a psychopathic madman, bent on revenge against humanity. In a larger social environment he would surely be in a maximum security prison. But not here. There was no judge, no jury, no higher authority to stand up to El Gordo. Only Larry now, a bystander forced to take action for the common good. One orphan against another.

Larry stood and hurried back in the direction he had come until he was out of sight of the village. He stared at the spear in his hand. It wasn't a weapon yet. Just a stick with a sharp end until it cut human flesh.

Larry approached a tall fat cactus and stabbed at it again and again and again as thin streams of juice oozed out from it. He tasted the juice, expecting the metallic pungency of blood, but it tasted like sweet water.

Larry set down the spear and shield and practiced using the slingshot. He turned his body sideways and found that smaller round stones worked best. He hit close range targets with frequency until his index and forefinger ached.

He returned to the shade of the rock cluster at the southern end of the island to sort out the scrambled thoughts running rampant in his head.

There was no delaying the inevitable. Tomorrow he would have to use his limited talents against the man turned monster.

CHAPTER 53

Larry woke suddenly, tucked away in the shade of the rock ledge, his armor, spear and helmet by his side.

He saw the silhouette of a woman, kneeling over the three graves, arranging cactus flowers on the stones. How long she had been there, he didn't know. Her thin sun dress was tattered, arms and legs covered with scratches and patches of dirt. She removed her straw hat and set it to the side, revealing an alluring copper face and dark silken hair. She was raw and wild and beautiful. Larry recognized her immediately. She was Jack Douglas's model, the woman on the stamp.

Ismelda.

She turned her head towards him, bright violet eyes sparkling. She spoke in a soft, soothing voice. "I didn't mean to wake you."

"I didn't mean to fall asleep," said Larry.

"But then, I was about to wake you."

He crawled out from under the rock and stood. Ismelda rose up from the graves. They faced each other in the soft light of fading sun. One pair of kind eyes matching the other.

Ismelda smiled. "Dario brought you, I see."

"How did you know?" said Larry.

"The Cuacalati, the helmet made of feathers and bones. It is Dario's handiwork. How is everyone?"

"Surviving at sea."

"What is your name?"

"Larry."

"Hello, Larry. I am Ismelda."

"I know who you are," said Larry. "I was sent here to find you."

"By Dario."

"Yes and no. Dario recruited me to slay the giant, but it all started with a message in a bottle with your painted image inside."

Ismelda looked at him quizzically. "But Jack did that so long ago."

"I met Jack in his cave. I think he would agree that some things take time to run their course. Jack's portrait brought me to Mexico. Otherwise..." Larry gave her a brief history of the events that brought him to la isla.

"So you did not volunteer to slay our giant," said Ismelda. "You came for your friend, me and Jack?"

"And along the way I was recruited for this '*kill the giant*' business which I will give my heart to. But now I know what really brought me here."

"What?" said Ismelda.

Larry stepped up to the graves and looked down. "I was a different man when I started my journey. Now I realize I was chosen by fate or destiny, whatever you want to call it. You, these graves, your people below."

"I was a different woman before the madness," said Ismelda. "I liked to sing and dance and to laugh."

"I have been doing it for you," said Larry.

Ismelda smiled softly. "You are not like the other men who came to face El Gordo. Like him, they believed in conquest, I think. But they did not succeed."

"What do you know about conquest?" said Larry.

"I read hundreds of history books and encyclopedias before the pig burned them. They are filled with conquest. One ruler outwits or kills the last ruler but with time, they become like the man they replaced."

“That isn’t important today,” said Larry. “All that matters is avenging the dead so the rest of you can keep on living.”

“Perhaps you and I are alike,” said Ismelda, “if we compare our souls and character.”

“My nobility is still under construction,” said Larry. “I spent years cataloging my weaknesses and flaws only to discover how irrelevant they were.”

“So you came here with a shield and spear to pick up a challenge that is not yours.”

“I think if a person is able, he or she needs to take a stand against cruelty.”

“I made my stand,” said Ismelda. “Have you seen him yet? The pig?”

Larry nodded. “Even at a distance he is a frightening thing to behold.”

“A *thing* yes. All evil tucked under human flesh.”

”He moves slowly,” said Larry.

“He will move slower tomorrow when he starts drinking the pulque we have made.”

“From drunkenness?”

“The mescal is cooked with wood poisoned by varnishes, paint thinners, epoxies and kerosene, whatever we could find. El Gordo’s beloved drink will be his enemy soon.”

“Maybe I won’t have to kill him,” said Larry.

Her eyes fell on the graves. “To let him die a slow death is too generous. When you see the pig up close, when you can smell him and he casts his cold dead eyes on you, you will feel the devil inside him.”

“Does he have other weapons besides the machete?”

“No. Everything else he destroys so we cannot harm him.”

“If I do kill El Gordo, what then for you and the others, Ismelda?”

“We will make costumes from old rags and build castles from the piles of rubble. But it will take hard work and we will have to eat fish until we’re past hating it.”

“And if I should meet a desperate end tomorrow? What will you do next, Ismelda?”

She knelt again and faced the graves. “I may find myself stepping off a cliff to end my desperation.”

Larry took a knee next to her. “But I’m told you are too strong for that.”

"What does anyone do when the grief of life becomes unbearable? We close our eyes to the world finally, once and for all."

"Dario says you are the last of your kind, the maker of mermaids."

"Look at these graves," said Ismelda. "This has been the future for my kind."

"Your children?" he said.

"Yes. Mateo. Jadzia. Taina. I named them after the leaders who led my people over the Mexican mountains long ago."

"How did they die?"

"The pig killed them when they were born. He smashed them against the rocks."

Larry shook his head in disbelief. "Why?"

"Because they were beautiful and made for the sea. And what am I to the pig? My body is his prisoner but never my soul. If I don't sacrifice myself, he hurts or kills the old ones."

"Not anymore," said Larry.

"If you are willing to face Gordo it must be tomorrow," said Ismelda. "When the pig drinks the pulque the monsters inside him will free themselves. He will prey on the weak then, your friend

Pharaoh first, waiting for his execution, locked in a cage like an animal."

"Can you give Pharaoh a message from me?"

"Yes."

"Tell him I will visit him tonight."

She rose and turned to stare at the sun dropping in the west. Her eyes were ablaze with fire.

"Such a beautiful sunset. Do not be afraid tomorrow," Ismelda reassured him. "You are not alone. There are angels behind you or you would not have come."

"I was raised believing in angels," Larry said.

"Then embrace them one more time with me. If tomorrow we do not succeed, we know how things will end for us."

"Badly," said Larry.

"I must go now, Larry. The pig will be looking for me."

"Tomorrow then?"

"Maybe tomorrow we begin new lives," smiled Ismelda.

She hurried away. Larry followed her to the circle's entrance and watched her run until she was but an illusion on the horizon.

Such a creature, filled with flaming hope despite despair. How was it possible? How could she still smile? She needed to be set free, to run wild again with happiness.

She had come to him as a message in a bottle tossed in an endless sea. *But now she was real.* Ismelda had been touched too roughly and Larry had not been touched at all, two souls pinned together with an uncertain future.

CHAPTER 54

High gray clouds danced across the ceiling of the night sky. Larry moved in complete darkness down the hillside towards the shacks below. His spear and shield were ready in his hand, the slingshot swinging against his side. He heard his pounding heart ricocheting against his shield. He reached the edge of the tiny village and stood silently, listening for movement until he was satisfied with the eerie quiet. He caught the glint of the steel cage and took slow steps to it.

Pharaoh was in there, propped up, waiting for him.

"Larry?" he whispered.

"I'm here," said Larry.

A few clouds opened overhead. Larry could see Pharaoh's face, gnarled and raw like something burned in an oven.

"Oh, Pharaoh," he whispered.

"I'm a sight, ain't I?"

"A beautiful sight, my friend."

"Listen to you. I know I'm a mess," Pharaoh almost laughed.

"I'll get you out," said Larry.

"Not now," said Pharaoh. "I can't run, much less walk. We got enough peril here." He pointed at El Gordo's shack. "Have you seen him?"

"Yes."

"Scariest mofo I ever saw. But what can we do?"

"Kill him."

Pharaoh put a wrapped fist up to his mouth and stifled a laugh. "You crazy, Larry? He ain't a man. He's extra terrestrial. Like some kind of predator sent to earth to have sport with us."

"He's just a man," said Larry.

"Say you. Besides, you're Larry Settlebottom. Leave us, Larry. Go back to Chicago. Lock yourself in your house and play yourself some music. There ain't nuthin' for you here."

"Everything's here, Pharaoh."

"What? You sayin' we got on the wrong train for a reason?"

"It's called fate."

"It's called waiting to die. Go on now, Larry. You can't face that man. Maybe I could if I was straight but I ain't."

"Then it's on me."

Pharaoh's whisper rose. "Leave me, Larry. I don't deserve your kindness. I deserve to die. You don't know what I done."

"What? Leaving me in Puerto Vallarta? I'm sure you had your reasons." Larry pulled the satchel off his shoulder and showed Pharaoh the burned money in the fanny pack he had found at the crash site. "But most of the money is still here. Burned like you, but..."

"Goddamnit, Larry! What else is in there? In my wallet? Did you read it?"

"Read what?"

"The newspaper article."

"That's your property, Pharaoh."

"You a fool, Larry. Go on. Take it out of the wallet. Maybe then I can get you to skedaddle."

Larry pulled out the newspaper article.

"Go on. Read it," said Pharaoh. "Read it out loud."

Larry read the headline. "Woman's Body Found In South Side Home After Burglary."

"Keep reading Larry. What's her name?"

Larry squinted in the darkness. "I can't read it. The type is too small."

"I'll tell you her name, Larry. It's Alina. Ring a bell? She was your girlfriend. I was the one who robbed your house and kilt her."

Larry folded up the article and stuck it back in the wallet. "The police say she died of asphyxiation. They ruled it an accident."

"I'm the one who put the duct tape on her mouth. I kilt her."

"She had asthma. You did me a favor, Pharaoh. She was in my house to clean out my bank accounts."

"That don't change things. I ruined your life then. I abandoned you in Puerto Vallarta. I tried to set things straight. I even went to church and prayed on it. I followed you for months to find a way to make my amends. But I'm no good, don't you see? I can't be trusted, I got a selfish hunger inside me, I need to be punished. Now go, Larry. Leave this place before you get yourself kilt."

"You and I are better men than we were yesterday."

Pharaoh's head swooned. "Dammit, you're crazy! You got to leave this island and take all that noble bullshit with you!"

"Well, I'm not leaving. I'm going to face the pig tomorrow and send you home."

Pharaoh pulled himself up, examining Larry. He seemed taller than Pharaoh remembered. He was tanned and stood erect, his slouch gone.

"Why you dressed like that?" asked Pharaoh. "You think you're some kind of ninja? Where the hell have you been Larry?"

Larry backed away from the cage. "It's a long story. Time for me to go."

Pharaoh leaned forward and hissed at him as he crept away. "Wait, Larry! You can't stand toe to toe with the pig and his machete! At the plane wreck there's a pistol in a metal box. Find it and use it if you have to."

He watched as Larry turned and raced up the hill, his feathered helmet bobbing until he was swallowed up in the dark.

Pharaoh leaned back and shook his head. "Goddamned Larry dressed like a rooster! We all dead for sure now. Every last one of us."

CHAPTER 55

The pig stood outside his shack, making his presence known by clearing his throat with swatches of phlegm. He crossed to a bell hanging from a metal pole and rang it with the side of his machete.

"It's time," he yelled. "Our big day! Let us taste the fruit of your labors!"

Ismelda brushed past him, clapping her hands. "Ándele! Ándele!"

The old men and women appeared from the smaller shacks, pulling on faded shirts and torn clothes to cover their bodies.

The pig went to one of the fermenting barrels and raised the lid. He scooped out the liquid with a fat hand, tasted it and smiled. "This one is ready," he decided. He grabbed one of the old men. "Find me a cup," he ordered. "A big clean one."

The old man hurried inside a shack and returned with a silver trophy cup he had saved from one of the sunken boats. It was shaped like a chalice. He handed the cup to Gordo. The pig rubbed the English engraving on it.

"What does this say?" he asked.

The old man answered with a nervous smile. "First Place."

The giant smiled. He scooped the chalice in the barrel, filled it, and raised it to his lips. As he drank, thick white foam spilled from his chin. When he was done he raised the cup in the air and shouted. "Look at me! First place!"

Ismelda and the old ones nodded politely as he refilled the cup. He carried it to his favorite rock and sat. A king on his throne. El Gordo took the locker key from around his neck and tossed it at Ismelda's feet.

"Today we celebrate. Give the old ones food."

Ismelda picked up the key and unlocked the metal locker. She passed out canned goods to the eager old ones. After they received their rewards they hurried away to hide in their shacks and eat.

Finished, Ismelda locked the cabinet and returned the key to the pig.

"You did not take anything," he noticed.

She picked up a fishing pole next to his shack. "I will eat fish today."

The pig watched her closely. “Fish. Always fish. We are surrounded by fish. You can have some mescal instead.”

“It is all yours,” she said. “Drink made for a king.”

“Yes,” El Gordo smiled, “today I am a king!”

He drank down his second cup. Ismelda took it from him, refilled it from the barrel and handed it back to him.

Gordo poured a few drops of drink on the back of his hand, waved it in the air and sniffed at it. “Ah! I can smell the process - the firewood, the rock, the earth and fire. So complex!” He held the cup with both hands, inhaling the aroma. “Grassy and fruity. An explosion of flavor. I can taste the flowers!”

“Then you are no expert,” said Ismelda. “The soil here is weak and dry.”

“Enough of your sass,” El Gordo spat. “I waited two years for this. Now I have gallons and gallons to drink. Drums full! Enough to last until next year!”

“It is all for you,” said Ismelda. “Only you. The king!”

“But not too much in a day. I will pace myself.”

“Start tomorrow. Today you must celebrate your harvest.”

“Yes! I must...” He paused, studying her with a curious look. “Why do you talk with such encouragement?” He twisted his body and stared out to sea. “I think I did see a boat yesterday.” He stared at the cup in his hands. "I think maybe I won't celebrate too much today." He stood, grabbing her by the arm. "I think you are up to something, Ismelda. Maybe there is someone on the island? Another one of Dario's assassins? I think maybe today I will kill the black man in the cage. And if a stranger comes, then I will kill him too, eh?"

"Then drink some more," said Ismelda. "Drink to build your courage to strike down a man caged like an animal. Or will you let him out to stand before you cut off his head?" She pulled herself away from him. "I have listened enough to your stupid talk. I will fish now."

He sat on his rock again. "Yes. You go catch your fish."

He sipped his pulque slowly now, his gluttony in check as she made her way down the hill to the twisted dock. She always needed watching, that one. He raised his machete and sharpened it against the rock, eyes fast for anything unusual around him.

Larry poked through the plane rubble looking for the gun Pharaoh mentioned. He found a charred metal box and opened it. Inside was a small black pistol. He had never fired a pistol, never held one. It was light in his hand. He pressed a release button and opened the swing-out cylinder. He counted the rounds. Eight.

Enough to kill any man at close range. As he tucked it in the pocket of his shorts he found the coin Mrs. Chumley had given him. He flipped it in the air, caught it and returned it to his pocket.

"I'm done with luck," he decided.

He wasn't lonesome Larry anymore. Today he had an army of angels and mermaids behind him.

He dressed himself in his makeshift armor. Now all he had to do was walk down the hill to put things in motion. Shoulders back, chin raised, he stepped in place. He had a gun, a spear, a slingshot and shield.

Larry remembered a cold hard fact about himself. He could whistle. One afternoon at school he had whistled in the hallway and was sent to detention for it. He needed a good theme song to play in his head for marching into battle. Something to dismiss the terror, a good confident ditty to confuse his enemy.

"The Fishin' Hole" theme from *The Andy Griffith Show* was too casual. Beethoven's "Ode to Joy" was much too happy. "Dueling Banjos" from the movie *Deliverance*? Too many change-ups. *The Good, the Bad and the Ugly* theme? Too hard on the tongue. He chose "The Colonel Bogey March", the theme song from an old movie he remembered as a kid; *The Bridge on the River Kwai.* It was defiant. Perfect.

He started to whistle and marched along the ridge towards the village with short choppy steps on the uneven ground, arms swinging mechanically, the shield in his left hand, the spear in his right.

There was no turning back now.

When he saw the village below, he sat down in a cluster of scrub trees and surveyed the situation for almost an hour.

The giant returned to the barrels only twice to refill his cup. All but Ismelda remained in their shacks, out of sight. Had she warned them of Larry's arrival? He could see her down by the shore. She was fishing.

Larry stood. He started whistling again and marched down the hill, eyeing the unaware pig as he approached. The pig's back was to him. Larry reached the outskirts of the cluster of shacks and loaded the slingshot with a smooth rock. Still whistling, he aimed at the giant and released a shot. It pinged off the rock where the giant sat.

The pig stood, brandishing his machete, adjusting his eyes. Where had the shot come from?

Larry reloaded the sling and shot off a second stone. It hit the pig in the stomach, stinging him.

The pig let out a yelp. He seemed disoriented. Was the alcohol taking its toll? The pig took a few unbalanced steps, circling.

"Who is there?" he yelled.

Larry kept whistling.

The pig faced him, eyes narrowing. "Ah! There you are," he said. "Come closer."

Larry reloaded the sling, aimed and released a third stone. It hit the pig in the leg. He didn't flinch this time.

"I am made of stone," shouted the pig.

Larry walked past the shacks, a handful of old people in their doorways on his right, hope in their eyes. He raised a finger to his lips for them to remain quiet. He saw Pharaoh in the cage. His friend was standing, watching events unfold.

The pig raised the machete in his hand. "Come closer," he demanded.

Larry released a fourth stone, hitting the giant in the forehead, stunning him. A trickle of blood appeared. El Gordo's knees buckled but he did not fall.

"Just a mosquito bite," laughed the giant. His eyes narrowed. "Ah! There you are, rooster man!"

Larry kept whistling. Instead of closing in on the giant, he circled around him at a safe distance, shooting stone after pesky stone. Many missed but a few found their mark.

The giant was enraged now. "Mano a mano!" he shouted. "Enough play! Stop whistling!"

The heat of the day was upon him, the poisoned alcohol burning from within. The giant picked up a handful of rocks and hurled them at Larry. They bounced off his raised shield.

Larry kept whistling, marching in cadence.

El Gordo spun around and around, his breathing irregular. "Come and fight!" said the sweating giant, choking on his words.

Larry went to the barrels. He set down his spear and rocked one of them until it spilled over on its side. He picked up his spear and danced away, whistling.

The giant ran towards the barrels, his feet tripping under him as they splashed through a puddle of dumped liquor. He fell but rose up again. Next to the barrels, the pig took several heavy breaths. He removed the lid of one of the barrels and scooped up several handfuls to quench an uncommon thirst, ignoring his inconvenient enemy for the moment.

Larry ran up to Pharaoh's cage and swung open the meshed entrance.

"Run to the water!" Larry ordered Pharaoh. "Find a safe distance!"

Pharaoh exploded out of the cage, the searing pain of his burns forgotten for the moment.

Larry faced the shacks and yelled again. "Everyone, run to the sea!"

He watched as the old ones scattered from the shacks and ran past him. A few stopped and aided Pharaoh down the hill.

The pig watched, still scooping up the pulque until he was satisfied. He started to laugh.

"You are only one man," the pig roared. "You cannot dance all day. After I kill you I will go below and slice the rest of them to pieces. See what you caused me to do?"

The pig pushed away from the barrels with amazing speed, machete raised. He raced towards Larry slicing at the empty air.

Larry backpedaled and moved behind the cage.

The giant fell against it, a rattle of strung metal between them. His thick fingers reached through the cage and he shook it viciously.

"There you are," smiled the giant. "I can see you now. You are no soldier. You are tall and skinny. I will whittle you down into shaved pieces."

Larry started his annoying whistling again.

"Stop it!" shouted the giant. "Stop the noise!"

Up close now, Larry saw mounds of sweat bubbling from the big man's face and body.

"Come around the cage so I can poke you," El Gordo shouted.

Larry pushed away from the cage to the open ground between the dock and the village. He saw the villagers below, huddled around Ismelda, nursing Pharaoh. Everyone watched in silence as the play continued.

The giant moved away from the cage and faced Larry. Larry reached in his pocket and retrieved the pistol as the giant took several steps towards him. Larry raised the gun, closed his eyes and pulled the trigger. It fired loudly. The giant hesitated in his tracks, inspecting himself for wounds.

But there were none.

Larry opened his eyes, aimed again and fired off all the rounds in the pistol. Seven more popping sounds came from the barrel, but no bullets.

"What trick is this? A gun with no bullets?" laughed the giant.

Gordo trotted towards him like a bull unleashed, releasing a guttural scream as he raised the machete over his head.

Larry stepped back and tripped, landing on his back. He raised his shield.

The giant came up on him, swiping with the machete.

Larry blocked it. The machete dug deep in the shield. As El Gordo wrenched it free, Larry saw a pair of feet appear behind the giant. He heard the pig scream in pain. Larry rolled away and regained his footing.

Standing behind the giant was Jack Douglas holding a blood-stained rock in his hands.

Gordo turned on Douglas with his machete. As he raised his arm to strike, Larry stood and lunged at him with the spear. A long swath of blood oozed from the giant's back.

"Move away!" Larry ordered Douglas.

Douglas ran to a safe distance.

"Come on fat boy," Larry said. "This is our fight."

The pig turned and faced Larry again. "We are out of music then?"

His mouth was a mess of froth, lips thick. The giant's eyes glazed and he puked suddenly, falling to his knees.

Spear raised, Larry stepped towards the big man reduced to a heap of helpless blubber and sinew, the evil pushed out of him.

Larry's arm seemed stuck in the air. He could not strike the final blow.

Ismelda came up on him, grabbed the spear and sliced the pig across the neck. Blood spurted out in a large pool. The giant fell into it, face down, drowning in his own body fluids. His muscles shuddered and twitched in a final death throe until he moved no more.

Larry looked at Ismelda. The mother of mermaids. How fitting that she struck the final blow against the evil that had ruined her people. Her face was a blank of mystery.

"The devil is dead," she said.

Larry saw Jack Douglas step into view. He poked at the dead man with his foot.

"The cave got to me. I needed a break," said Douglas. "Hope you didn't mind my joining in."

The old ones came up from the sea with Pharaoh and surrounded the dead beast. Their nightmare was ended.

Ismelda tossed the spear on the ground and went to the pulque barrels. "Come," she told the others. "Give the devil back his brew."

One by one, the barrels fell; a stream of liquid running downhill to be captured by the sea.

Larry sat on the pig's rock and watched it all, Pharaoh and Douglas joining him.

"I never thought I'd see this day," said Douglas.

Pharaoh shook his head in disbelief. "Good ol' Lawrence Settlebottom. Who would have thought? You come a long way since that first day at the train station."

Larry remembered what Dario had said if the giant fell.

Hang a white sheet on the dock.

It took old Calista a few minutes to find him one. She led Ismelda and Larry by the hand down to the shore. Together they secured the sheet to the dock.

They sat and waited, but not for long.

The gypsy catamaran sailed in from the west; Nina, Pinta and Santa Maria waving and shouting with frantic delight off the bow as they dropped the sails.

Dario was at the rudder, a plume of smoke erupting from the pipe in his mouth. He ran the boat up on the beach.

Calista waded through the surf and pulled Dario to her in the water.

Dario smiled at her. "Look at you, woman! So beautiful!"

Calista shook her head stubbornly. "Go on with you, husband. Have you gone blind?"

"In a week you will be fat again."

"I was never fat," said Calista.

Dario swept his arms wide and shouted, "We bring food! Tonight we feast!"

Jack Douglas and the old people came down from the village pushing Pharaoh in a wheelbarrow.

Nina, Pinta and Santa Maria bounded off the boat and hugged the old ones; aunts and uncles and cousins and daughters finally reunited.

Dario picked Calista up in his arms and carried her to the shore. He noticed Larry and Ismelda holding hands on the dock.

Dario smiled at Larry. "You found your mermaid, I see. I forgot to mention I am her uncle."

Ismelda raced to his arms. Dario held her close to him, afraid to let her go.

While the women carried provisions off the gypsy boat to the village, Larry, Dario, Douglas and the remaining old men wrapped Gordo's body in a tarp and carried it down the hill to the beach.

"What next?" said Larry.

"A proper send-off," said Dario. "He was a confused man, angry at himself and the world but still a man."

"And one of us," said one of the old men.

"I recommend a Viking farewell," said Douglas, "a dishonorable send-off adrift on a burning pyre to the pagan realm of Helheim. Agreed?"

"Agreed," said the others.

"Not much to burn with," said Dario.

"Use the mescal barrels," Larry offered. "It seems fitting."

Pharaoh watched their progress from his seat on Gordo's old rock. The men rolled the barrels to the beach. Dario grabbed an axe from the catamaran. The men took turns splitting down the barrels. It was hard work.

Larry and Douglas visited the plane crash site and found a damaged pontoon. They dragged it down the hill to the beach and made a raft of it. Together, all the men placed Gordo's covered body on it and arranged tiers of wood.

"Now let us eat," said Dario. "We will set him off when night falls."

T he men joined the women in the village. Nina, Pinta and Santa Maria had prepared a feast. It had been a long time since the gypsies were together. There was joy and laughter again in the village.

Larry couldn't help following Ismelda with his eyes. Despite her tragedies she was gracious and affectionate to all, a woman who lived for today and the expectations of a better tomorrow.

After sunset everyone went to the beach. Gordo's pyre was lit and set adrift into the west. Many tears were shed; tears of relief and human loss. A violent chapter in their history was finally over.

"What is next for you?" Larry asked Dario.

The old man turned and stared at the decrepit village. "We will rebuild this place; save water, hunt rabbits and pluck gifts from the sea. It will be hard, but our lives have always been difficult."

It had been a long and exciting day. Before they turned in for the night, the women tended to Pharaoh's wounds and made him a comfortable bed under a lean-to.

Larry went down to the dock. Douglas was there, dragging his feet in the water, admiring the celestial night.

"Thank you for helping today," said Larry. "I was almost a dead man."

"No big deal," said Douglas. "It was a thing that had to be done." He looked over his shoulder and saw Ismelda, waist deep in the water off the beach. She was washing her hair. "But it's Ismelda we should thank. She struck the final blow. Fitting, if you ask me."

"What now?" said Larry.

Douglas stood. “For me? Back to my cave. I have work to do.”

“Art for art’s sake?”

“Yeah.”

Douglas walked up the path to the village, grabbed a handful of sweets and hiked back towards his cave on the cliffside trail.

Larry went down to the beach and watched Ismelda in the water. She was humming in a soft voice that reminded Larry of a child’s lullaby. He had never listened to lullabies as a child, never been rocked to sleep with the soothing love of a parent.

Ismelda shook her hair loose and came up the shore to him. “Today was a good day, Larry?”

“A very good day.”

“Tomorrow will be better,” she said.

“Much better,” he answered.

She leaned in to him and kissed him on the lips. He shivered from her touch and embraced her. They sat down in the sand together, holding hands, listening to the wild sounds of the ocean, the whistle of the wind, and the soft caress of the tide running along the sand.

Music.

CHAPTER 56

Weeks passed. Pharaoh could walk again. Day by day, his burns healed, but he would always bare permanent scars. He thought about wheelchair man, the plastic surgeon who rescued him in the bar fight. What would he recommend?

He watched Larry, busy at work, tearing things down with his bare hands, erecting new shelters with the others. Ismelda was always at his side, showing him things, teaching him survival techniques in the wild. Pharaoh had never noticed Larry's laugh before. It sounded like a giddy young boy's.

Most nights Larry sat down on the dock, a notebook and pen on his lap, writing things down in the moonlight. He was planning something.

One day, a big yacht named *The Wile E. Coyote* arrived and anchored offshore. A dinghy carrying five men ran up on the beach of the island. The entire village turned out to greet them.

The leader of the small expedition was a cool dude wearing a tee shirt, shorts and flip-flops. Pharaoh recognized him but he couldn't place his name.

"I'm Travis Spinner," said the man. "The country singer?"

"Not a fan," said Pharaoh.

"Maybe you know one of my songs then? A party hit called 'Rum-A-Tum-Tum'?"

"No."

"It went platinum. How about 'She Gets the Whiskey On'?"

"No," said Pharaoh. "What about you, Larry?"

"Nope."

Spinner had a big grin. "I got four platinum albums under my belt and a wall full of CMA and Grammy awards, but no mind. Guess I've been a star too long. I forgot there's real people in the world.... We're looking for a plane. A musician I ran into down in P.V. named Joey Grillo got an SOS text alert on his cell phone when his plane disappeared. He tracked its final destination here with a Spidertracks satellite app. Me and my band mates are taking a month-long cruise from Miami to Los Angeles and Joey asked us to maybe take a peek."

"The plane's here," said Pharaoh. "Up over the ridge. Not much left of it, I'm afraid."

Larry, Pharaoh and Dario led the country singer's expedition up the hill to the wreckage. While Spinner's crew plucked through the debris Pharaoh explained how the plane got there.

"Damn," said Spinner. "You fellas have been through some shit. I have to cut a new album in L.A. next month. Problem is, I don't have any material. That is, until now."

"I got some ideas," said Pharaoh.

"You a song writer?"

"Everybody's a writer when they put their mind to it," said Pharaoh. "How's this for a title? 'Loose Lips'."

"I like it," said Spinner. "Good hook."

One of the band members ventured a hundred yards behind the wreckage and returned with an unscathed box of TAIL PIPE caps. He passed them out to everyone.

As the group made their way back towards the village, Spinner admired the island. "I'm lookin' for a getaway. My own private island. Kenny Chesney has one. So does Tim McGraw. This one for sale?"

"Sorry," said Dario. "It's taken. Besides there's no water. A man like you, wouldn't you prefer a tropical island? One with palm trees and a lagoon for snorkeling and jet skiing."

"Now you're talking," said Spinner.

"I like palm trees," said Pharaoh.

"Maybe there's a song in that too," said Spinner.

"Probably," said Pharaoh.

Spinner liked their company. They were the real deal. "Listen, I got a sea chest full of steaks and chicken with all the trimmings on my vessel. Corn on the cob, too. Maybe have a barbecue down on the beach with me and my crew? Everybody's invited."

Travis Spinner had his stories. He didn't like being famous, but he was stuck with it. His private yacht had stopped in the Grand Caymans, Costa Rica, Panama and the coasts of Mexico. It was a crazy trip so far. He had been boarded three times by navies and coast guards looking for drugs or bribes.

"Pissed me off," said Spinner. "I thought the ocean was a free place. All they found was beer and rum. Besides, we're all drug free now, except my drummer. He takes the needle for his diabetes."

During the barbecue some of the band members broke out acoustic guitars with Spinner singing some of his hits: "Love for

Rent", "Girl on Fire", and "Burned Again but Love the Pain." They were amusing songs.

Nina, Pinta and Santa Maria danced with a handful of groupies who came ashore from *The Wile E. Coyote.* One by one, the old islanders were pulled to their feet to join in. It was a glorious night. Even Larry danced, teaching Ismelda "The Twist".

As the band packed their instruments back in the dinghy, Pharaoh approached Spinner.

"Think me and Larry can hitch a ride to Los Angeles tomorrow?"

"No problem, bro. Maybe we knock some songs out together. 50-50 royalty split. You own a guitar?"

"No," said Pharaoh.

Spinner handed him a guitar case. "Take my Les Paul. I got plenty more." Spinner visited Larry and Ismelda at the dock next. "Man, I thought I had the life, but you all got somethin' here. Your own private paradise. I wish I could trade places, but I got my own tribe to look after. Mine won't last forever. The day I don't chart a top ten hit, the walls of my Jericho will come tumbling down."

After Spinner and his friends returned to the yacht for the night, Larry and Ismelda led Pharaoh to the secret circle and showed him the three graves.

"Mrs. Chumley needs to hear the whole story," Larry reminded Pharaoh. "Every detail so she can sleep at night."

"You can tell her yourself," said Pharaoh.

"I'm not going back," said Larry, hugging Ismelda. "We have work to do here." He produced his notebook and handed it to Pharaoh. "I wrote down all I could remember; Jack Douglas, the pirates, the ship, the giant, these graves."

"It's a hell of a tale," said Pharaoh.

"If the widow Chumley is willing, we can use some fresh supplies to rebuild here. I made a list."

"What about your job at the museum?"

"A trained monkey can do my job. My house in Chicago? You take it. Lots of music, lots of wine."

"*Take it,* Larry?" said Pharaoh. "It's yours. I'll just sit on it until you come back home."

Larry showed him other papers. "These are signed affidavits, legal powers-of-attorney to protect you. I have plenty of money in the bank. Get your face fixed if you like. The house key is under a water tap by the back door. There is a car in the garage I never drove – a Buick. You might have to buy a battery for it. Keys are in a kitchen drawer. "

"Damn, Larry," said Pharaoh. He was full of guilt. "You're giving me shit like a man dying of cancer! You'll be back some day, you'll see! I kilt your girlfriend, remember?"

"If she didn't die, do you think I would be here?" said Larry.

"Probably not," said Pharaoh.

"Most definitely not," said Larry. "I'd already be dead from poisoning. See how things work out Pharaoh? The great mystery of it all? One thing bumps into another thing and everything changes. Maybe for a reason, maybe not. But isn't it wonderful?"

"Sometimes it's wonderful," said Pharaoh. He turned to Ismelda. "You really are sumpin'," he said. "Your eyes on that little stamp brought us halfway across the world. But can I tell you sumpin'?"

"What?" said Ismelda.

"You're even more beautiful in person. Larry is a lucky, lucky man."

After everyone had gone to sleep, Pharaoh sat on Gordo's rock, the guitar case at his feet. There was one last thing to do before leaving the island in the morning. It was an ugly decision, but necessary to tell the whole story. He picked up the guitar case and hiked back to the secret circle where the graves stood.

Early the next morning, Travis Spinner arrived in the dinghy loaded with food and water for the villagers waiting on shore for Pharaoh's send-off.

"Come on, fellas!" Spinner shouted. "I got a new song burning a hole in my head. You guys ready?"

"It's just me going," said Pharaoh.

After hugs and kisses from everyone, he climbed in the dinghy with the guitar case. Pharaoh looked back at Larry. *Good ol' Larry Settlebottom.* The first brotherhood either of them had ever known. No more trench coats and concrete for Larry. He had a tan and a hot girlfriend.

"Any last words?" Pharaoh asked him.

"Go find your own beach," said Larry. "And don't forget the palm trees." He dug his hand in his pocket. "I almost forgot!" Larry produced the Double Eagle and tossed it to Pharaoh. "For luck. Whatever you do, don't spend it."

Pharaoh turned the coin over in his hands. "You sure about this?"

"I'm sure."

Spinner pushed off and started his engine. "If you all ever get a jukebox on this island, don't forget to stock my records!"

As the dinghy bounced over the surf, melancholy Pharaoh stared back at Larry, waving goodbye from the shore. It was a sweet parting. Pharaoh started crying.

"You gonna miss him?" said Spinner.

"Best friend I ever had," said Pharaoh.

"Sounds like a song," said Spinner.

CHAPTER 57

They sat in the gazebo, enjoying the rustle of leaves in the brisk autumn air.

Rosemary Chumley was liberal with the Jameson pour, listening to handsome Mr. Williams spin his fantastic tale.

"By gum," she laughed, "Larry had his adventure, alright! Mad dogs, musicians and mermaids! Priceless!"

Pharaoh placed the rare coin in front of her. "I believe this is yours," he said.

"Nonsense," said Rosemary. "Possession is nine tenths of the law."

"But I had it appraised," said Pharaoh. "I know the value."

"Then don't lose it," she said.

"I don't need the money," said Pharaoh. "I got two hit songs comin' out on the radio with Travis Spinner. The advance paid for my new face, too."

"All that remains for me is the final mystery," said Rosemary.

Pharaoh guessed the question. "Do mermaids exist?" He placed the guitar case in front of her. "There is an old proverb, Mrs. Chumley - 'the proof is in the pudding'. See for yourself."

Rosemary unbuckled the hinges of the case and opened it. Inside was a small finned skeleton.

"You can look at it one of two ways," said Pharaoh. "Is it wonderful or a freak of nature?"

"What did my Larry see?" said Rosemary.

"*Wonder,*" said Pharaoh.

"Then I prefer wonder, too." She offered him chocolates on a silver tray. "Try the Black Flag fudge. It melts in your mouth."

Pharaoh took one, savoring the flavor on the roof of his mouth.

Mrs. Chumley took a sip of whiskey. "I have one final question, Mr. Williams. This Ismelda — was she worth dying for?"

Pharaoh finished the chocolate before his reply. "She was to Larry."

"Well, then. That's all that really matters," said Rosemary. She leaned back in her chair and laughed with delight. "Oh, if Georgie only knew the mischief he caused!"

ALSO BY BARRY JAMES HICKEY

THE FIVE PEARLS: A true portrait of throwaway kids in today's America as a mysterious teacher challenges five angry students in an after-school program.

CHASING GOD'S RIVER: On a whitewater adventure, everyone wants something from Wade Jones that he can't provide. And then there is the river - a snarling, whitewater snake. It wants something from him too - maybe his life.

THE GLASS FENCE: A female employee with wanderlust confronts a luxury hotel's entrenched management staff to start an employee rowing team and discovers dark secrets about her employers.

WAKING PURGATORY: All Hallow's Eve is approaching. Once again, the citizens of Purgatory, Illinois will attempt to open the door between heaven and hell. Never wake the dead. Never!

THE WATER LAWYER: A new attorney unravels a murder-for-hire scheme at a Colorado law firm and becomes the target of corrupt killers. Is water worth killing for? It is in the modern day Wild, Wild West. (With Kevin Donovan)

THE PENDRAGON PROPHECY: Convinced he is the last heir to King Arthur's throne, an American farmer has one summer to prepare for The King's Challenge, a secret tournament between knights to determine the world's future and rid the world of evil wizards, monsters and magic. Lucky for him Merlin is still alive!

www.ingramcontent.com/pod-product-compliance
Lightning Source LLC
Chambersburg PA
CBHW060553310726
48982CB00008B/1105/J

* 9 7 8 1 6 4 5 1 6 7 3 1 0 *